Changeling Press LLC

ChangelingPress.com

Gunnar/Knuckles Duet
A Bones MC Romance
Marteeka Karland

Gunnar/Knuckles Duet
A Bones MC Romance
Marteeka Karland

ISBN: 978-1-60521-953-0

Publisher:
Changeling Press LLC
315 N. Centre St.
Martinsburg, WV 25404
ChangelingPress.com

Printed in the U.S.A.

Editor: Jean Cooper
Cover Artist: Marteeka Karlend

The individual stories in this anthology have been previously released in E-Book format.

Table of Contents

Gunnar (Kiss of Death MC 1)
A Bones MC Romance
Marteeka Karland

Pippa is the unexpected twist in my life, a complication I never saw coming.

Pippa -- My life has been shaped by some kind of underworld scheming I don't really understand. Or maybe I don't want to know. But now I'm living in darkness and violence, unable to break free but unwilling to succumb to the drug induced stupor my captives force on me. Then Gunnar, a fierce man with a dark relentlessness, charges to my rescue like a black knight, taking vengeance on those who have hurt me. Our first meeting isn't a rescue out of a fairy tale -- it's pure chaos. Gunnar may be an ex-con, but he protects me with a ferocity I never knew existed.

Gunnar – Pippa's quiet resilience clashes with the violent life I know. With just a look, the woman claims my heart and life takes on a brand new meaning. I've done time -- fifteen long years behind bars, to protect my sister. Now I'll protect Pippa with a ruthlessness she can't even imagine. My past is dark, my future uncertain, and every moment with Pippa makes me realize the lengths I'll go to keep her. Fate has brought me to the one woman I know I can't live without.

Prologue

"No, Gunnar. You can't do this."

"It's done, Hannah. Go home before anyone sees you here." I tried to keep my voice soft, but there was an almost overpowering rage inside me threatening to explode. My sister, my twin, should never have to be exposed to something like this.

Hannah sobbed and threw herself at me. "Please don't do this, Gunnar. Please. I can't not have you with me."

"I'm so sorry, Hannah. And no matter what, I'll always be with you. Go home and clean up. Don't say anything to Mom or Dad."

"I can't do that. Dad has to know."

"NO!" I snapped the command hard at her. "This can't come back on you." I pushed her back slightly but framed her face with my hands. "Go clean up. Burn your clothes."

"He was going to r-rape me, Gunnar." Her voice was so soft I barely heard her. Had I not been looking straight at her I would have missed her words.

"I know. But he didn't. Right?"

She shook her head. "No. I s-stopped h-him."

"Good. That's all that matters. Now go. Do as I say." I tried my best to be gentle with her, but the fact was, this was really a shit show.

"Daddy told me he didn't like him." Now, Hannah turned to look at the man she'd stabbed to death ten minutes before. Thank God I'd been close when she'd called. Just like our father had taught us, Hannah's blade had found his left kidney several times and he'd bled out. The result was a Godawful fucking mess. There was no way for me to clean it up without leaving evidence behind and the only way to ensure it was completely clean would mean getting Bones MC involved. Which I would never do. Not for this. Yeah, there was some sketchy shit going on from time to time in Bones, but Dad and Bohannon tried to keep it clean. This was *anything* but clean.

"I know. Don't worry about that right now. Just go home and do what I told you. And not a word to anyone. Go home. Go to your room. Take a shower and scrub all the blood off. Don't forget to get under your nails. Use peroxide on your hands. It will bubble if it touches even dried blood, so you don't miss anything." She held my gaze with her fearful, pain-filled one. "Burn all your clothes, Hannah. Take them to the woods deep inside the compound, away from everyone. Everything. Including your underwear and socks. Be careful, but use gas or lighter fluid. You have to get it all and sift through the ashes to make sure everything is burnt. Understand me?"

She nodded before hugging me once more. "I'm so sorry, Gunnar. So sorry…"

"None of this is your fault. He crossed a line and was asking to get killed. Just take care of yourself. I'll talk to you soon."

I watched her go. At sixteen, she should never have had to go through this. Now it was up to me to protect her, and I would. With everything in me. I'd give up everything to protect my twin. Even if I called my older brothers, I wasn't sure they could fix this. Not without risking the club and I'd never put my dad in that situation. Every single member of that club was like family to me. I'd known them all my life. So, the only way to protect Hannah without risking any more of my family was to do this myself.

I gave Hannah a few minutes to get on her way. I spent that time getting my hands bloody. I had no intention of them doing a thorough job investigating this crime scene, but I wiped down the blade Hanna had used before covering it back in blood and making sure my own prints were on the knife.

By the time I'd prepared for my next call, I'd had time to think about what I was doing and consider the consequences. No matter which way I looked at it, the only path I could see to keep my sister, brothers, my father, as well as Bones MC and my father's company, ExFil, away from risk was to take responsibility myself. My decision would probably cost me my relationship with my father and the club I'd grown up in, but Dad could take care of himself as well as Mom and my sister.

The legal battle that followed was short and painful. Short because I pled guilty from the first and would not let anyone convince me to do anything different. I never wavered from my story that I'd killed the bastard, but I'd told them it was because he'd threatened my sister. I think even the judge was baffled by my refusal to allow my lawyer to negotiate for a lesser charge. Or go to a fucking trial!

Dad was pissed as shit. I think he knew something was up, but I wasn't saying anything and, just like I'd instructed her, Hannah didn't either. When she'd visited me and could get me away from Mom and Dad, she'd plead with me over and over to change my mind. To let her tell Dad what happened and have him sort out the whole mess. I'd refused and she'd respected my wishes, but I knew what her decision cost her. She felt doubly guilty. Hannah would never survive incarceration of any kind. She was too gentle and empathetic. The juvie population alone would eat her alive. I couldn't even contemplate her in an adult female prison.

My mother said Hannah cried a lot for no apparent reason. She asked me if I thought she loved that bastard enough to mourn. I told her I had no idea. I let them think Hannah was mad at me and she likely was. Just not for killing her boyfriend. She was angry because I was going away to prison, running headlong like I was looking forward to it. The reality was, I was fucking terrified.

"Son, I can't help if you don't tell me what's goin' on."

"What's goin' on is I killed a man who threatened my sister. I did the crime. I'll do the time." I didn't mean to be belligerent, but it was either that or break down and give it all to him straight. Along with a lot of tears and snot. I knew what the consequences of this were. My childhood ended today.

Deep down, I knew I needed to tell Dad. He could take care of all this. You know. If I'd told him to begin with. Looking back, keeping him out of this might not have been the best decision of my life. Oh well. Done was done. I'd do this for my sister because she deserved to be happy and to not be punished for killing the son of a bitch trying to rape her. I absolutely would not take a chance on some overzealous prosecutor painting her as the victim. She'd been through enough. I'd do this, because I wanted to be the man Dad raised me to be.

As someone once said, if you pray for the rain, you have to deal with the mud too.

"They're talking about sentencing you as an adult which means twenty *years*, Gunnar. More if they decide to sentence you on murder instead of manslaughter. You didn't even negotiate what you were fucking confessing to!" Dad stood abruptly and paced across the room before returning. In what was probably a fit of frustration and anger, he smacked the chair over so it skidded across the narrow strip of floor between the table and the wall. "Christ! Have you even thought about what that means? You'll get to do your first couple in the juvie camp, but the day you turn eighteen, they'll put you in with the big boys."

"Yeah, Dad. I thought about it. I went over everything with my lawyer."

"Did he also tell you this prosecutor is going for the maximum sentence? You killed an unarmed man with a knife. You did it in private so it looks like premeditation, and no one can dispute your account of the story."

"I know." I was starting to feel like a kid. My dad was a bit overprotective, even with us boys. Though I was only sixteen, my dad had raised all his kids to be men and women. I'd come this far so it was time to man up.

After this, I'd never make my father proud, but maybe he wouldn't be ashamed of me.

Chapter One

Gunnar
Present Day

"This the day?"

I glanced at my cellmate, now a close friend. I was packing up my personals in our cell, getting ready to leave prison after serving fifteen years of a twenty-year sentence. "Yep."

"Thought you had a few more years left."

I shrugged. "I did."

"Interesting." Knuckles leaned against the end of the bunk. I paused in my packing to find him watching me intently.

"Yeah," I drawled slowly. "Thought so myself."

"You think it was your old man?" Knuckles knew about Cain and ExFil and Bones. He knew my dad had some pull and was likely thinking I'd held out on him.

"If you're implyin' I've been down-playin' people I know, I haven't been. This is as much a surprise for me as it is you."

"I know."

OK, now I stopped what I was doing altogether and took a step toward Knuckles. "What's goin' on?" Clearly, I'd missed something important.

"You're a solid guy, Gunnar. I had an... opportunity."

"What kind of opportunity?" I was preparing myself for a fight, but I had no idea who'd I'd be fighting. Knuckles didn't usually play politics inside, but one thing I'd learned while in USP Terre Haute was that there wasn't much men wouldn't do for a few amenities.

"The kind where I had to make a choice."

I narrowed my eyes at him. "Are we gettin' ready to try to kill each other, Knuckles?"

"Depends on your answer."

I held my arms out from my side slightly so he could see I wasn't armed. "Gotta know the question first, man."

"I was told there was a one-time opportunity for me to get myself or one person of my choosing out early. Call it a favor from someone in the position to make this happen."

"What's that got to do with me?"

"If you agree to do something for me, you get to go back to your life a couple years early."

"I suppose it depends on what it is you want. There are things I won't do. Even for my freedom. I take it me getting this early parole wasn't my father's doing."

"Even for the man who kept you alive when you first got to the real prison outta Camp Hilton?"

There was nothing easy about the camp and the bastard knew it. He also knew I'd agree with him I was alive now because of him. "Yeah, Knuckles. Even for you. But I hope you know I'd never deny you something without a fuckin' good reason."

Knuckles studied me for several seconds before nodding his head slowly. "Yeah. I do know. It's why I went ahead and pushed the order through. You're a good man, Gunnar. Of all the people here, I believe you are the one man who has never been a danger to society. Anyone who fucks with your family isn't considered society and is asking for whatever you dish out." He snorted out a laugh. "You're leaving whether you agree to help me or not."

"What's the ask, Knuckles?"

"My daughter," he said. "She's been taken. One

of my enemies found out who she was and used her to get revenge on me." Knuckles handed me a few photos of a young woman bound and gagged with an expression of abject terror on her face. The thing striking me most about her were her bright green eyes. They shimmered with tears, but there was something about them. A quiet acceptance of what was about to happen, maybe? Not in the sense that she'd given up, but like she'd accepted the experience wasn't going to be pleasant, and was determined to make it through so the task was complete.

"Pippa?" Knuckles had told me of her often enough. He was so proud of his baby girl. He'd managed a fling with one of the nurses in the prison before I got here and the woman had kept in touch over the years, even going so far as to let the girl meet Knuckles. The visit had gone well, but Knuckles had come back to the cell angry and agitated, afraid his enemies might use her to get revenge. That had been about five years ago. I knew there was nothing in the Goddamned world Knuckles wouldn't do for Pippa, whether it be killing or dying for her.

"Yeah. I've had some stuff sent to the Bones MC clubhouse for you. I can't rescue Pippa on my own and I have no idea if my own club would back me after what happened. The fallout of killin' those bastards put Kiss of Death in a pretty bad position."

OK, the name of his club got my attention. "Kiss of Death? Motorcycle Club in Nashville?"

Knuckles nodded. "You know of us, then?"

"Yeah. You could say that." I had to be careful here. I had no idea how I had managed to form a strong friendship with this man over the course of fifteen years and not realized he'd had ties to Kiss of Death.

"I was vice president before I got put in here. After I went away, things went to shit. Ain't even sure at this point if they'll still accept my patch. Damned sure ain't vice president anymore. So my chances of gettin' her back on my own are pretty Goddamned slim."

"You think I have a better shot?"

"Know you do. The new prez of Kiss of Death came from Bones. Vice president too. I can tell by the look on your face you know this."

"Yeah. What I don't know is why you kept your ties to them a secret from me."

"There's a reason I hadn't called in that favor before now, Gunnar. I set this in motion the day I found out Torpedo had taken over Kiss of Death. It took a few months for my guy to pull it off, so I used that time to gather as much information on the fuckers who took her."

"I assume the information is in the package you sent back to Bones?"

"Yeah. Let whoever you need see it. Do whatever you have to. But get Pippa away from those bastards."

I didn't hesitate but stuck out my hand to Knuckles and he took it. "On my life, brother. I'll bring Pippa home."

"No," he snapped. "You take her back to Bones or Kiss of Death if Torpedo and Bohannon are men you trust. But get her behind locked doors and do not let her out of your sight. If that means you take her as your old lady, then you do it. That's the ask, Gunnar."

It took a moment to comprehend what I'd just heard. "Me? You want me to make your daughter my old lady?"

"It's the only way she's safe, because you're not the kind of man to let anyone harm someone who belongs to him. You rescue her, charm her, then claim her. And you will treat her with fucking respect and coddle her like the fuckin' princess she is. Or, so help me and by God, I will *bury you*."

"I'll give her my property patch, Knuckles. I'll protect her with my life, but that's as far as I can promise. If she don't want me, she don't want me."

"Take it as a challenge, then. Make her want you." Oh, the man was good…

"One thing I've always said is my dad taught me you didn't lie to people who meant something to you. So I'm not gonna lie to you. No matter how much you bully me. I will give her my property patch so she has my protection, but I'm not promisin' anything beyond that."

To my surprise, Knuckles grinned and clapped me on the shoulder. "This is why you're the only man I trust with my baby girl. You don't cave under pressure when it's somethin' you believe in."

"My dad taught me you can't trust a man who doesn't respect his old lady. That means you don't cheat on her. Any man who does can't be trusted. I won't make her my old lady until I know it's what we both want. Even patchin' her is splittin' hairs, but I'll go that far to give her all the protection I can and defend her with my life."

"Your dad sounds like a smart man. I wish I could have met him."

"Neither of you are dead. It could happen someday."

Knuckles snorted. "Not on your life, kid. Ain't meetin' a man like Joe "Cain" Gill wearin' what amounts to chains."

"Can I ask you something?"

"Name it, kid."

"Why'd you kill those three guys?"

Instead of answering right away, Knuckles indicated for me to take a seat on the lower bunk, which was his. He pulled up a box with tattoo supplies. Once he'd taken out what he needed, he indicated I should put my right hand on top. He spread my thumb and forefinger apart and started working. The image was small and incomplete, looking like a Celtic knot with half of it missing. The ink extended from where the webbing at the corner of my thumb folded in when my fingers weren't parted to the very edge of the webbing. Where the center of the knot would be if the image were complete was an what looked like an upside-down V with one side straight while the other was at an angle.

He wiped down the image and put some goop on the fresh ink, then extended his hand to me, wanting me to take it in a handshake. When I did he gripped hard. "Look at it." I did. Where our hands locked, the knot was completed. In the center of it was a capital K. Mine completed the bottom part, his the top. The tattoos were basically identical, but his half of the K had a crown where mine didn't. "Anyone loyal to me will have the same tattoo. Mine has a crown because I'm in charge."

"I'm loyal to you, Knuckles. You know that. But I'm also loyal to my family and I have no intention of ever coming back to prison once I'm out. I'm not doing illegal shit for you or anyone else unless there's a fuckin' good reason." I held my ground, grasping Knuckles's hand as hard as he did mine. "I'll do anything necessary to get your daughter out safe, includin' killin' a bunch of motherfuckers if they need it. But that's as far as I go. I won't deliberately go against you unless I feel it's morally wrong."

Knuckles was silent for a long time, holding my gaze. When he spoke, he gripped my hand even tighter. Given the way his eyes seemed to bore into my soul, he was probably looking for any sign of a reaction to whatever he was getting ready to say or do. "They raped and murdered my sister." There was a slight flinch to the muscle under his eye when he spoke. Like the mere memory affected him viscerally. "The men I killed. When I learned Pippa had been kidnapped, it felt like fate intended for you to go after her. You protected your sister despite the cost to you. Not many men would commit to something that hard. So, if you tell me you'll get my daughter back, I'm puttin' my faith in the boy who chose to be a man to protect someone he loves. I'm hopin' you've still got that determined kid inside you somewhere."

"On my life, Knuckles. I'll get her back and keep her safe. If I die, one thing I know with absolute certainty is that Cain would never let an innocent suffer once he knew of it. Torpedo was his second long before I was born so I've known him my whole life, too. I know them all. Once I get them on this, as long as one of them is still alive, they will never stop trying to bring Pippa home." It was as big a promise as I could make, but I knew my dad and his club. Even in fifteen years, they might not accept me back into the fold, but their integrity would never break.

"Then get your ass outta here. You tell me when she's safe."

"I'll give you regular reports. We'll have to research and plan, but I won't take any more time than strictly necessary before going to bring her out."

"Plan it well, brother. Get her out safe."

"You have my word."

* * *

Pippa

They were coming. I could hear heavy footfalls and raised male voices. It was part of the torture I'd endured for the last month. At least, I thought it had been a month. I'd scratched a notch into the wooden floor for each day I'd been there. Might have missed a day or counted one twice. It was hard to tell with the drugs and the fact that there was only one window and I wasn't even sure if it faced the morning or evening sun. I never knew what my captors were going to do, but it was never pleasant. Usually, it meant someone was drugging me or a beating when I fought the drugging, but things had been escalating recently. I got the impression they were waiting on something. I wasn't sure what, and the natives were getting restless, so to speak.

"Is Boss lettin' us play with the bitch today?"

"Not yet." The voices were distinctively different. While the first one had a squeak and a whiny tone, the second voice was deeper and more sinister. It was the man who came in to shoot me up. While I sometimes got a little dizzy, whatever they were using wasn't as strong as I'd have expected. I was never completely under and had, so far, been able to fight them off whenever they got handsy. Probably more because they obviously didn't have the go ahead to do whatever they wanted. As to who "they" were, I had no idea.

The door opened and I huddled into an even tighter ball on the floor in the corner. There was only a dingy mattress for me to sleep on and a bucket in the corner for me to go to the bathroom in, and that was it. Not a blanket or pillow or anything. I was naked, cold, and filthy, my hair a tangled, nasty mess. If I made it out of here, I was sure I'd have to cut it. Which was the least of my worries.

It was dark, and the light spilling into the room hit me squarely in the eyes. I whimpered and lifted a hand up to block out the light. Which was exactly what the man wanted. He snagged my arm and extended it so my elbow wasn't bent.

I struggled but he didn't smack me around this time. Probably because I was no match for his greater strength. Plus, they hadn't been feeding me regularly and it had been a couple days since I'd had any water. The fight was rapidly running out of me. Rather than waste energy on a futile effort, I did my best to conserve my strength. Unless he hit me with a lot more than he usually did, I would still have enough awareness of everything around me to be able to fight if this was a prelude to another assault. What these guys didn't know and what I'd taken great pains to hide from them, was I had never been overly susceptible to narcotics. Why? No clue. But other than taking away the pain, I didn't get high. Which, in this situation wasn't exactly a blessing.

There was a sharp prick in the bend of my elbow as the guy found a vein, even without a tourniquet. He pressed the plunger and the sharp burning sting left in its wake made me cry out. Every time they did this, I was certain my arm was going to turn black and fall off. A few seconds later, euphoria warmed me from the inside out. They'd definitely hit me with a stronger dose, but it still wasn't enough to put me out. I wasn't sure if being awake was a blessing or a curse, though.

The second he pulled the needle from my arm, the guy let me go and stomped out, just like always. The whiny-sounding guy lingered, but the other man snagged him by the upper arm and dragged him to the door. He slammed the door shut and I heard the click of the outside lock. Once again, I was alone.

My head was actually spinning, but the disorientation I'd thought might follow didn't happen. Everything was just… soft. God only knew how much the bastard had hit me with to get this effect. Good news was, my face didn't hurt where he'd hit me anymore.

It wasn't long before the door opened again. Just like I knew it would. They never waited long between injections before they came in with people to look at me. Men. Women. Mostly men, though. It wasn't hard to put together they were there to inspect goods. Which meant, I was being sold to the highest bidder. Or something.

"The side of her face is swollen." This guy sounded different than the others who'd come to look at me. Less refined. I thought I smelled gasoline. Kind of like when I'd been brought here. The dizziness combined with the bright light in my face made it impossible to see him clearly, but one thing was for sure. He was a big motherfucker if the unfamiliar blurry double shadow I was seeing was the guy speaking.

"Bitch shoulda laid still."

"Where else's she hurt?"

"Dunno, man. Don't fuckin' care either. Do you wanna make a bid on the bitch or not?"

There was a small *pop*. Nothing big, more like a snap firecracker. Then two more. I heard more voices, then hands grabbed at me, tugging at me. I screamed and kicked out as hard as I could, panic driving away the lingering effects of the drug I'd been given.

"It's all right. It's all right. You're safe, Pippa. I'm here to get you out." The words did nothing to calm me down. Especially when something was shoved over my head.

"NO! NO! Bastard!" I fought. Hard. But I'd been starved and drugged, not to mention taking beatings any time I fought back. I didn't have a chance against this guy. Then my head was free and my arms soon followed. That's when I realized he'd put a shirt on me, covering my body in soft material.

"I know, honey. But I promise I'll be better." He sounded like he was only half paying attention to me even as he slipped my feet into some loose, soft pants.

"Be better?" I know it was a stupid conversation and probably not one we had time for, but the question slipped out before I could even think of censoring it.

"At not being a bastard." He put socks on my feet before slipping shoes on.

"I'm, uh, not really sure I can walk. I haven't been on my feet much since they brought me here." I took in a shuddering breath as flashes of the early hours of my captivity flew through my mind. I heard myself whimper. "I'm not… I c-couldn't e-even go to the b-bathroom…" My thought trailed off, and I shuddered again, barely biting back a sob of despair and humiliation.

"Didn't figure you could walk out, and I don't plan on you having to. I just believe in being prepared. Besides, the socks and shoes might help get your feet warm." He continued to move around the tiny space with efficient movements. "I know you're hurting and scared. But I'll keep you safe. On my life."

I looked up at him and knew I was going to cry. No tears came, but I could feel great sobs inside me wanting to break free. "I don't think I'll ever be warm or clean again."

"Christ." The man pulled me into his arms and

held me for long moments before wrapping an arm around my waist to pick me up and carry me outside. Instinctively, I wrapped my arms and legs around him and hung on tight. "When I get you to safety, I may well kill Knuckles for this fuckin' stunt."

"Knuckles?"

"Yeah, honey."

"Why would you kill him? Did he do this to me?" My heart started pounding again and I knew a panic attack was imminent. I pushed away but the man only held me tighter, wrapping his other arm around my back to hold me more securely as he continued walking. "My mom s-said h-he wasn't a good m-man, but…"

"He is, honey. He's the reason I'm here to get you. He sent me to get you because he knew you were in trouble."

"Y-you had other th-things to do. I'm so s-sorry!" I sobbed out a cry, unable to stop myself.

"Stop it!" He snarled at me, and I flinched. He climbed into the back of a big Humvee with me still in his arms. Instead of sitting me beside him, he simply thumped on the seat in front of him with the side of his fist. "Move out."

The vehicle jerked into motion and his arms tightened around me. "Just hold on, honey. I've got you now. You're safe." His words and tone were kind, but I doubted he wanted to be in the situation he found himself in. He held me with one arm while he fished around in a pack with the other hand. Moments later, he pulled out a bottle of water.

"I'm so sorry." I sobbed against his shoulder where I'd buried my face. "I appreciate you c-coming for me, but I'm s-sorry you h-had t-to."

"None of this is your fault, Pippa. Understand?

None of it."

"But you're angry at Knuckles because he sent you after me."

"He did and I *am* angry, but not at him. Certainly not at you."

I breathed out another small sob. "Thank you," I whispered. "Thank you for getting me out of there."

He grunted and opened the bottle of water before giving it to me. "Drink up." The man simply could not help but be in charge. In any other situation, I might have smiled. He tugged a thermal blanket from his pack and draped it around my body. Then his arms tightened around me and the blanket and he sighed, his chin resting on top of my head. "Just rest if you can. The girls'll get you something to eat and help you clean up when we get to the clubhouse. Then you can rest. I'll be watching over you the whole time. You're safe now, Pippa. I swear it."

I had no idea why I believed this man, but I did. I didn't even know his name, but he was being kind. Maybe it made me stupid to trust him so completely, but one second I felt my body relax into his embrace, the next… nothing.

Chapter Two

Gunnar

"She's out." I told the contact Knuckles had given for me to get a message to the other man.

"Condition?"

"Banged up and likely drugged, but she's coherent. Passed out when we got underway."

"I want a detailed list of her injuries."

That got my attention, but I knew better than to ask now. The convo had to be short and to the point. "Copy that." Then I disconnected the call.

The woman in my arms was nothing like what I'd expected. And I'd expected quite a lot. There was a palpable gentleness about her I'd never associated with Knuckles. Despite her nature, she fought when she had to. I got the feeling I was gonna lose my shit when I found out all she went through. Yet, despite her trauma, she could still fall asleep in my arms.

I was under no illusion that all the shit Knuckles spouted in prison about him wanting me to take care of his daughter was the only reason he chose me for this task. Knuckles wasn't a complete monster, but he wasn't above using whomever he had to, including family, to get what he wanted. Unfortunately for him, I was going to ignore his duplicity and keep his daughter, and there wasn't a Goddamned thing he could do about it.

We rolled into the Bones MC compound an hour later. I'd already been here before heading to Pippa, but I'd come in secret. Scout and Goose, a couple of guys in Bones I'd known as a kid, had helped me get in and get the package Knuckles had sent for me. I'd left and pored over the information he'd sent in a hotel room for two days before calling Torpedo. Much as I wanted my brothers to help me, I wasn't ready to face them. Especially while bringing something like this to their door. Torpedo had sent two of his men and the Humvee to help me with this mission. Chains and Hawk had proven to be solid all the way around, offering their military insight to my brute force approach. I'd soaked up the knowledge, seeing it as a critical skill I was sorely lacking. I could learn. I'd just have to not be too proud to ask for help. In the end, we came up with a good entry and exit strategy that had worked perfectly.

Pippa hadn't moved but was breathing steadily and easily. One small hand curled into the material of my shirt, and I covered it with my own. This was the woman I was going to make my old lady. She didn't know me. I didn't know her. But somehow, I was going to make this happen.

The second we stopped in front of the clubhouse, my adopted brother, Ice, opened the door and held it for me. I stepped out with Pippa cradled against my chest, sound asleep. My other adopted brother, Cyclone, moved close to us and brushed a hank of dirty hair away from her eyes where it had fallen. "I've got Mama waitin' for you, Gunnar. She'll take care of your girl."

I nodded my thanks, then turned back to Ice. "What do you know about an MC called Fire and Steel?"

Ice frowned. "Bad lot, that bunch. Pretty sure the members Torpedo and Bohannon didn't kill in Kiss of Death migrated this way. Most of them moved on northward, but a few settled near Richmond. Outside our territory, but when you called with this" -- he indicated Pippa – "we started digging. Data, Zora, and Suzie are still investigating, but there's no doubt they're trafficking."

"I confirmed that myself. I got in to get Pippa by posing as a buyer. Bastards ain't real smart. They didn't even make me put down a deposit or pay in full before seeing the merchandise."

"Did you leave any of them alive?" Ice gave me a hard look, and I wasn't really sure what the correct answer was.

I was my own man, especially after the time I'd spent in prison. But Ice was still my big brother. And Cain was still my father. Lying wasn't even an option. "Not inside or in the immediate vicinity of the compound. Anyone left alive in that club wasn't home."

"Were you careful?" That came from Cyclone. Ice gave him a hard look too, but Cyclone didn't back down.

I wasn't going to lie, especially to myself. This hurt. Horribly. "You don't want us here." It was an accusation, pure and simple, without even a hint of a question. I'd told them the situation when I realized I'd have to get Pippa seen to before making the trek to Nashville. It hurt like a motherfucker knowing they didn't care enough about me now to offer us their protection for more than a few hours, but I got it. Didn't mean I liked the idea of my own brothers kicking me and my woman out to save the club. Of course, I hadn't really claimed her as my woman in front of others. Also, Pippa needed to know the score, too. Once she was sober.

"Dawn and Willa are both pregnant again." Cyclone was talking to Ice. Not me.

"And we don't turn away defenseless women. *Or family*. What the fuck's the matter with you?" I don't think I'd ever seen Cliff or Daniel seriously argue. They were always on the same page. Obviously more than a few things had changed since those two took over as president and vice president.

"We didn't even know you were out of prison until you called to tell us you were rolling in!" He turned back to his brother. "You can't tell me you're completely comfortable with this. We've got more than just us and our family to worry about, Cliff. We've got the whole fuckin' club and all their families to worry about, too. If he's brought trouble back with him and someone gets hurt…"

"Then you deal with it." Mama appeared from the shadows and moved to me and Pippa. As she passed Cyclone, she smacked him on the back of the head none too gently. "You don't abandon family, boy," she snapped. "Your father taught you better than that."

"The fuck, Mama!"

"The fuck indeed," she muttered as she ran her hands over Pippa. "I can't believe you'd even entertain the thought of turning your brother and his woman away." She shone a light in Pippa's eyes, pulling up her eyelid as she did.

Pippa cried out and turned her face into my chest, ducking her head. I held her tighter, which seemed to be what she needed. She settled, then turned her head and met Mama's gaze.

"I'm sorry, child," Mama soothed. "I'm a doctor. I only want to make sure you're OK." Mama smiled kindly at Pippa before looking up at me. "Bring her to my clinic, Gunnar." She looked back at Cyclone. "You can stay here, young man. And if you think that just because I love you like a grandson I won't make sure you're stripped of your rank in this club, try pulling a stunt like this again." She gave Cyclone a derisive sniff before turning and heading back to the clubhouse.

I didn't look at my brothers. I wasn't sure I could. Not right now. Instead, I followed Mama and carried Pippa inside, shifting her around so her front was to my chest as I held her close. This wasn't the homecoming I'd envisioned.

"Lay her here." Mama put the head up on the stretcher and put a pillow under Pippa's knees for comfort as well as one behind her head when I did as Mama asked. Pippa whimpered and clung to me when I tried to back away from her. "Don't worry, sweetheart." Mama brushed her fingers over the bruise on Pippa's cheek. "Your man's not going anywhere without you."

Pippa whimpered again, but nodded her head slightly, then took a deep breath. "I'm sorry," she whispered as she let me go.

I took her hand in mine and brought her fingers to my lips. It was an instinctive move on my part, an attempt to soothe her when I didn't really know how. I'd not been in female company for fifteen years. I'd love to say I went out and got laid my first day out of prison, but I had a job to do and I was determined to do it as safely and quickly as I could. Which didn't leave time for learning to be around women. Giving comfort was something I forgot how to do a long fucking time ago.

"You got nothin' to be sorry for, Pipsqueak."

She wrinkled her nose. "Never heard that before."

I grinned at her. "You haven't? Good. That was some of my best work."

"I was being sarcastic." She gave me a tremulous grin.

"Oh, little Miss Sassy?"

She shrugged. "Maybe." Then her smile wavered and her chin quivered as she valiantly fought to keep her composure.

"I like sassy. Lets me know you got fight in you."

She was trembling like a leaf now. I glanced up at Mama and she shook her head slightly, keeping her watchful gaze on Pippa. "I tried to fight them. It's why they hit me."

"Did they..." I trailed off, clearing my throat. "Did they rape you, Pippa?"

She shook her head. "No. A-at least, I don't think so. I-I got hit on the head when they first took me, so I don't know for certain, but I never felt like I'd been touched." Her voice was barely above a whisper. "They tried to keep me drugged, but I can't get high from opioids."

"You seemed like you were pretty high when I found you." I frowned at her, not sure if she'd been hallucinating or maybe trying to convince herself she didn't have any memory gaps. Kind of a self-defense mechanism.

"I was really fuzzy. I know they hit me with a higher dose than normal. My guess is, it was enough to knock out a horse because I don't really have a whole lot of pain. So, yeah. I was really out of it, but I could still process what was happening. I was more startled by the sudden light in the darkness than I was disoriented." I could tell she understood what I was concerned about. I knew she had to be heavily drugged. "I swear, I'm not being delusional. I really do have a resistance to opioids. They take away my pain, but I don't get the euphoric effects."

"When did you need narcotics, child?" Mama had a stethoscope in her ears and placed the bell on Pippa's chest.

"When I had my appendix out. They gave me something to help me relax before they tried to put me under, but it didn't work. Neither did the gas they used to put me under before the procedure. The fact I was affected at all by what those bastards drugged me with means they really hit me hard."

"I'm going to take some blood, honey." Mama tied a tourniquet around Pippa's upper arm before swabbing her inner elbow with an alcohol swab and quickly inserting the needle to take her blood into several tubes. "I've got a friend who'll process this for me with a comprehensive drug screen. I'll know what they used on you in a couple of hours."

"Will you, um, you know." She twisted her fingers together nervously. "Check for other things, too?"

Mama studied her as she finished labeling the tubes with Pippa's name. "I can do the standard HIV/Hepatitis screen. Do you want me to do a swab? Just in case?"

Pippa gave me a sad, resigned look. "I think maybe it's a good idea."

"I'll step just outside the office door and give you privacy, Pippa. But I promise I won't leave. I'll be right back when Mama tells me it's OK." I have no idea why I said that. She might not have cared. Probably didn't care since she didn't know me from Adam. But I had this driving need to take care of her. Maybe it was because I'd already started thinking of her as my old lady. I'd learned how a man should treat his woman from my father and how he treated our mom. What I said to Pippa was something my dad would have said to Mom.

"You promise?" Pippa's gaze was both hopeful but resigned. Like she didn't really expect much, but needed to believe she could have it all.

"Yeah, honey. I promise. All you have to do is holler for me and I'll be in here before you shut your mouth." That got a small smile from her. So I put my hand on her head, leaned in and kissed her forehead. "Not much, but I'll take it. I'm just out here."

"Your name's Gunnar?"

"Yeah, honey. Gunnar Gill."

"Thank you. Thanks for rescuing me." Two tears fell from her luminous eyes, and I felt like I'd been stabbed in the heart.

"You never have to thank me for that." My voice was husky as I tried to swallow the sudden lump in my throat. I pointed to the door. "I'm just out here." She nodded, and I stepped out of Mama's office and shut the door behind me.

I turned around to find Ice and Cyclone standing from where they'd been waiting in the small outer office. I scowled at them, keeping my arms loose at my side in case I needed to defend myself. "Post a guard outside if you want, but I don't want you here."

"Gunnar, we're sorry," Ice offered. Cyclone looked down at his feet, not meeting my gaze.

"Yeah. I can see that. If it makes you feel better, we're only staying until Mama says she can leave. I've already talked to Torpedo and Bohannon. They're gonna take me in at Kiss of Death."

That finally got Cyclone's attention. "Kiss of Death MC. You'd leave Bones? Your home club?"

"This hasn't been my home for fifteen damn years, Dan."

"And whoes fault is that?" Ice -- Cliff -- stepped toward me in an aggressive move. If he thought I would back down from him because he was my older brother, it was time he learned just how wrong he was.

"It's the fault of that son of a bitch Hannah was dating," I snapped back, taking my own aggressive step forward. "One of us had to do it. I happened to be the one there at the time."

"And yours." Ice shoved me back, but I stood my ground. "All you had to do was call Dad. Tell him what happened, and he'd have taken care of it. Why didn't you do that, huh?"

"I had my reasons, and would do the same thing in the same situation. I don't regret one single second of my time in prison."

"What reason could you possibly have for not letting Dad take care of that killin'? No one would have ever found the body or known what happened to that fuck. They certainly wouldn't have been angry with you for killin' him. Why didn't you just let the club do what needed done?"

"Not your business and not something I'm ever gonna tell anyone." I thought I heard Pippa whimper and realized I wasn't calming her anxiety by yelling at my brothers.

Cyclone tilted his head and narrowed his eyes at me. "You don't have to." He and Ice exchanged a look. "Hannah knows."

"Yes," I conceded. "And if she's not told you in the last fifteen years, she's not telling you anything now."

"We'll see." Ice gave me a superior smirk that had made me want to hit him in the head with a rock when I was a kid. Had pretty much the same effect now.

"So, after all these years, *now* you want to know what happened? You guys came by at Christmas and that was it!"

"Dad came every week, askin' for the truth of it.

Begged you to tell him. He's on his way here now, you know. Was on the ground with ExFil in France on some high-profile babysitting detail. I called him right after you called me, and he was on the company jet back to Somerset as of twenty minutes ago. Dad will get this out of you. If he doesn't, I'll get it out of Hannah."

"No. You won't. And neither will Dad. It's done. I served my time. I'll finish my parole and try to find a normal life for myself."

"You can do it here," Ice urged.

"Not happening. Not after the warm welcome I got."

"Why would you expect anything other than the reception you got?" Cyclone was pissed as shit, but he wasn't the only one. "You've been out of prison for *weeks*. You didn't bother to let any of us know. Instead, you dragged a half dead woman into the compound, not knowing if you were followed or not, and you still expect a warm welcome?"

I lunged for my older brother, driving the heel of my hand into his chin. From the way his eyes widened the split second after I moved, Cyclone had thought he'd see any move I made in time to defend himself, if not get the jump on me and go on the offensive. What he hadn't realized was, telegraphing your movements like that in prison would get you killed. I'd gotten good at being unpredictable and fast. Another strike out with my hand smashed his nose.

This time Cyclone stumbled backward, backing off to reassess the situation. He wasn't giving up, but neither was I.

"What the fuck is going on out here?" Mama threw open the door and stomped between me and Cyclone. She shouldn't have bothered because Cyclone was shaking his head as he backed off. "Daniel Gill, get your ass outta my office! If you can't be a decent fuckin' human being, don't come in here anymore. And this is your *only* warning." Mama stomped the two steps separating the two of us and jabbed her finger against his chest. "Next time you say or do something utterly stupid, I will call for your fuckin' patch."

"How do you know it was me who was stupid?"

"Really, Cyclone?" I drawled. "Are we twelve?"

He rolled his eyes. "You know what I mean. Why assume it was me?"

Mama smacked the side of his head. "Because when you get something in your head, you won't leave it alone. You're pissed at your baby brother because he grew up faster than you and doesn't need your help anymore. And while you're trying to take out your anger on Gunnar, you're also taking it out on a young woman who doesn't deserve anyone's anger. Gunnar can take care of himself. Right now, Pippa cannot."

Cyclone winced. "Fuck. I didn't think about it that way."

"You didn't fuckin' think at all," Mama snapped. "Now stop being such a fuckwit and admit you missed your brother."

Cyclone rubbed the back of his neck, glancing between Mama and me with a pained expression. "I... fuck. You're right," he admitted grudgingly. "I've been an asshole."

I clenched my jaw, seconds from walking out, leaving Bones for good. I mean, I *was* leaving. How long I stayed gone and to what extent I kept in touch was still up for debate. The tension was palpable and the absolute only reason I hadn't already gotten the hell outta Dodge was because I wasn't leaving Pippa behind. Not even with Mama and Pops.

"I'm only here until Mama says Pippa is OK to travel. Last thing I want to do is bring trouble to your door." I did my best to keep the sneer out of my voice but wasn't sure I managed. "Torpedo and Bohannon said we could hole up there as long as we like."

"Stay here, Gunnar." Ice held out a hand to me, wanting me to take it. I wanted to, but I wasn't ready. I knew everyone was angry with me for how things went down. Not because I'd confessed to killing the man who'd assaulted my sister, but for me not even trying to fight the charges and mount a defense. But mostly for making my mother cry.

"I don't think that's the best idea. For so many damned reasons I don't even want to think about them." We were all silent for a long moment, them studying me, me studying them. All three of us trying to figure out how to get the upper hand. Finally, it was Cyclone who broke the silence. I'd never wanted to hit my brother more in my life than I did in that moment.

"You want to get out of here before either of them can get here." Cyclone sat back in a chair and crossed one ankle over the opposite knee, all smug like he'd won this round. Which he might have. "Who are you afraid of seeing most? You know. Now that you're out of prison and all the monitors and guards and inmates listening aren't a factor?" That smug expression on his face was nearly my undoing. "Mom? Or Hannah?"

"Fuckin' Christ." Mama grabbed my upper arm and tugged me back inside her clinic before I could attack my brother again. "When Angel and Hannah get here, the two of you are on your own. You've effectively ruined any chance of convincing Gunnar to keep Pippa here instead of leaving just when Angel got him back." She shot my brothers an angry, exasperated look. "God help you when Cain finds you, because this time, it's not Gunnar who'll make your mother cry. And your father will be less tolerant with the two of you than he was with Gunnar because your infraction was completely uncalled for." She shoved me toward Pippa where my woman lay on the stretcher, then shut the door behind us.

Chapter Three

Pippa

I could hear Gunnar arguing with the men outside. It sounded like they were pissed as shit, but I couldn't make out much of it because my ears were ringing and the room was spinning. "Why did I have to experience my first time being high like this?" I had no idea who I was talking to or even if anyone was there.

"Not to worry, dear." An older woman with steel-gray hair and piercing blue eyes leaned over me and gave me a kind smile. "I'm sure there will be other, more enjoyable times to explore."

"No, there won't." I was emphatic, shaking my head, which only made the disorientation worse. "I'd never be able to afford the amount of drugs it took to get me this high."

She handed me a bottle of water. "Drink up, child. The more fluids you get in you, the better you'll feel."

She was right. I was thirsty as shit so I took a long pull, savoring the cool liquid sliding down my throat like I hadn't been able to before. In the Humvee I'd been hurt, scared, and more than a little nauseous. I know I managed to drink some, but not nearly enough. Now that I'd had a moment to register just how delicious it was, I gulped down several more swallows. Mama helped me undress, making sure to always keep me covered. I swear, the woman was a saint. Gunnar had put clean clothes on me when he'd found me, so my clothes weren't soiled enough they needed to be thrown out. It was more the thought of what they represented. Mama tossed the garments in the trash and tied the bag shut without a word.

"The night they took me, I was at a party for a friend's birthday." I wasn't sure why I was telling Mama this, but I wanted to get it out now for some reason. "We'd all gone to a local bar and I snuck in. Since I hadn't planned on ordering myself anything other than water or soda, I figured I'd be OK as long as I stayed away from anyone who might check an I.D. after I got in. A guy struck up a conversation with me and handed me a drink. Obviously, those were my first and second mistakes all rolled into one."

Mama raised an eyebrow at me. "Which were?"

"First, I'm not old enough to drink and had never drunk before. I thought I was prepared but I grossly underestimated the atmosphere. The first time, in a bar, by myself, was not the place to experiment with alcohol, but I liked the guy and wanted to fit in. My second mistake was also because I'm not old enough to drink and I had to rely on someone else to purchase my drinks. Which meant accepting something intentionally mind-altering from a man I didn't know, that I couldn't verify hadn't been laced with something."

She stared at me for several seconds before I spoke. "That's a bunch of lessons."

I huffed out a breath. "You know what I mean!"

"Of course, I do. So he *did* drug you."

I shrugged. "I don't know."

"You... don't know?"

"We were at that bar for hours. He kept ordering me drinks and I kept accepting them. We laughed and flirted. I'd indicated I'd be interested in sex, but he hadn't taken the step to take me outside. Probably because I was nowhere near drunk.

"After a while, he got agitated. I thought he was mad at me and told him I thought it was best if I leave, but he smiled and said he'd had a stressful day at work. He did a double shot of whisky and soon after was back to his charming self. Anytime I thought he was going to lose his temper, he'd take another drink.

"I caught him stirring my drink with his finger once. He said they'd shorted me on the alcohol, and he'd topped my glass off with some of his and was mixing it so it would blend properly. Again, I should have been suspicious, but I was having fun. It was the first time I'd ever been to something like that party and I wanted to experience all the moment had to offer."

"You're too reckless with your own life, sweetheart. You need someone to have your back." Mama sat on the edge of my bed and took my hand in hers. "What happened then?"

"We just... kept drinking. He was matching me drink for drink after a while. After he'd touched my drink before, I watched him closely. I knew I wasn't going to get drunk, judging by the fact this guy was about to fall off the barstool and I was starting to seriously believe I'd been drinking the foulest tasting water known to man. Because I've decided I'm seriously not a fan of whisky. It burns. And I *still* wasn't drunk."

"I think I see what you mean. You said this was the night they took you. How did they get you out of that bar and to their compound?"

"Three more guys approached us after that. I got up to pretend to go to the bathroom so I could bolt, but two of the men dragged the first guy off while the biggest of the three clamped a hand over my mouth and pulled me around the corner of the bar and out the back, then one of them hit me in the head and knocked me silly long enough to get me inside their van.

"They shot me up with more drugs in the back of

a van on the way to the place Gunnar found me. I kept fighting and they kept shooting me up. It took them five tries before I was finally incapacitated. I heard them complain while they held me in that place how keeping me drugged was going to seriously eat into their profits if they had to hold on to me long."

Mama looked equal parts pissed as shit and slightly amused. "Impressive. Did they keep you drugged the whole time you were there?"

I shook my head. "I don't think they could have. Every time they drugged me, the more it took to put me under. At some point, I'm sure I'm going to withdraw from whatever they gave me. At least, I guess that's how it works. I don't feel the need to have more, and I'm really glad the fog is lifting. The conversation with you helped to brush back some cobwebs."

"Good. Now. Let's see if we can get the worst of the grime off you before putting clean clothes on." She had a basin of warm, soapy water and a couple of washcloths. She took one and I took the other. I worked on my front while Mama was behind me working on my back. She let me do what I could, but I was still really weak, and in the end she had to help me finish. Once done, she brought me some soft cotton shorts and a T-shirt, along with an unopened pack of underwear. "Let's get you dressed, then we can check on the boys before they start World War Three in my lobby."

The voices of the men outside the door got louder. I recognized Gunnar's voice, even though I hadn't had a real conversation with him. I doubt I'd ever forget his voice.

"Oh, for heaven's sake." Exasperated, Mama stomped to the door and yanked it open. "What the fuck is going on out here?" She closed the door firmly behind her.

I sat up, turning to let my legs hang over the side of the small bed. My head still had a few cobwebs but the conversation with Mama had helped. Other than kind of being sick to my stomach, I didn't hurt anywhere else. Though, I was pretty sure I looked terrible and smelled like shit. I thought it funny that I felt safe enough to worry about my appearance and personal hygiene given everything I'd gone through.

Of all the people I expected to make any kind of appearance in my life, Knuckles hadn't been on the Bingo card. Of course, my mother had told me about him, and I'd be lying if I said even the thought of Knuckles didn't terrify me, but given the circumstances, if he'd sent Gunnar to rescue me, then I'd trust him and Gunnar until they proved to be untrustworthy.

Besides, I was fairly certain Knuckles would do whatever he had to, to get me to safety. He'd told me once he'd always watch over me. Now, I knew exactly who I could trust to have my back. But only Gunnar and Knuckles. Everyone else could kiss my ass and lick the hole. Even Mama. She projected nothing but calm and reassurance, but it wasn't hard to see there was something dangerous about her. Even though she had to be in her seventies, she wore a tank top that showed her arms and a flash of midriff when she moved. Sure, her skin was aging and not as tight as a younger woman's, but Mama was more fit than most women less than half her age. She was definitely not someone I wanted to underestimate.

Mama opened the door, tugging Gunnar with her by his upper arm. "Inside, Gunnar. Go sit with your woman." OK, *that* tone of voice from Mama was new. She'd seemed like the soft-spoken grandma type. Not so much now. She gave a little shake of her head. "Hard-headed bastards. All of 'em." She fixed her gaze on me and pursed her lips. "I'm sorry, Pippa. We're not usually so unwelcoming to newcomers. Especially when they come to us with one of our own." Her tone was back to being gentle and sweet, but now that I'd seen that small peek of who this woman really was, I couldn't unsee it.

"I don't want to cause problems. Especially not with family." I wanted to look at Gunnar, but couldn't bring myself to do it. If I saw regret or condemnation in his eyes, it might well be my undoing. And I really had no idea why I'd latched on to this man. Because, logically, I knew it was the idea he represented. The black knight on a white steed. The bad guy tempered with the smallest bit of good. A man who could keep me from ever getting kidnapped again, and who would punish those who took me in the first place. That was Gunnar. I knew I could trust him, no matter what.

"Trust me when I tell you, Pippa, my dear, none of this is your fault. It's this one refusing to let his family help him when he was little more than a child, and those knuckleheads out there for being knuckleheads." Her dry tone was the perfect reflection of the look she leveled on Gunnar. "Now. Here's what's going to happen."

"Uh-oh." Gunnar dropped his head. "Here it comes."

"Excuse me, young man?" If there was ever the stereotypical image of a cross Catholic nun, Mama looked every inch of her. Well, except for the tank top displaying toned, leathered skin, the thick, steel-gray hair in a long braid down her back, the leather pants and motorcycle boots. But hey! The pants were black and the top white. Same colors.

Gunnar raised his hands in surrender. "Nothin', Mama. Nothin' at all. Please continue."

Mama let her disapproving stare linger on Gunnar until he lowered his gaze in surrender. "Pippa." When she turned her focus back to me, her gaze was once again warm and welcoming. The sweet little granny about to impart the most insightful advice imaginable. "You go take a shower and clean up. I'll help with your hair when you get out. We'll get you feeling more like yourself in no time."

Gunnar sighed heavily. "Mama --"

"No arguments, Gunnar. This is happening."

"You know why I want to get us out of here."

"I do. And it's time you sucked it up and told your father and mother what happened. Not for yourself, but for Hannah. She isn't the type to keep anything from Cain and Angel and her guilt has been eating her alive for fifteen years. And not just because she didn't tell them what happened. She stabbed a man to death. Sure, he was trying to rape her, but she took his life. Up close and personal. Because you told her not to say a word, she felt like she owed you whatever you asked of her. Hannah's kept everything bottled up inside. She's going to destroy herself. I know you tried to take all the blame and the punishment, but she lost the same fifteen years of her life as you did."

Gunnar grunted like she'd struck him, and I immediately reached for Gunnar's hand. "Please don't be mean to him. I don't think he's a bad person. I don't believe you think he is either."

Mama gave me an impatient glare. "Of course, he's not a bad person. He confessed to murdering his sister's boyfriend because he said the guy had threatened to hurt Hannah. The fact was, Hannah had killed the bastard when he tried to rape her. She had a knife her father and brothers insisted she keep on her. When things got rough, she stabbed the bastard in the kidney. Gunnar took the rap so nothing would touch his sister and, in the process, cut his parents out of the decision-making process and pled guilty. Those, my dear, are not the actions of a bad person. Maybe someone a little shy in the brains department, but not a bad person at all."

There was a soft gasp, and I noticed a striking, petite woman with soft brown hair streaked with silver. She looked to be in her early- to mid-fifties. At first, I thought I must look worse than I thought, but she wasn't looking at me. She was staring at Gunnar with a heartbreaking mixture of shock, pain, grief, and love.

"Mom, this isn't a good idea." Ice tried to grab his mother's arm. Cyclone was right behind them. Both men glanced at Mama, who leveled her gaze on them like the strictest teacher known to man. "Gunnar and, uh, his, uh, friend there, will be out in a minute."

The woman shoved herself away from her sons and moved toward Gunnar in a daze. "You're home?"

"Yeah, Mom. I'm home."

She lunged for Gunnar, throwing her arms around him and sobbing like her heart was breaking. I knew she'd heard what Mama had said, but she didn't comment on it. I was pretty sure that would come later.

Mama moved to my side and put her hand on my shoulder and squeezed. She gave me an encouraging look but said nothing until Gunnar's mother finally pulled back to look at her son. She framed his face in her hands and stroked his face like he was the most precious thing in her world.

"Angel?" When Gunnar's mother looked back at Mama, she continued. "This is Pippa. Gunnar rescued her from a rival club at the request of his cellmate."

Angel gasped before her gaze darted to me. "Oh, no. Are you hurt, Pippa? How can I help?"

"I..." I had no idea what to say. Was I hurt? Maybe not physically, but I wasn't sure I'd ever be the same person I was before I was taken. The more people I didn't know surrounded me, the more anxious I was. "I'm fine."

"Mom, I promise I'll sit down and talk to you later, but I'm taking Pippa to Nashville. Torpedo and Bohannon have agreed to take me in at Kiss of Death."

"You're not staying here?" Angel looked from Gunnar to me and back. "There's no reason you both can't stay." She looked at me, taking a step toward me as if pleading for me to tell Gunnar to stay with his family. "I might be able to help you. You know. Talk. Me and Suzie both were taken by a member of Kiss of Death before Cain and Torpedo decided to take it over. That was years ago. But I know how terrified and helpless I felt before I escaped."

I gasped before turning to look at Gunnar for some context because Kiss of Death sounded like the kind of place I wanted to avoid at all costs. He shrugged. "The men who were responsible for takin' women and children are dead. The club was purged. Torpedo and Bohannon kept the name because it was established in the area already. Despite being run by murderers and pedophiles, Cain said their reputation for doing business was impeccable. Besides, apparently having it known that Bones cleaned the scourge that was Kiss of Death without a trace left helps keep rival MCs and local gangs in line."

Then Gunnar gave Cyclone a hard look. "And

there is a reason we can't stay, Mom. I'll be in touch, and you'll know where I am. I already texted you my new number, but I'll do it again in case you missed it or didn't recognize the number and ignored it."

It was obvious Gunnar was doing his best to remain calm around his mother. It was also obvious how much he was hurting with every second he was in her presence. Angel seemed like a good person and was super concerned about Gunnar, but if she'd made him feel like he was an embarrassment to her because he'd been in prison, I might have to hurt her. No matter how much Gunnar loved her, I wasn't about to watch the man who'd risked his life to get me out of hell, then saw to my safety be degraded or belittled.

"I've not even had a chance to talk to you. Surely you can stay tonight." Again, she smiled in my direction. "Besides, you haven't had the chance to introduce me to Pippa." Angel's eyes glistened with unshed tears, and I softened toward the other woman. Yeah, there was no need to worry Angel thought her son less somehow for what he'd done and gone through. This was a woman who was just grateful to have her son back.

Gunnar pulled his mother into his arms and held her tight. "I've missed you, Mom. I'm sorry about what happened."

"Is what Mama said true? Did you take the blame for that bastard's death?" Angel didn't let go of her son or insist on looking him in the eyes when she asked. It was almost like she didn't really want to know. I could imagine it, because it sounded like Gunnar's sister was carrying a boatload of guilt.

"Does it matter, Mom? I mean, *really* matter? I'm out. I'm OK. Now, I'm trying to be the kind of man Dad always expected me to be."

"Honey, you *are* the man your dad wanted you to be and have been for a long time. Since before you went to prison. What you did was something your dad would have done. If he tries to tell you how he'd have been smart and asked for help, he's lying." Angel finally pulled back and smiled at her son, laying her hand on his cheek again. "When I came to see you a few weeks ago, and they told me you weren't there, I was scared out of my mind." She took in a shuddering breath. "Especially since the last time I saw you, we fought."

Gunnar sighed. "I wasn't angry at you, Mom. I was worried about Hannah and took out my fear and frustration on you. Every week you came to visit, you asked me to tell you what happened. Without exception. Every week for fifteen years. I'd have been worried if you hadn't asked." He glanced away. "It would have felt like you'd given up on me."

"I've missed you so much, honey. I know Hannah didn't come often, but I see now she felt guilty. I could see it in her every day and thought it was because she looked at it as you going to jail because she ratted out that bastard. Now, I know why."

"Is she with you?"

"Yes. She's probably standing outside the door wringing her hands. It's what she's done since she found out you were out of prison. Each day that passed without us hearing from you, the more she withdrew from us."

Gunnar gave me a helpless look, like he didn't know what to do, when I'd bet my life this man was never indecisive.

"Go hug your sister," I said softly. "Sounds like you both got shit on, and she's hurting just as badly as you are."

He hesitated but reached over to squeeze my hand. "I won't be long."

"No. You *need* to spend some time with your mother and sister. You need this. Sounds like they do too."

"How about we compromise." Gunnar stepped closer to me, holding my hand in both of his. "You take a bath and clean up. Take as much time as you want. Lay down and sleep the rest of that drug off. I'll come get you in a couple of hours and we'll head south."

"They said your dad was out of the country or something, earlier? Did I hear that?"

"Yeah. He's on his way back now, but it's a long-ass flight."

"I think you really might be avoiding your father." I kept my expression as blank as I could until Mama barked out a laugh before clapping a hand over her face. Then Angel and Mama both started laughing and I couldn't help but smile.

Gunnar shook his head, but he was grinning. "Wait until you meet my dad. You'll understand."

Chapter Four

Gunnar

I had no intention of waiting around until my dad got here. Not necessarily because I didn't want to face him yet, though I'd admit to being a little... apprehensive. If my brothers had given us this kind of welcome, I had no idea if they were playing off my father or simply protecting their families. I could kind of understand the second, but if that was the case, they didn't see me and Pippa as important as the rest of the family. I was already roiling on the inside. The last thing I wanted was confirmation of how badly I'd fucked up with my dad.

Pippa squeezed my hand and gave me a small smile. She was doing this for me when I could tell she didn't want to be by herself. But she didn't know me. I thought she might trust me since I'd been the one to rescue her, but she had to be questioning everything around her after finding out what I'd done. It was just one more blow to my chest, because I intended to keep my promise to Knuckles. I would claim Pippa as my old lady whether she wanted me to or not. With that claim, I'd treat her with the respect an old lady deserves. If she didn't want me in any other capacity, that was her choice, but I'd always be there to protect and care for her until I died, or Knuckles revoked the privilege.

"Mama, is there somewhere Pippa can have some privacy to clean up and rest?"

"You can bring her home," my mother interjected, reaching out to take Pippa's hand. Mom looked like she was barely holding on to more tears. Though she was trying to give Pippa a welcoming smile, her lower lip trembled and her eyes were glossy with unshed tears.

"I don't think that's a good idea, Mom." I tried to be as gentle as I could while trying to do what I felt was best for Pippa. I wanted her comfortable. While my mother and sister would be nice to Pippa, I knew my brothers didn't want us here, not really, and having us stay for any length of time would cause friction between my mother and sister and my brothers. And I hadn't even seen Hannah yet.

"Just until you get ready to leave." Mom gave me a pleading look. "That way you won't have to leave Pippa in a strange place by herself." Trust my mother to cut to the root of the problem. She had always known me better than anyone else.

"I have a better idea." Mama crossed her arms over her chest and glanced to the door where my brothers were just outside. "You can bring Pippa to my house. Pops can keep out anyone you don't want to talk with, and you will be close to Pippa."

"Surely you don't think someone would hurt Pippa while she's inside this compound." My mother looked from me to Mama. "This is the safest place she could possibly be."

"Angel, the president and vice president of Bones are under the impression they are protecting the women and children in the club. Given both their wives are pregnant, their protective instincts are on high alert."

Mom narrowed her eyes at Mama before looking back to my brothers. "Gunnar would never put this club or anyone inside it in danger intentionally. He's family. Anyone he says needs our protection will get it." Her fierce defense of me chipped away at the ice around my heart. It was hard enough to see my mother this upset, because I knew how much her family meant to her. She would be horrified that my brothers would even consider turning us out on our own.

"Like it or not, Mom, they're doing what's best for the club and everyone inside. I can take care of Pippa. I have a plan in place. We'll be all right."

Mom's gaze flitted to Pippa, then back to Mama before reluctantly nodding. No doubt she'd hoped to get me home so she could convince me to stay. If I was honest, part of me wanted to go with her. I'd been sixteen when I'd gone to prison. I wasn't a kid by any means, but I still missed my mother. Seeing her on the other side of bulletproof glass or in a room with a dozen or more people I didn't know where half of them were convicted felons just wasn't the same. I hadn't been able to give her a hug in fifteen years. Or Hannah.

"I thought Pippa was your woman." Mom looked confused as she looked back at Mama. "You said she was his woman."

"She's his." Mama didn't sound the least bit unsure. "He just hasn't told her yet."

"This isn't the place for this." My soft tone was deceptive because I was starting to get pissed. Mama was the best of the best. She'd helped raise me and all my brothers and sisters, but she was deliberately pushing me, trying to bully me into telling my parents everything. The truth was, I wasn't ready. But more importantly, the last thing I wanted to do was frighten Pippa.

"What haven't you told me?" Pippa met my gaze with wide, guileless eyes when I suspected she was anything but. She was trying to pretend there wasn't a possibility she was in a worse situation than what she'd just escaped.

"I swear I'll tell you later, but I think you really

need some food, a shower, and some rest. But I promise you, you're safe. And you have the right to refuse any claim I have on you. This is as much for your protection as it was to keep a promise to a very good friend."

"Knuckles?"

"Yeah, baby. Knuckles asked me to rescue you and protect you after I got you free. He told me to make you my old lady, so that's what I'm gonna do. How much you want to be involved with me is up to you, but you will have my property patch and the protection of my club."

"Isn't this your club?" Her expression was carefully neutral, but I could tell she was trying to make a point. Bones should have been my club. Cain had been letting me go with them on runs and teaching me how to handle myself in combat, all trying to prepare me for taking my place in the club and in my father's paramilitary organization, ExFil. I had planned on putting in my time in the military, maybe even doing teams training and serving an extended enlistment. All with the goal of taking my place with the rest of my family as part of Bones. In a way, Bones MC was more important to me than anything on that list of life goals because Bones was family. Until everything changed.

"It was." I smiled to soften the blow those words caused to myself. "And it will always be important to me. But I chose this path. Now I have to accept the consequences and follow it. Kiss of Death has some family too. Just as close as everyone here. Mom knows that. Everything will work out."

Pippa's gaze shifted to the door where Ice and Cyclone stood just outside the open clinic door, listening and whispering to each other. "I think you're right." When she met my gaze again, she held it. "I'll trust you. You know what's best. They might not want us here, but they've not said anything to indicate you're like the people you rescued me from. Besides, you've been really nice to me. I'd probably be…" She trailed off and the color drained from her face. "I don't want to think about it."

"You don't have to because it's not going to happen. I swore to Knuckles I'd protect you with my life, and that's what I intend on doing." I grinned at her before addressing Mama. "We'll take you up on your offer, Mama." When Mom gave a distressed whimper, Ice went to her, putting his arms around her. "I want you and Hannah to come with me and Pippa. I need to spend as much time with the two of you as I can before me and Pippa leave. I've missed you, and I want Pippa to know you guys."

Mom gave me a watery smile. "We missed you too. Mama, me, and Hannah will come to you in a bit. I need to make a stop to pick up some clothes for Pippa." Mom smiled at my woman. "I don't have time to get anything expensive, but I can get you new underwear, socks, and shoes, as well as a couple pairs of jeans and three or four T-shirts. If you have to leave, we'll make sure you're ready for the trip." Mom brushed a tear from her cheek as she reached for Pippa, pulling her into a warm embrace. "Please don't judge us because Cliff and Daniel are being assholes. They're not bad men either. Just… hurt their little brother didn't need their help."

Mom let Pippa go but not before she spilled more tears as she traced one dark bruise on Pippa's face with gentle fingers. "I'm so sorry this happened to you."

Pippa shrugged, trying for a tremulous smile but coming up a little short. "It worked out. At least, I hope it has." Pippa lowered her gaze. She obviously had her doubts -- and I didn't blame her -- but I thought she was probably too weak and tired to worry about it.

"Good, then." Mama had been busy moving around the room getting supplies she thought she might need. I knew she had things at her house, but all her medicines were here where she used them most. "I let Pops know you'd need your own room and he's making sure you're all set. If you don't mind, I'd like to give you a tetanus shot and a shot of penicillin. When I get your test results back, I can give you something else if need be."

Pippa nodded. "Absolutely. I was gonna ask if you thought I needed something."

"I've got you covered, dear. Before you leave, Pops will bring you a phone. It will have mine and Angel's numbers in it. I want you to promise to call one of us if you don't feel well, or if you just need some female backup. We'll round up the old ladies in force and burn that place to the ground if they don't treat you right."

"I'd like to think you're kidding, but I really don't think you are." Pippa's smile was genuine this time. And so fucking beautiful I almost fell to my knees and worshiped her. She had to be terrified out of her mind, but she was easily the most beautiful woman I'd ever seen. It was at that moment I knew I'd do anything to have with this woman what my mother and father had. What Mama and Pops had. What so many of my friends had found while I was locked away.

This woman was my destiny. I knew it like I knew my own name. My life was finally coming into focus with a clarity I'd never expected. Now all I had to do was prove myself worthy of her which… That ship had already sailed. No way a man who'd gone to prison for murder was good enough for the angelic vision before me.

Fine. I might not be worthy of her, but I'd be the most vicious protector anyone could find for her. She'd be my most treasured possession, the person I kept safe and close at all times. I'd be the demon to her angel. And I'd give my last Goddamned breath to see her safe and happy for the rest of my life.

* * *

Pippa

Gunnar helped me into the big-ass Humvee we'd used to get to this place. His touch was gentle as he made sure I was settled comfortably in the back seat next to him. I didn't buckle my seat belt because, now that it had been a while since I'd been drugged and all that shit was finally getting out of my system, I was starting to feel every ache and pain I had from my extended stay in hell. I was exhausted and sore, but determined to stay awake for the drive to Mama's house.

"It's not far." Gunnar put his arm around me in an awkward gesture. It was almost like he didn't know what to do with himself. Like he wanted to touch me but was unsure how to go about it. "Just a couple minutes and you can get some decent food in you and rest."

I nodded, giving him a small smile. "Just tired. And really looking forward to that shower."

He chuckled, leaning in to brush a kiss against my temple. It wasn't a gesture he seemed comfortable with but either felt like he should, or he wanted to and wasn't sure how to go about it. "I bet. Everything's gonna be fine. I'll take care of everything."

I couldn't lie, even to myself. The idea someone had my back and would protect me until I could get my life back was comforting on an elemental level. I hadn't had the meltdown I needed, and I knew it would come. I suppose when the time came, I'd find out exactly how serious Gunnar was about this whole old lady thing. Assuming that was like a wife or a permanent relationship. I wasn't savvy with biker lingo. After the last month of my life in that horrible place, I wasn't as alarmed by Gunnar inserting himself into my life as I probably should be.

As we drove, I couldn't help sneaking glances at Gunnar. He was incredibly handsome in a very edgy, even deadly, way. With his shaggy dark hair and intense eyes, he had my attention. But more than that, there was a quiet strength about him that made me feel safe. Probably because he'd rescued me and I knew getting in and out of the place had been more of a feat than I had been able to appreciate at the time. I knew I shouldn't trust him so quickly after everything I'd been through, but I couldn't help it. Simply being near him made me feel safe. No matter how awkward his gestures. The man was trying. The more I thought about it, the more I kind of found it charming.

He was right about the ride. It was less than two minutes. It actually took longer for the men who brought us here to get out of the vehicle with all the crap they had on their tactical vests. Gunnar didn't have a vest on now, but I had vague memories of being juggled around so he could shrug his vest off once we were on the road after my rescue.

We pulled up in front of a ranch-style house. It was by far the biggest in the area, and the whole compound seemed to have been built around this house and the main clubhouse where we'd met Mama.

The main building was more like an older resort hotel or something. There was even a courtyard in the back. Mama's house wasn't far from the main building, but far enough there was room for other houses to spring up near it, making Mama and Pops -- whom I had yet to meet -- the center of the club.

"I thought you bastards would never bring that sweet girl here so she could eat and rest." A man who looked to be a few years older than Mama exited the house and skipped down the three steps from the porch like a youngster. He had on faded jeans and a tight, white T-shirt. He had to be at least as old as Mama and, again, though his skin was aged and sun-leathered, he had firm, bulky muscle underneath. He wasn't as big as the other men around us, but there was something in his gaze that told me he was more dangerous than he seemed. "I've got burgers and dogs hot off the grill with all the fixins. Best I could do in a couple of hours."

Mama got out of the Explorer the women had come in as the man spoke. "I think that will do just fine, Pops. Can't go wrong there." She smiled and went to the older man. He pulled her to him with one arm and kissed the top of her head before letting her go. Mama looked up at him and gave the man a soft smile, then she came to me. "Come on, Pippa. Do you want food or a shower first?"

"I think the crackers you let me nibble on earlier along with the water will let me get clean first." I cringed as I fingered my hair. "I'm not sure even a shower is gonna fix this mess."

Mama put her arm around me, effectively removing me from Gunnar's reach with little effort. I looked over my shoulder and whimpered before I could stop myself.

Gunnar immediately stepped closer, his brow furrowed with concern as he reached for me, taking my hand in his firm grip. "What's wrong, Pippa? Are you in pain?"

I shook my head, feeling foolish. "No, I just... I don't want you to leave." The words tumbled out before I could stop them.

His expression softened. "I'm not going anywhere, Pippa. I'll be here when you're done getting cleaned up. If it will make you feel better, I'll stand guard outside the bathroom. You need me -- for anything -- call out and I'll break the Goddamned door down to get to you." The more he said, the fiercer his expression, the tighter his hold on my hand until he tugged me away from Mama and wrapped his arms around me in a tight embrace.

Mama patted my arm reassuringly, trying to extract me from Gunnar's hold, but he simply growled at her. Instead of backing down, this tiny, grandmotherly woman pulled me away from Gunnar with gentle encouragement. "Don't you worry, dear. Gunnar will be waiting for you when you're ready. Now let's get you that shower so you can feel more like yourself."

I nodded, allowing Mama to guide me into the house. As we walked, I glanced back one more time to see Gunnar watching me intently. The intensity in his gaze made my breath catch.

Once inside the house, Mama led me to a bedroom in the back of the house. "There are fresh towels and unopened toiletries in the bathroom just there." She pointed to a door in the back corner which was slightly ajar. "Take as long as you need. I've brought you a few things until Angel and Hannah get here with more for the longer haul." She dropped a small bundle of items on the bed just as Gunnar entered the room.

"Thank you," I said softly. "For everything."

Mama patted my shoulder gently. "You're safe now. That one will see to it you stay that way." She nodded in Gunnar's direction. "If there's something you need that I missed, let Gunnar know and I'll bring it to you." She handed me a small flip phone. "It's not fancy, but it will let you do what you need. It's also easy to part with if you get in a pinch and are afraid someone is tracking you."

"I hadn't even thought of that," I whispered. Looking up at Gunnar I know I looked wide-eyed and afraid. "Do you think they'll come after me?"

"Honey, we didn't leave anyone alive in that fucking hellhole, and Torpedo's people cleaned any evidence *anyone* was ever there. Even if someone suspects what went down, there's no proof of anything, digital or physical."

"But --"

Gunnar cut me off. "*But* if someone comes after us, we've got backup. And I'll protect you with my life. No one's gonna hurt you again, Pippa."

The sincere determination on his face settled something inside me. I was still kind of numb -- I was still a little woozy from the lingering effects of the drug I'd been given -- but it was easier to relax. The shower I was getting ready to take might actually make me feel human on the outside now that my insides were feeling better.

"OK." It was an inane thing to say, but I believed everything Gunnar said. With my whole being.

He gave me the most heartbreakingly gentle smile I'd ever seen, and tears threatened to overwhelm me. "OK," he whispered.

I took the clothing Mama had given me into the bathroom and shut the door, leaning back against it. I took in great gulps of air as I slid to the floor, my legs no longer able to support me. I wanted to cry. Wanted to scream and rage against the whole fucking world and people who could do such evil to other people for money. Maybe I had more of my dad in me than my mother wanted because, right now, I wished those bastards were still alive so I could kill them myself.

I forced myself to take several deep breaths, trying to calm the storm of emotions threatening to overwhelm me. The urge to break down was strong, but I knew if I started crying now I might not stop. And I desperately wanted to feel clean again.

With my body trembling, I pushed myself up off the floor and started peeling off the clothing I'd been given after Mama's exam. The need to feel human again overrode my exhaustion. If I sat on the floor of the shower and fell asleep, at least some more of the grime would be gone.

I avoided looking in the mirror, not wanting to see how awful I looked or how badly my hair was tangled. Instead, I focused on turning on the shower and adjusting the temperature. My hair hung below my waist in a long, thick mass of curls. There was no doubt in my mind I'd have to cut at least some of it, if not just fucking shave it all. Which, as I touched the tangled, knotted mess now, I admitted to myself wasn't the worst idea. In fact, I'd put the likelihood of me buzzing it all off at some point in the coming minutes as more probable than possible.

As I stepped under the hot spray, I let out an involuntary sob. Yeah, I needed that breakdown to happen later rather than sooner because I had the feeling if it happened now, I'd have a man I didn't know in the shower with me whether I wanted him to be or not. Though I'd admired him earlier, I wasn't in any shape mentally or physically for what would happen if he decided to make good on the old lady stuff.

The water felt heavenly against my skin, washing away any lingering grime and fear. Needing to feel clean, I'd turned the water as hot as I could stand it. I stood there for several long minutes, just letting the water sluice over me before reaching for the shampoo. Three washings later, my hair started to feel clean again, though I probably would have to do it again later. My arms were too heavy to continue. I did manage to work some conditioner through what wasn't matted together, but only because I knew there wouldn't be a snowball's chance in hell of working the knots out otherwise.

As I turned the water off, there was a knock at the door. "Pippa?" *Knock.* "You all right?" Another knock.

"Um, yeah." My voice shook. More from exhaustion than fear. "Just a little wobbly."

"Did you fall?" There was alarm in his voice. "I'm coming in!"

"No, wait!"

The door was shoved open. I'd locked it on reflex, but this guy broke the door facing with alarming ease. His gaze tracked the small room, looking for threats before focusing on the floor. He read the room so fast it had to have been instinct. "Did you slip? Are you hurt?" When he brought his gaze to me, he eyed me with a clinical gaze until he realized I wasn't hurt.

I stood sideways with one arm over my breasts and one frantically reaching for a towel, which was when I finally did lose my footing. With a cry, I toppled sideways. Right into Gunnar's waiting arms.

Chapter Five

Gunnar

I was gonna die. And I was going to hell. I had a naked woman in my arms. One who had been the sole focus of my existence for four weeks. The same woman I'd sworn to my only friend I'd give the protection of my property patch and make her my old lady. Everything in me was screaming to take care of her, not to objectify her or even look at her as anything other than a young woman who was hurting and vulnerable. Unfortunately, my dick didn't get the Goddamned message.

"I'm so sorry!" Pippa clung to me, breathing hard. She kicked out, trying to get her feet under her, but I lifted her with my arm around her waist. She sucked in a breath, her eyes going wide. "Gunnar?" That breathless whimper was the only thing keeping me from seeing how far she let me take us. But there was no way she was able to consent to anything. And I wasn't nearly ready my own damned self.

"Are you OK?" My voice was a husky groan as need punched through my body like a spear.

She nodded, looking up at me. I couldn't tell if she was frightened or not, but instead of resting passively in my arms, she gripped my shoulders and pulled herself closer to me. Her breasts were mashed against my chest, and I couldn't stop myself from shuddering.

"Words, honey." I cleared my throat. "I need words."

"Yes."

I sat her on the vanity and snagged a towel from the shelf over the toilet. I wrapped the towel around her shoulders and snagged another one to wring her hair out. She tucked the terry cloth under her arms to hold it in place.

Pippa trembled slightly as I gently squeezed water from her long hair with the towel. Her eyes never left mine, wide and uncertain. I tried to focus on the task at hand and not on how soft her skin looked or how badly I wanted to touch her because no matter how much I wanted to, it simply wasn't happening.

"Thank you," she whispered. "I'm sorry for causing you so much trouble." Her lower lip trembled even as she smiled. "And for getting you wet."

I grinned back at her. "You could never cause any trouble, honey. And I'm the one who barged in here." I winced. "Probably overreacted."

"You were worried about me?"

"Yeah. I was."

"Because you promised my dad you'd protect me." Where before there might have been a budding desire in her eyes, now Pippa looked lost. Resigned even.

I shook my head slowly. "No. And no, I can't talk about it right at the moment because I don't know what to tell you. But it's not because I'm obligated." It was her turn to shiver. She sucked in a breath, and I knew she felt the pull between us too. She gave me a shy smile, lowering her gaze so her eyelashes lay like dark crescents under her eyes. "Do you think you can stand, honey?"

"Yeah." Pippa nodded and slid off the vanity as I stepped back. I kept my hands on her hips to steady her. Good thing too, because she swayed slightly and I realized she was drooping with exhaustion.

"You gonna be able to eat? I think you'll feel better with something in your stomach, even if it's just a bite or two."

"I'll try. I'm hungry, but I'm dead on my feet."

"Figured."

"I'm going to have to cut my hair." The sad look on her face told me her hair represented more than just hair to her.

"Maybe not. I bet we can save most of it."

"Are you good with getting mats out of a woman's hair?"

I shrugged, a smile tugging at my lips at a memory. "I used to be. When me and my sister were little, she had hair so long she had to be careful not to sit on it. She was all the time getting knots in it. No matter how hard she tried to keep it brushed, she would always end up crying and bringing me her brush to help her."

"How old were you?"

I shrugged. "Maybe seven or eight. She said Mom was too rough. Just like Mom was always too rough cleaning our faces. Like every spot of spaghetti sauce was a personal affront to her."

"I think that's a mom thing. Mine was always too rough too."

"Anyway, Hannah refused to cut her hair, and I hated listening to my sister struggle with taming the wild mass. So, I took care of her."

"Just like when she defended herself and killed her attacker?"

I should have expected the question, but she slipped it in there as skillfully as any investigator. "Yeah, I guess so." She didn't flinch away from me at the reminder of my prison time. I thought I might see fear or something in her expression, but there was only a deep longing. "Did you ever have anyone help you with your hair?"

"No." She looked away.

"No sisters? Surely your mom helped you."

She shrugged. "My mom wasn't what one would call overly demonstrative. If she ever helped me with anything, I don't remember it."

I reached for the clothes she'd set on a small make-up table so she didn't have to walk on shaky legs. "That doesn't sound very pleasant."

"I guess it's what happens when your mother gets pregnant by a prison inmate but has a husband on the outside."

"Knuckles didn't tell me that part."

"That's because I doubt Knuckles knows. If he does, he's got Mom completely fooled. She seduced him, intentionally got pregnant by him, introduced us and suckered him into thinking of me as his daughter so he cares about me. At least, that's what she believes she did."

"You think your mother had anything to do with your kidnapping?"

"I can't say for sure either way. And you have no idea how bad that hurts."

I grunted. "To know the whole reason you were conceived was to hurt someone else."

"Yeah. The only thing I know about my father is that Mom says he's a killer and that if he suspects for a moment I'm playing him, he'll kill me without hesitation."

"Pippa, Knuckles would never hold you responsible for your mother's actions. Even if you were guilty of tryin' to take him out, he'd still give you every benefit of the doubt until he couldn't."

"But after that, he would kill me if he thought he had to."

"Honey, I'm not going to lie and say that, no, he wouldn't kill you if he thought he had to. But I can't say he would kill you either. I've known him for fifteen years. The only time I ever seen the man show fear was right after he came back to his cell the afternoon he met you. He said the whole prison knew he now had a weakness."

Pippa gave me a strange look. "I don't like being a weakness. To anyone."

"You're only his weakness because he can't have anything happen to you. Especially not because of him. Your dad has a lot of enemies, but he's still as solid as they come. Ain't gonna say he's a good man, but he has a strict code he lives by."

"You trust him?"

That startled me. I hadn't expected the question. "Yes. Like I said. He's solid. He might not do something for the reasons you think and he will always find a way to use any situation to his advantage, but he would never intentionally hurt an innocent."

"Then I'm going to choose to believe Knuckles is better than my mom. Do you know if anyone has been looking for me? Did Mom file a police report or anything?"

Yeah. This girl was smart. And it was going to get her hurt. "You're so tired your words are slurring, Pippa. We can talk about all this later. I'll give you as many answers as I have once you've had a chance to rest. Get dressed and I'll see if I can work through your hair while you eat something."

"There's no way I can eat while you attempt to detangle this rat's nest. Notice I used the word 'attempt.'"

As I'd hoped, I distracted her from the line of questioning she'd opened. Because the answer to her question was a resounding *no*. Her mother hadn't filed a police report. She also knew full well her daughter was missing because I'd spoken with the woman three weeks before I finally found Pippa, then again just before we executed the rescue. Both times, the woman claimed to have seen her daughter just the day before.

"We makin' bets?"

"I don't have any money. Since I've been gone a month, I'm sure my bank account is overdrawn." She tried to sound flippant, but I could tell she was doing her best to keep reality at bay. She needed to break down and have a good cry or primal scream or something. Instead, I watched as she bottled up all the pent-up fear, anger, and grief inside her and tried to bury it in dark humor. But this woman was hurting.

"How about, if you manage to accomplish anything on my hair without me calling you a son of a bitch while I'm eating, I'll talk Knuckles into getting you out of babysitting duty."

"You're not getting out of this as easy as that, Pippa. I promised Knuckles and, now that I've met you and spent some time in your company, I'm not sure I'm ready to quit this job."

She stared up at me and, in her eyes, I saw the same longing I felt. Then she closed her eyes tightly. When she opened them, her face was blank.

"Do *not* shut me out, Pippa." I didn't mean to snarl at her, but I did. She didn't recoil, but her eyes widened and she sucked in a breath. "You tell me what you're thinking, and I tell you what I'm thinking. If we do that, we can get to know each other faster. Now, what are you trying to keep from me?"

"Nothing. Just…" She took a deep breath. "Gunnar, will you kiss me?"

Chapter Six

Gunnar

I'm not really sure what happened. One second I was looking down at Pippa in shock, the next I was kissing her. Just like she'd asked. Once her tongue brushed against mine tentatively, I groaned and did something I never thought I'd do. I surrendered. Not in a submissive sense, but to the woman I'd claimed as mine. To Pippa. She needed something to fill her mind with besides fear and terror. If she wanted a little pleasure with someone to make her feel safe, who was I to deny her? Which brought up a new subset of problems, but I'd figure it the fuck out.

I wasn't sure what I was expecting, but the silky feel of Pippa's lips, soft and warm against mine, surpassed anything my mind could have dreamed up. The feel of her lips and tongue sliding over mine was the most exquisite, beautiful sensation ever. Nothing in my wildest imaginings could have prepared me for this kiss. *Nothing.* I cupped her face gently in my hands, deepening the kiss as she melted against me. Her fingers curled into the fabric of my shirt, pulling me closer.

I poured everything I was feeling into that kiss -- my desire to protect her, my growing feelings for her, my need to chase away her pain and fear. Pippa responded with equal intensity, her body pressing flush against mine.

Christ! I wanted to snatch the towel away from her and look my fill at her beautiful body. I also needed, with everything inside me, to look over every single inch of her. Not for admiration. OK, so, not only for admiration. More than anything, I needed to see any visible signs of what those bastards did to her.

Everyone in the clubhouse where she'd been held was dead, but there were more people responsible. I had the feeling once I got Knuckles' request for a complete list of every injury she had, I'd be required for another task. It was the thought of still having that report to make to Knuckles that helped me get myself back under control.

When I finally ended the kiss and we broke apart, both of us were breathing heavily. Pippa's cheeks were flushed. "Wow." Her hoarse whisper was full of awe, and I wouldn't try to pretend I didn't puff out my chest a little.

I rested my forehead against hers. "Yeah. Wow."

"I've only kissed a couple guys before, Gunnar. That wasn't... I didn't expect..." Pippa trailed off, looking as dazed as I felt.

"Then you're a couple up on me. I went to prison when I was sixteen." The second I spoke, I realized what I'd said. Heat rose to my cheeks and my gaze snapped to hers. My chin rose defiantly as I waited for her derision. She'd either scoff and call me a liar or, worse, laugh at me for being a fucking virgin in my thirties. Instead, her eyes widened and she stared into mine, searching for the truth of my statement.

Then she shook her head, a smile giving her lips a delicate curve. "If that was your first kiss, you're a natural." She wasn't ridiculing me or even amused. Instead, she looked just as shell-shocked as I felt.

I brushed my fingers over her lips, then her jaw. "Ain't had time to find a woman since I got out, so yeah." I spoke like I was in a trance. It was quite possible I was.

"Why?" Her innocent question caught me off guard. Why? Because I'd been too focused on finding her than looking for a woman to get laid. But was that really the reason? Or was it because I'd claimed her the second I'd seen her picture? And that had been long before Knuckles had asked me to make her my old lady. That was when I realized I'd committed my life to this woman before I even met her.

I was stripped bare. There was no way to hide the raw pain and hunger inside me. Or the embarrassment. Yet, I couldn't make myself leave her or to allow her to not choose to stay with me. The thought of parting from her couldn't even completely form in my mind before I shut it down.

"Why? Why what?"

She reached up one small hand, trembling to give my bearded face a tentative touch, stroking gently when I didn't stop her. I tilted my head and sighed as I soaked up her touch. "Why didn't you find a woman after you were set free?" For some reason, I liked the way she phrased her question. It *did* feel like I'd been set free, and not in just the literal sense. Because I was very much afraid that kiss had been the thing to truly set me free.

So I gave her the most honest answer I had. It wasn't something I'd thought about or even really acknowledged to myself, but the second I uttered the words, I knew they were true. "Because they wouldn't have been you, Pippa."

"But we've never met."

"Knuckles showed me your picture. I think the one he gave me when he told me to find you was the last picture your mother sent him." I fished it out of the pocket of my inner shirt and handed it to her. It wasn't the one of her tied up and terrified. It was one where she was staring off into the distance with a soft smile on her face.

"I don't understand." She smiled up at me,

obviously confused but not concerned.

"I fell in love with the woman in that picture, Pippa." I looked at her helplessly, unable to give her anything but the strict truth. "From that moment, there was never going to be another woman for me." I thought I might have scared her, but her grip on my shirt tightened and she clutched me closer to her.

"Gunnar…"

"Look," I said roughly, "I need you to understand something. I may not have experience in anything to do with women, but I know what I want. And what I want is you. Not just because of my promise to Knuckles, but because I'm drawn to you in a way I can't explain. I want to protect you, care for you. I want what my mom and dad have together, and I want it with you. But only if you want me too."

Pippa bit her lip, looking uncertain but interested. "Maybe… What if we did that?" She picked at my shirt with one hand while still clutching one small fist in the material.

"Did what, honey?"

"You know. If we decided to be a couple. You're right that I need rest and to get settled. Go to therapy and see if I can get medicated to the nines or something. But you're right. There is a definite connection between us. And…" She trailed off, glancing away from me.

"What is it, honey? Don't be afraid to tell me what you're thinkin' or feelin'. 'Cause I'm shit at readin' women." My attempt at humor wasn't great.

"Gunnar, I don't… I don't want you to leave me alone." Her voice was a mere thread of sound. Had I not been so close to her and staring at her lips, I probably wouldn't have known what she said.

"No one said I was goin' anywhere, Pippa. Truth

is, I feel better when I can at least see you. I'd prefer to be within arm's reach." We stared at each other for a very long time. There was so much to say but I'm not sure either of us knew where to start. I liked the fact she wanted me close. "Whether or not you agree to my claim, I won't leave you unless you tell me to go. Even then, you might not see me and I won't interfere with your life, but I'll always be watching over you." When she opened her mouth to say something, I plowed on. "Not because of anything Knuckles wanted me to do. Because you're it for me."

The relief in Pippa's eyes was immediate, and she actually sagged against me. "Good." She patted my chest. "That's good. Glad we got that straight."

I tightened my arms around her, tucking her head under my chin. "Yeah, honey. I'm glad we got that straight too."

Pippa trembled slightly in my arms, whether from exhaustion or emotion I wasn't sure. I held her close, savoring the warmth of her body against mine. After a few moments, I reluctantly pulled back.

"As much as I'd like to stay like this, you need to get dressed and eat something," I said gently. "Then we can work on your hair and get you into bed for some real rest."

She nodded, looking a bit dazed. "You're right. I'm just… I don't want to let go yet."

"I know, honey. I don't either. But you need to get dressed." Then something occurred to me. "Are you steady enough to dress? Do you need me to… I don't know… *help*?"

She smiled again, rubbing her hand up and down the left side of my chest. Over my heart. "I think I can manage myself. Thank you for offering, though."

I sighed, feeling something I hadn't experienced

in a very, very long time. I was content. I'd saved this woman. Gotten her out of danger and brought her to the place that had once been my home. She was looking to me for comfort and security. Pippa wasn't mine yet, but it wouldn't take long for her to be all in with me. Hell, maybe she was already. I didn't know enough about women to know. But even now, she still clung to me.

I leaned in and brushed one more soft kiss to her lips. Stopping myself from going further was harder than I'd thought. Now that I'd experienced kissing Pippa, I wanted to do it more.

Pippa nestled closer to me, her body relaxing against mine. I could feel her exhaustion in the way she leaned heavily into my embrace. As much as I wanted to keep holding her, I knew she needed rest more than anything.

"Get dressed, honey. Then we'll get some food into you."

Pippa took a deep breath and nodded again. Her eyes were pleasantly glazed as I lifted my head from hers. "OK, I can do that."

Reluctantly, I pulled away from her. Her lower lip trembled and she whimpered softly, but nodded her head. I left her there but leaving her alone went against everything inside me. I needed to comfort her. To help her. To be there for her in case she needed me for anything. But she needed privacy. Not a strange man looking at her naked body, lusting after her.

Once outside the bathroom, I leaned against the door as I shut it. The door between us felt like prison walls and I hated it on principle. Sure, I could open it and go to her, but she needed to know I'd do anything for her, even if it was hard. At least, that's what I hoped she took away from this, because if that's not what I was giving her, I had no idea why I was denying us both what we wanted.

I took a breath. No. This was what my dad would do. It's what my brothers would do.

Instead of vacillating on whether or not I was doing the right thing, I looked at my phone and pulled up the number Knuckles had given me. Mama had confirmed that, if she'd been raped, it wasn't recent and there were no physical signs. She wasn't pregnant. The STD testing was still pending. I saw some bruising on her torso and one side of her face was discolored, but considering where she was and what they'd wanted her for, she was Goddamned lucky.

I sent off a text. I'd actually spoken to Knuckles when I'd called the last time, so even though he was still in prison, I knew he had a simple burner phone smuggled into his cell. Which didn't really surprise me. Knuckles was nothing if not resourceful.

The text was brief, giving the bare details. The last thing I wanted to do was to set off any red flags on some super secret government server and have the feds come after me. If he wanted more, he could contact me.

The door opened as I hit send. Immediately, my attention was focused on Pippa. I straightened, tucking the phone back into my pocket.

"Knuckles wanted a detailed list of your injuries. I didn't talk to Mama, but other than being knocked around, I didn't see anything major in the brief glance I got." I tried to smile at her, but at the moment, she was so exhausted, the bruise on her cheek stood out like an accusation.

"I'm sore and stiff, but I suspect that's more from inactivity. My injuries are more mental than physical, I think. I'm OK." She didn't meet my gaze, and her lower lip trembled.

"Yeah, baby. You're nowhere near OK."

Pippa's eyes welled up with tears at my words. She bit her lip, clearly trying to hold back the flood of emotions. I stepped closer and gently cupped her face in my hands.

"You don't have to be strong right now. You can let it out if you need to."

She shook her head, blinking rapidly. "I can't. If I start crying now, I don't think I'll be able to stop and we're not at a stopping point. We're still going to that other place. Right?"

"Kiss of Death?" When she nodded, I did too. "Yeah. I wanted to head out tonight after Mama checked you over, but that was for my own benefit. You need rest more than I need to avoid my father."

"I can sleep on the way."

I reached out to her and brushed my thumb gently over her bruised cheek. "Yeah. You could. But you're not goin' to. At least, not in place of proper sleep. You've been through a lot. Sleepin' in a strange place is gonna be hard enough without tryin' to sleep in a vehicle. And we both know that Humvee ain't the most comfortable ride."

My attempt at humor fell flat. She gazed up at me, tears swimming in her eyes. One of the offending drops of poison spilled from the corner and down her cheek. She said she didn't want to cry, but I thought a breakdown might be a relief once she started. But, shit. What the fuck did I know?

"You're right, Gunnar. I'm not OK." Her voice cracked on the last word, and she swayed slightly on her feet.

I immediately stepped forward and wrapped my arms around her, pulling her close. She buried her face against my chest and let out a shuddering breath but still didn't let go of all the grief and pain. Pippa held back as much of the crying as she could and other than the occasional shuddering breath in, she didn't make a sound.

"It's all right, honey. You don't have to be OK right now," I murmured, running my hand soothingly up and down her back. "You've been through hell."

She nodded against me but didn't speak. I could feel her trembling and knew she was fighting to hold herself together. Part of me wanted to tell her to let it out, to cry and scream if she needed to. But I also understood her need to stay in control, at least for now.

It took a while. I was afraid to move, not wanting her to think I was rushing her. I was willing to do whatever it took to help her feel better. When she finally pulled back, her eyes were red-rimmed and tears streaked her cheeks. She wasn't nearly done, but she'd released all she could for now.

After a long moment, I leaned in and kissed her again. One long, soft, lingering kiss meant to comfort instead of arouse. But fuck me, it was arousing as hell. Her lips were soft and trembling. I could taste the salt of her tears and longed to kiss every inch of her face to remove any lingering moisture. There should never be a reason for Pippa to cry. Ever.

I pulled back and watched her face carefully. Her eyes opened slowly. There was a dreamy expression on her face that made her even more beautiful than I'd first thought. Instead of telling her that and risking sounding like a complete idiot, I smiled gently at her.

"You think you can eat while I work through your hair?"

"I still don't think you can manage it. It'll be easier to just cut it." She didn't really want to cut her hair. I could see that plainly. I thought that maybe she didn't want to have hope only to have it ripped away from her. That's when I realized there might be more going on with her than I'd first realized.

"Easier isn't always better." I had to be careful. Phrase my words carefully. "I'm sure I'll hit a few snags. It might hurt a bit. But I think it's worth taking a chance to fix it, rather than cut it."

Her eyes widened and her lips parted. "You really want to try?" She was guarding her words as much as I was, so I decided to take the first leap.

"I do, Pippa. I meant what I said when I told you about Knuckles. Yes, he asked me to make you my old lady and give you the protection of my name and my club, but if I'd met you on my own, even not knowing you were Knuckles' daughter, I'd have done everything in my power to make you mine." More tears filled her eyes, spilling over and sliding down her face. "I know I must sound creepy as fuck to you, but I can't sugarcoat it and tell you I'm gonna be your fairy tale prince. That ain't me."

Pippa let out a small giggle even as another tear fell. "You don't sound creepy, Gunnar." She reached up and touched my lower lip with her fingers. "You sound just about perfect to me."

Chapter Seven

Pippa

Supper consisted of the yummiest hamburgers and hotdogs I'd ever tasted. The burgers were juicy with just a hint of smoke taste from the charcoal grill, and the dogs were just this side of burnt. *Delicious!* Sure, there were other things, but the burgers and dogs were my main concern. I ate three. Of each. Now I was so sleepy I could barely hold my head up while Gunnar continued to work on my hair.

"Almost finished, baby," he murmured as he continued to pick at a few of the tangles. He'd only had to cut out a couple of very stubborn knots he couldn't get out. Just a few strands here and there. I'd call it a win, but I was just too tired to celebrate.

"Yay..." My gratitude was great, but my enthusiasm was somewhat lessened. Not for lack of trying. I was dead where I sat.

His warm chuckle filled me with contentment. How had this man sucked me in so completely? I'd been in his company a few hours -- not counting sleeping off the drugs I'd been full of -- and I already couldn't imagine my life without him. "The best part is, your hair will be completely dry by the time I'm done. You can go to sleep without a wet head."

"Yay..."

We were sitting on the bed in the back bedroom Mama and Pops had given us to clean up and rest in. Gunnar was at my back with one leg bent beside me, the other hanging off the side. It probably would have been more comfortable if he'd had both legs on the bed and me between them, but he was taking great pains to not pin me in. I was more grateful to him for recognizing I might be a little claustrophobic. I had my knees tucked under my chin with my arms wrapped around my legs. My eyes were closed, and I was drifting as Gunnar made pass after gentle pass with the brush over my hair.

He chuckled, leaning in to kiss my cheek before whispering, "You think you can sleep now if you lie down?"

"Yes. Would you mind staying with me for a while? Maybe hold me or something?"

He paused before setting the brush aside on the nightstand. I thought he might be going to refuse me. After all, he was supposed to be talking with his mother and sister. Then he urged me to lie down and, to my surprise and more relief than I should have been comfortable with, wrapped his muscled, tattooed arms around me in a warm, soothing embrace. "I'll stay with you as long as you fuckin' want, baby." I loved the gruff tone of voice. He sounded like he might be as emotional as I was.

I wrapped my fingers around one of his forearms where they crossed in front of me, holding me to him. He grunted once. The second I settled, I took a deep breath… and I was out.

* * *

I woke to voices in the distance. I thought there was tension in the conversation and I gasped, sitting upright and scooting back until I felt the wall at my back. Only, the wall had some give to it. Not much, but it felt off. Besides, there was something in the back of my mind telling me to calm the fuck down. That's when I realized I was actually in a bed, and nothing stank like dirty feet and excrement.

I took several deep breaths, trying to get my heart rate under control. The spike of adrenaline left me shaky and out of sorts, but everything came back to me in a rush. I was safe. One of the voices outside the bedroom was Gunnar's. There was more than one woman's voice talking over each other and one was now sobbing uncontrollably.

I was dressed in a pair of soft cotton pants and a T-shirt. Since I had no idea who else was out there, I took time to find the items Angel had brought for me and dug through them until I found a cotton sports bra. I slipped it on before putting the shirt back on, then opened the door carefully.

Our room was at the end of the hall. To get to the living room, I had to turn a corner that led out of the hallway. Instead, I stood at the corner and listened.

"But you don't understand, Mom! This is all my fault!"

"Hannah, you're not thinking straight." I recognized Angel's voice and heard the tears when she spoke. "None of what happened was your fault."

"But it was! It was! Gunnar, I'm so sorry!" I heard Gunnar grunt and Hannah's sobs were muffled. She was likely hugging him.

"No, Hannah!" her mother snapped and I peeked 'round the corner. Gunnar had his arms around his sister and Angel stood with them, forcing Hannah's face up so Angel could look into her eyes as she spoke. "I know what happened. I know Gunnar protected you. He made a choice. Don't dishonor that sacrifice with regret."

"Gunnar lost fifteen years of his life because of me, Mom!"

"No, he didn't." I stepped around the corner, my attention focused on the two women, but I couldn't help a glance at Gunnar. He looked like he was helpless in the wake of his sister's tears. I seemed to remember a similar look when I was a hair's breadth from my breaking point.

Hannah turned her face away from me and into her brother's chest while she hastily wiped at her face with the sleeve of her shirt. It took her a couple of seconds, but she heaved in a shuddering breath, then turned to me. "He spent fifteen years in hell when he should have been living his dream. He was going into the military so he could be part of ExFil with Dad and my other brothers. Because he's a convicted felon, Dad can't hire him and Gunnar can't help Dad run the place when Dad finally retires. Everyone lost out. Because of me."

"Sometimes life throws a kink in your plans." I didn't want to make light of Hannah's feelings, but I had a very different opinion of Gunnar's sacrifice. "If Gunnar hadn't gone to prison and met my dad, I'd be wishing I was dead right about now. I hate that Gunnar had to go through what he did, but while he was there several things happened to change the course of both our lives. Mine for the better. His? I don't know. But if he hadn't met my dad, hadn't learned how to fight dirty and relentlessly, I wouldn't be sitting here today. I'd have been sold to the highest bidder and probably killed shortly thereafter once they realized they couldn't control me with drugs.

"So, as much as I would never want anyone who didn't deserve to be there to go to prison, I'm glad Gunnar is the man he is. And that man took a prison sentence for his beloved sister so she could have the life he thought she should have. I suppose, in a way, he sacrificed himself for both of us. Thank him. Love him. But let him have the credit for his sacrifice."

There was silence in the room. Then someone to my left sniffled. Then Angel let out a small sob. Then it was on. Snotfest of epic proportions. Turned out,

Mama was the one who let loose that critical sniff. She soon pulled all of us into a circle and everyone had a good cry before we all laughed.

Gunnar hugged his sister for a long time. They spoke softly to each other while Angel and Mama fussed over me.

"You should still be asleep, child." Mama brought me a glass of water and I smiled as I took it from her. Pops appeared behind her with a tray of cheese and crackers. He looked disgruntled, but winked at me as he sat the tray down. "You couldn't possibly have rested enough."

I caught Gunnar's look and shrugged. "Once I metabolized the rest of the drugs, I felt much better. And to be perfectly honest, the bath did me more good than anything. Gunnar was even able to get most of the knots out of my hair." I tugged at one curl gently as if to illustrate my point.

"He was always good at getting out tangles." Hannah gave me a watery smile. "I'm sorry if it seemed like I was making light of your situation."

I shook my head. "I never thought that. Not at all. I have a different take on the situation and hoped it might bring you some comfort to know I owe him my life. You too. If you hadn't let him take charge, I would never have met Gunnar. He'll have to decide if I was worth the years he spent on the inside with my dad, but I intend to never make him regret doing what his instinct demanded of him. And that was protecting his sister."

Hannah hugged me close and whispered next to my ear. "Take care of my big brother."

"I will."

When we parted, Hannah smiled and wiped her eyes again. "Are you waiting on Dad to get here?" She spoke to Gunnar, who had been talking to Pops. The two men shook hands, clapping each other on the shoulders.

"No," Gunnar said. "If Pippa's rested enough, I want to get on the road. I'd like to reach Nashville before daylight."

"Why the hurry?" Angel was back to wringing her hands. It was obvious she wasn't comfortable with Gunnar leaving. Not yet.

"Because, like it or not, there could be half a club full of angry bikers ridin' for my head. I told Ice and Cyclone I had no intention of letting this touch Bones, and I meant it." As if on cue, the men in question entered the house.

"Christ on a crutch," Mama swore under her breath. "Angel, did you not raise these boys to know it's rude to enter someone's home uninvited?"

"She did, Mama." Ice continued into the house without so much as pausing. Cyclone closed the door behind them and both brothers went to Gunnar, enveloping him in what was probably an embarrassing hug, but it didn't seem like any of the men cared. This was two older brothers welcoming home a brother they thought was lost to them.

Hannah openly wept while Angel hugged her close. Mama put her arm around me and I started. The older woman raised an eyebrow and I smiled back at her.

"You're a remarkable woman, Pippa." Mama kept her voice soft, for us alone. "You're the perfect woman for Gunnar. You're what he needs in more than one way. I have a feeling that, unless you curb him, that one is going to live his life to please you and fuck everything and everyone else. You're either going to need to rein him in, or let him run amok, in which case he will eventually take over your life."

I shrugged. "He will anyway. It's what overprotective cavemen do. Besides, he would never take over my life to control me, but to keep me safe and happy. And how do I know this?"

Before I could answer, Mama waved me off. "Pfft. You know it because you've been paying attention to the man who's had you in his care."

"He's done nothing but what he thought was best for me, Mama. I don't think he wanted to come here at all, but was afraid I was hurt worse than he could tell."

"I know it was." Pops moved to Mama's side and put an arm around the older woman. "That's who Gunnar is. He has more of his father in him than either of them will admit. At least in public."

"Did they have a strained relationship before everything happened with Hannah?"

"They butted heads from time to time, but that's just because they're so similar. I think Gunnar needed to get away from Cain so his father didn't smother his personality. Gunnar is too much of an alpha to roll over. It's hard for an alpha father to let his own alpha son be his own man when he raises the kid."

"I'm sure there could have been a better alternative than prison." Mama slapped at Pops' chest, a gentle chastisement. "He was going to the Marines. They would have straightened him out."

Pops turned to Mama then. "Really. Do you honestly think the damage wouldn't already have been done? One of two things would have happened. He and Cain would have come to blows, or Gunnar would have submitted out of respect for his father and been a shadow of the man he is now."

"Dramatic much?" Mama raised an eyebrow.

Pops crossed his arms over his chest in a belligerent stance. "You tell me I'm wrong, I'll admit to being a drama queen."

Mama grumbled. "Shut up." Yeah. She knew Pops was right.

It wasn't long after the guys broke it up. They continued to razz each other and do that strange male bonding thing all men seem to delight in. I watched intently for my own reasons. I could see the force of personality Gunnar had. I hadn't noticed before, because I'd been too focused on merely surviving, but if I had to judge the three of them, there was no doubt in my mind Gunnar was the natural alpha. It was in the way he took charge of me in that awful place where he'd found me. And how he did the same with his brothers when he first arrived with me at this place. Now, though they hadn't seen him out in the wild in more than a decade, it almost seemed like the president and vice president of Bones deferred to Gunnar. It was subtle, to be sure, but I could see it.

"She gets it," Pops said, nudging Mama. I glanced at them to find the couple smiling at me.

"Of course she does." Mama sniffed. "That boy would never pick a woman who wasn't intelligent."

"It's not about how smart I am. That man's a predator. And not just any predator. He's an apex predator. There might be men who could fight him, but I don't think there are many who could best him."

"I'm impressed." Mama didn't look impressed. She looked wary. Which was odd.

I checked Pops, then went back to Mama. While Pops was relaxed, he still watched me intently. "What?"

"You have training?" Mama tilted her head. "Because you were very specific in your description.

That's a lot for someone to pick up in no more time than you've been together, especially when you were at least partially messed up from the drugs you'd been given when he first found you."

"I was going to school to be a zoologist and to study sociology in animals. I'm literally trained to recognize social traits in animals, including identifying the alpha."

"You couldn't be that trained." Mama shook her head, frowning slightly. "You haven't been out of high school that long."

I huffed out an exasperated breath, rolling my eyes. "I took college courses in high school and was fortunate enough to go to a high school with a veterinary pathway. My senior year, I took night classes. Plus, I got in a full semester before this happy horseshit happened. So I'm greener than goose shit, but recognizing an apex predator for me would be like you recognizing a lethal heart rhythm. It's pretty basic stuff in the field."

Pops barked out a laugh before sitting down on the couch, his stout body shaking with humor. When everyone stopped to look at him, he guffawed outright, wiping tears from his eyes as they streamed down his cheeks.

"I don't see anything so very Goddamned funny." Mama crossed her arms over her chest, looking for all the world like a pissed-off cat.

"She got you that time but good, Mama. You don't admit it, I'll call you a liar in every language I know."

"You don't speak anything other than English!" Mama barked at him. Had she used that tone of voice with me, I'd probably have scurried away and hid.

Pops just shrugged. "Stupid smart phone has a

translator on it. I'm sure I can fumble through several different languages."

Mama finally gave up trying to look stern and gave a small chuckle as she shook her head. "Fuck all y'all."

"Well, what do you expect when you automatically jump to conclusions about someone?" Pops still wiped tears from his eyes and occasionally shook with quiet laughter, but his declaration was clearly a point of contention between the couple.

"It's happened before! I'd rather piss someone off and apologize later than get caught with our pants down."

"Christ." Ice scrubbed a hand over his face. "You thought she'd infiltrated the club. What? Did you think she was CIA again?"

"The woman is scarily good at profiling. At least, she's got your brother pegged better than me or Pops ever could."

Gunnar's gaze shifted to me. "You do?"

I shook my head, not liking the attention focused so completely on me. "I know animals. You just reminded me of some traits of animals at the top of the food chain."

"Humans are at the top of the food chain." Gunnar waved me off but didn't dismiss me outright.

I studied him for several seconds, trying to figure out his angle. "You want to know what my response to that statement is?" I raised my eyebrows. "Fine. No. Humans aren't at the top of the food chain. At least not with all things being equal. Technology allows us to be at the top. Technology we invented but have become so dependent on we can't survive without it. You take a small group of people and put them in the wild. Even give them decent shelter, but make them go without any sort of technology, and they might last a short while, but the environment will get them every time. And that's not with a big cat hunting them. There aren't many people who can survive on their own in the wild for long. Maybe a few months. Maybe as long as a year. The skills to do that are no longer bred into us." I lifted my chin at him. "That's your answer. The more feral a person is, the farther up the food chain he goes."

Gunnar cocked his head, amusement on his face. "You sayin' I'm feral?"

"Tell me you didn't feel feral at times when you were in prison, and I'll take it back."

That got his attention. He glanced from me to Mama and back. "All right. I see your point. She is good." He grinned. "Ought to make life interesting."

Chapter Eight

Gunnar

Surprisingly, my father didn't make an appearance before me and Pippa took off with Chains and Hawk. I sat in the back with Pippa and she'd leaned against my shoulder and slept most of the two-and-a-half-hour drive. If the situation had been different, I'd have loved to have made this ride with Pippa on the back of my bike. You know. If I had a bike. Something I'd have to make a top priority if I was gonna live in an active MC.

The sun was just peeking over the horizon when we rolled into the Kiss of Death compound. I had no idea how the club had acquired this area or how much land and construction it owned, but the compound consisted of fenced-in city blocks. Multiple blocks. Nothing but three-story warehouses occupied the spaces. Not in neat rows to maximize the space, but set up seemingly at random. Each building looked exactly alike, though each building had a different purpose. You couldn't tell from the outside what was on the inside. From what I could tell, Torpedo ran a tight ship. There wasn't a vehicle outside on the paths or in any kind of parking lot not under cover. Even the paths were camouflaged from above. Once someone entered the compound, it was impossible to see where they went, even from the air.

Hawk wound his way under the fixed camouflage netting, the Humvee barely fitting between some of the buildings. He drove the vehicle like he'd driven this same route a million times, never hesitating when I just knew he was going to take off a mirror or get a wheel wedged at a corner.

"Fuck," I grumbled. "I only had my driver's

license like three months before I went to prison."

Hawk barked out a laugh. Chains raised an eyebrow at Hawk but said nothing. "Don't worry, kid. I'll give you a crash course, so to speak."

"You know, I'm not afraid to go back to prison."

"And miss your honey? I don't think so. I'll take my chances today. Tomorrow might be another story."

"Fucker," I muttered under my breath. And yeah, those two bastards heard me. Even Chains snorted this time.

"I never learned to drive," Pippa offered, lifting her chin. If I hadn't already been in love with the woman, I'd have fallen then.

I leaned in on impulse and gently nipped her earlobe. "Remind me to tell you what you just did to me when we're alone."

Pippa sucked in a breath, her gaze snapping to mine. Her vivid green eyes were wide with shock and hunger. I wasn't experienced in sex, but I knew what the look she was giving me meant. "Oh?"

Instead of saying anything else, I tightened my hold on her, needing to wrap her up in as much protection as I could. Not because I didn't trust the men riding with me. Because I was a jealous bastard, now that I had the woman I wanted. It wasn't something I'd ever known about myself, but there was no denying the monster inside me. Pippa had caught Chains' and Hawk's attention and I found I didn't like their interest in the woman in my arms.

"Calm down, you jealous bastard." Hawk chuckled. "We ain't gonna make a move on your girl." Then he addressed Pippa. "He don't treat you right, though, you come runnin' to one of us. We'll put the asshole on the straight and narrow."

Pippa looked up at me, curling her lips in to keep

from smiling too much. Which she failed at miserably. "I don't think I'll have anything to worry about," she said, finally giving up and giving me a dazzling smile. "Besides, I'm fully capable of making sure he treats me right."

"Yep," I growled. "Gonna have to have a long talk with you when we get inside our room."

"Can you guys at least wait to get mushy until Bohannon assigns you a fuckin' room?" Chains sounded put out, but he was fighting another grin.

"Nope," I quipped. "Sure can't."

I leaned in and took Pippa's lips with mine, thrusting my tongue inside her mouth once before pulling back. Her smile was glorious before she buried her face in my chest demurely. Kissing was as far as I'd ever go where someone might see, but I really liked staking that claim. Even if it was only two of the club members. Putting a claim on Pippa was the most satisfying thing I'd ever experienced to this point in my life.

"Honestly, Chains. It's like you do it on purpose." Hawk kept driving until he pulled into one particularly large warehouse. The door was easily wide enough for two semitrailers to back in side by side.

Once we rolled in, the doors shut behind us and we all climbed out of the cage. Bohannon and Torpedo both moved to me with identical grins on their faces. "Good to see you made it, kid. Everything go according to plan?"

I nodded. "That place was evil, Torpedo. We got Pippa out and killed anyone inside or on the grounds. When the other half of Fire and Steel gets back to their clubhouse, they're gonna go hunting."

"Ice and Cyclone know the score?"

I nodded. "Yep. We tried to drop any

breadcrumbs we could going away from Bones. If they decide to go hunting, they'll come here. Not to Bones."

"Good. I got Data involved. He and Knight are working together on this. Between the two of them, we'll have plenty of heads-up before those guys show up."

"Torpedo. Bohannon. This is Pippa. Her dad was my cell mate. He might contact you guys at some point. If he does, I'd appreciate you letting me know."

Bohannon glanced at Torpedo before speaking. "There a problem?"

"Not at all. But Knuckles, a convicted killer who, by his own admission, killed the men who raped and murdered his sister, told me to rescue his only daughter and make her my old lady. Last thing I'm gonna do is not follow up on any call he makes in case he thinks I'm avoiding him. The man will put a hit out on me if he thinks I'm trying to keep him from contacting his daughter to confirm my treatment of her. I ain't too ashamed to admit I'm scared as shit of the man."

Pippa chuckled before putting her face against my shoulder but continued to laugh. The other guys laughed outright, and I found I'd missed this so fucking much. The comradery. The ribbing. The brotherhood I'd never found anywhere else in my life. Not even when I played sports in high school. My gaze met Bohannon who was grinning like a loon. He nodded at me, reaching out to give me a firm handshake. "We got your back, brother."

Everyone else followed suit. Three of the guys I knew from Bones. I figured they'd followed Torpedo and Bohannon, probably to help get things set up around guys everyone was familiar with until they knew they had guys here they could trust. There were a couple from Salvation's Bane as well. Mostly, there were guys I hadn't met before. Most of those had rap sheets as long as my arm. And all of them were men I recognized as being loyal to Knuckles. How did I know this? That same tattoo in the webbing of their thumb and forefinger I had. To a man, everyone who had that tattoo gave me respectful nods.

Bohannon's wife, Luna, took us to the top floor of the warehouse we were in. The place had been converted into an open plan apartment. "All four of my sons are with Kiss of Death now." I thought that was as much for me as it was for Pippa. "They're looking forward to seeing Gunnar again and meeting you. Probably wanting to meet you more than they want to see that one." Luna gave me a little smirk. "For now, think of it as the presidential suite," she said with a cheeky grin. "Only special people get to stay here. Mainly because the guys think it's too comfortable. Somehow, it makes them less manly to have a place this big. They own enough of these warehouses to make everyone a top floor flat, but the guys are holding out. I think they're taking bets on who gives in first."

"It's that pesky Y chromosome. Does something to them." Pippa winked at me, and I'd never been so happy to see a woman flirt with me. She should be scared and fragile. Instead, once she'd slept off the lingering effects of the drug she'd had forced on her, she didn't seem worse for wear. Which set off all kinds of alarms, but I had bigger problems right now -- because Luna said her goodbyes and shut the door and that left me in this place alone with Pippa.

Speaking of Pippa. She stepped into my personal space and put her arms around my neck. She didn't kiss me or do anything other than cling to me, pressing her body against mine. Of course, my arms went around her as if I had no control over them.

I had no idea how long I stood there with her, but I had no desire to move. As long as Pippa was in my arms, I could stay close to her. I could protect and cherish her. Maybe it was because I'd been in prison so long, away from human affection. Yeah, I got to see my mother and father and occasionally Hannah or Mama and Pops, but we weren't allowed to touch, and until I'd held Pippa in my arms when I carried her out of hell, I hadn't realized how much I'd missed affectionate physical touch.

She looked up at me with tears in her eyes, and I felt like the biggest fucking asshole in the world. Here she was, hurting, and I was losing myself in the feel of her sweet body pressed against me.

"Fuck," I swore as I used one hand to gently sweep away her tears with my thumb. "I'm sorry, Pippa. You're hurting and I'm…"

She reached up and put her trembling fingers over my mouth to hush me. "I think we're both hurting. I also think it's time to start healing."

"Tell me what to do, Pippa. I'm gonna need some help here." I'd never been more serious in my life. I was totally out of my depth.

"Kiss me, Gunnar. Then, just do what feels good because I'm out of my depth, too."

That was a tall order, but I couldn't argue. People had been doing this as long as there had been people. I knew the basics. I'd figure it the fuck out. But that wasn't as much a concern as her well-being. "Are you sure about this, Pippa? We don't have to have sex now. Or at all, if you don't want to. I can hold you while you sleep. I can pleasure you. Whatever you need."

"I want you, Gunnar. Please. Kiss me. We'll

decide what happens after that together."

Maybe it made me a deplorable human being, but a fifteen-year prison sentence said I wasn't a fucking saint. Kissing Pippa was easy. My mouth claimed hers, tongue sliding into her mouth like it belonged there. God, did it feel good! Like coming home after a long time away. Maybe that was what Pippa meant. Like I'd found something that completed me.

Pippa tilted her head, inviting me deeper, and I took what she gave me. My hands slid down her sides, cupping her ass before pulling her against my hard cock. The sound that came from my throat wasn't human, but Pippa didn't pull away. In fact, she moaned into my kiss and pressed herself against me harder.

"Bedroom," I said, more to myself than to Pippa when I finally pulled back enough to breathe without gasping. She nodded and led me over to the door on the far side of the room with a room key dangling from a hook on the wall beside it.

I picked her up without thinking, Pippa giggled and wrapped her legs around my waist as I carried her into the room and onto the queen-size bed along one wall of the corner space. The sheets were soft, clean with only one pillow on the bed. I should probably have been embarrassed at how my cock stretched the shorts I was still wearing, but fuck it. I had my woman in my arms about to claim her. She was letting me, and she'd be the only woman I'd ever be with.

When I was a teenager, before my life had gone to hell, I'd looked at the men in Bones and watched them interact with the club whores in the clubhouse. Anyone not married or in a relationship -- men and women alike -- took their pleasures frequently and with whomever they wanted as long as the woman was willing and everyone was single. I hadn't had that opportunity and, thanks to Knuckles, had been able to avoid sex in prison. I thought I'd never be in a sexual situation with a woman for a number of reasons. Even once my time was served, what man wanted to admit to any woman he was getting ready to fuck he was a virgin? I'd decided I'd lived without it during my prime years, I could manage going forward.

Pippa let me go and moved to the center of the bed, shrugging out of her shirt and pants before rolling onto her side to watch me strip off my clothes. I'd never been completely naked in front of a woman before and I'd never been so nervous in my life. The thought of showing every inch of my body to this woman made my heart race and my breath catch in my throat, and I wasn't sure how much was anticipation and how much was dread. If she found me lacking, I knew I'd never recover.

Pippa tracked my every movement, her attention completely focused on me. I saw her body shimmer in the lights as sweat coated her skin. The bruising on her body stood out in stark relief and I paused in undressing.

"Are you sure you're ready for this? Much as I want you right now, I absolutely will not risk hurtin' you, Pippa. Not for any reason."

I swallowed as she moved to the edge of the bed, her knees bent so she sat back on her heels. Without a word, she pulled her bra over her head, revealing the most beautiful breasts I'd ever seen. I figured I'd seen more than my fair share in smuggled-in magazines, but Pippa was absolutely exquisite. Her breasts were small and tipped with dusky nipples my mouth watered to taste. I simply to God couldn't take my focus from her to finish shedding my clothes.

"I've kissed a couple guys," Pippa said in a soft voice. "But I've never been naked in front of one."

I scrubbed my hand over my mouth. "I've never been naked in front of a woman."

"So, another first for both of us?"

"Gonna be a lot of firsts." I let out a nervous laugh as I reached for her.

Pippa pulled me to her and kissed me until instinct took over and I took the lead. *Do what feels good?* I could definitely do that.

As Pippa's soft lips parted under mine, I took that as my permission to explore her mouth with my tongue, tasting her sweetness. I didn't even try to fight the groan bubbling up from my throat. I'd have been embarrassed, but Pippa's soft moan mingled with mine. Any reasons I thought I had for hiding my reactions from her became unimportant. She deserved to know how wonderful she made me feel.

I trailed my hands over her smooth flesh, relishing the sensation of silky skin against my roughened palms. She was so warm, so alive against me, it was intoxicating. I pulled her closer, needing her tight against me, her breasts mashed against my chest. Pippa responded by arching against me, her breasts rising and falling with each ragged breath.

I moved lower, trailing kisses down her neck and shoulders before taking the top of one breast in my mouth. I sucked, shuddering in pleasure when she cried out and thrust her chest toward me again. She tunneled her fingers through my hair and held me to her. The harder I sucked, the better she seemed to like it.

"Gunnar." Her soft gasp sent pleasure through me. My cock was hard as granite and I knew there was no way I would last very long.

"I'm gonna do everything I can to make you come, Pippa. But, please don't hold it against me if I can't. I promise you I'll figure it out."

She let out a small laugh. "I don't think you'll have to do much. I'm wound so tight I'm pretty sure a stiff breeze would set me off."

"Don't I know the fuckin' feelin'."

My hands shook as I continued to move down her body. My lips followed my fingers as I kissed my way down her beautiful body. I marveled at her sweet scent, at the salty taste of the sweat glistening on her skin. With every sigh or sharp inhalation Pippa made, my cock pulsed even harder.

When I reached the hem of her panties, I took in a shuddering breath. With trembling fingers, I pulled them over her slim hips and down her long legs until I slipped them from her feet and tossed them to the floor beside the bed. My heart thundered in my chest as I took in the sight of her perfect pussy -- smooth, pink, and inviting.

Pippa's eyes were lowered but she watched me intently as I dipped my head to taste her for the first time. We both seemed to hold our breath until the second my lips grazed her glistening sex. Her clit pulsed under my tongue as I lapped gently.

The taste hit me like a punch. I actually grunted as her flavor exploded on my tongue in a tangy, musky zest. I grunted at the same time Pippa cried out in surprise.

"Holy fuck!" She leaned up on her elbows. "Don't you dare fuckin' stop!"

With a growl, I fastened my mouth on her pussy and licked and sucked while she writhed underneath me, grinding her cunt against my face.

I wanted to put my fingers in her, to see how much more I could give her, but I wasn't exactly sure if I should. I didn't want to hurt her. As I brought my fingers to her pussy to circle her opening with my fingertips, Pippa's breathing grew erratic and ragged.

"Gunnar! Oh, God!"

Her body tensed beneath me, then she thrashed her head from side to side as she screamed. Her pussy quivered beneath my lips and tongue as she came. I was so relieved I got lightheaded and thought I might have sobbed in relief.

When her body relaxed, so did her grip on my hair. I kissed her inner thigh and lapped softly at her folds. Sweat coated my body, and I actually trembled.

"Gunnar?" She found my shoulders with her hands and tried to pull me to her. I took my time, kissing a blazing trail up her torso, between her breasts until I kissed her lips as I lay on top of her, my hips in the cradle of hers.

"Are you sure this is what you want, Pippa? I'm not strong enough to let you go once I have you."

She smiled at me, stroking my beard with her fingers. "Were you planning on leaving me if we don't have sex?"

I didn't even hesitate. "Fuck no!"

Pippa's laughter warmed my heart. After everything she'd been through, I had no idea how she could manage any sort of humor, but my woman wasn't a shrinking violet. She was brave. Strong. Once she found her footing with me and wherever we landed after this, I knew she'd be a force to be reckoned with. "Yes, Gunnar. I'm sure this is what I want. I want you to make love to me."

"Not sure I ever thought I'd actually make love with a woman. Always thought of it as just fuckin', but

I see the difference now."

She smiled up at me. "Don't make me wait any longer, Gunnar. I'm just as anxious as you are to do this."

I nodded and took a deep breath, trying to calm my racing heart as I reached between us and fisted my cock to guide myself to Pippa's entrance. The head of my cock brushed against her slick folds and we both gasped at the sensation. I froze. "I forgot a condom."

"I've got an implant. Mama said all the tests she ran came back clean. There's a couple pending, but she said…" Pippa's face flushed pink. "My hymen's intact," she finished in a soft rush. "And I was pretty sure they hadn't touched me like that before, but she confirmed it."

"I got tested when I got out on account of the ink. And I didn't have sex."

"Then if we're doing this, let's do it all the way."

"Nothing between us?" I raised a questioning eyebrow.

She smiled up at me. "Nothing between us."

"I'll be as careful as I can. You tell me if I hurt you."

"I don't think anything could hurt right now." Her eyes were glazed, and she looked like she was on the verge of another orgasm. Sweat dripped down her temple and also beaded on her upper lip. My own body shuddered occasionally as I shifted my weight. Anticipation was off the charts.

Bracing myself on my forearms, I slowly pushed forward, groaning as I sank into her tight heat. Her body enveloped me inch by inch. Pippa's breath hitched and her fingers dug into my shoulders. I paused, giving her time to adjust, but the effort it took bordered on superhuman.

"You OK?" My voice was strained as I summoned every ounce of willpower I possessed to keep from shoving the rest of the way inside her.

"Yes," she gasped. "Don't stop!"

I pushed again, easing the rest of the way inside her. Her pussy squeezed me so tight I thought I might lose my Goddamn mind. I tried to give her as much time as she needed as I strained to hang on to my control. Which was fast slipping through my fingers like the finest sand.

When I was finally seated inside her, I shivered, wrapping my arms around her as tightly as I could, holding myself still inside her as deep as I could go.

"Sweet God, Pippa." I buried my face in her neck. "You feel so fuckin' amazing!" It was the truth. Pippa's muscles clenched around me, milking my cock in the most incredible way. I had no idea how I hadn't come yet, but I knew there was no way this was going to last longer than a couple of minutes. No fucking way.

"So do you." Pippa shifted beneath me, urging me to move until we found a rhythm with each other.

I pulled back only to shove back inside her and she moved with me like we'd been doing this forever. Her body felt like a homecoming. As her moans and whimpers grew louder with each stroke, I knew I was exactly where I was supposed to be. With this woman. Pleasuring her. Protecting her. It was like everything in my life suddenly clicked into place. I would not be the man she trusted so completely with her heart and body if I hadn't gone through everything I had. She'd said as much before, but it hadn't really penetrated until this one perfect moment.

The bed squeaked beneath us as we found our pace. The sharp crack of thunder outside only punctuated our lovemaking, turning it wild and primal. I thrust into Pippa over and over again, with ever harder strokes. But it wasn't only me. Pippa planted her feet on my calves and lifted herself to meet me, crying out every time my body slammed into hers. She screamed my name, and her pussy contracted around my cock. The smell of sex in the air was something I'd always associate with this first time.

"I'm gonna come, Pippa. Tell me if you want me to pull out because I can't do it unless you tell me to." I thought that would be harder to admit, but not to Pippa. She already knew my flaws and accepted me. The least I could do was be honest with her and show her how much she affected me.

She dug her nails into my ass and pulled me to her. "Inside me," she whispered. "Inside me."

That was as long as I was capable of waiting. With a brutal roar, I emptied myself inside her sweet pussy. It made me a complete bastard, but I felt a sense of pride. Like I'd marked her for any other man to know she was mine. Then I collapsed on top of her.

As my breathing settled and my heart rate returned to normal, I nuzzled her neck and shoulder while she clung to me, her fingers once again in my hair as she held me to her.

"Thank you." Her voice was soft and drowsy. "That was so wonderful."

"Yeah. So worth the fuckin' wait. So fuckin' worth *everything*…"

I knew I needed to get up and help her clean herself or something. I definitely needed to pull out of her pussy, but I couldn't seem to make myself. Instead, I settled myself on top of her, my dick still firmly inside her, not softening one bit. I took a breath…

And I was out.

Chapter Nine

Pippa

"What the everlastin' fuck, Gunnar?!"

I let out a surprised squeak as something removed the most wonderfully heavy, delicious-smelling weighted blanket from my body I'd ever had the pleasure of sleeping under. After such a long time in hell, the loss was traumatic and I whimpered my displeasure.

"Get the fuck off my daughter!" The enraged roar was followed by a punishing fight. I sat up in shock, pulling the covers over my naked body on instinct.

"Stop it!" I screamed at the two men, but no one was paying me any attention. I reached for my phone, unsure who I was planning on calling, when another man sauntered into the room like he owned the place.

"For Christ's sake, Knuckles. What the fuck did you expect?" The other man didn't attempt to pull Knuckles off Gunnar. Instead, he leaned against the wall... drinking a cup of coffee? I could smell it from here! My gaze locked on the lidded cup and it was on.

"I've not had coffee in... Ohmigod!" I jumped from the bed and in the direction of the older man standing there all cozy with a grin on his face like this was all a big fucking joke, when I was still half asleep and hadn't had coffee in FOREVER! "Gimmie!"

"Oh, shit." The guy with the coffee straightened and I wasn't sure if he was trying to guard his coffee from me or hand it over, but he had both hands around his cup. All I could comprehend in that moment was a mean man was withholding my coffee. "Gunnar!" Gunnar's name was barked like a whip of command. Both Gunnar and Knuckles stopped fighting, but I couldn't be bothered. *Coffee!*

I snatched the cup from the guy's hands and popped the lid off, looking at the dark liquid from heaven and inhaled deeply. I moaned in pleasure even before I took a delicate sip. Even black and so strong the shit could probably jump out and walk on its own, it was the most delicious concoction I'd ever tasted.

"Christ." Someone wrapped a blanket around my shoulders and spun me around. "Bathroom, Pippa. Now." The order was sharp and followed by a swat to my ass which would have made me jump but I had bigger problems. Like how to walk and drink a full cup of coffee with no lid.

Gunnar guided me into the bathroom, one hand firmly on my lower back. I clutched the coffee mug to my chest, taking small sips as I shuffled along. My mind was still foggy with sleep and caffeine deprivation.

"Drink your coffee and get cleaned up," Gunnar said gruffly, though his touch remained gentle. "I'll deal with our... company." He winced as he finished, scrubbing the back of his neck before meeting my gaze and holding it.

I blinked up at him, finally registering his disheveled appearance and the red mark blooming on the side of his face. "Oh my God, are you OK?" I reached up to touch his face but he caught my wrist, hesitating before he relaxed and gave me a soft smile, letting me pet his damaged cheek.

"I'm fine. Just focus on waking up properly. I'll handle things out there." His eyes softened as he looked at me. "Take your time, sweetheart. I'll snag you some clothes."

"Might want to snag some for yourself, though I can't say I don't appreciate the view."

Gunnar glanced in the mirror at himself and his face flushed red under the forming bruise, which was kind of cute. "Fuck." He glanced back at me and shook his head. "Fuck." I couldn't help it. I burst into giggles and threw myself at him. Gunnar chuckled with me, holding me tight. "Yeah. Clothes for both of us. Though, if our dads don't want to see us naked, they shoulda fuckin' knocked." He pulled me up for a quick, hard kiss. Which turned into something a little hotter than either of us intended, but fuck those guys outside.

I urged Gunnar to deepen the kiss, thrusting my tongue into his mouth as his hands slid down to cup my ass. He pressed me against the bathroom counter and I moaned into his mouth, the coffee momentarily forgotten as desire flared between us. His erect cock pressed insistently against my stomach and I arched into him, craving more.

A loud *bang* on the door made us both jump. "Don't even think about it!" Knuckles' voice boomed from the other side. "Get your asses out here now!"

Gunnar pulled back with a frustrated groan, resting his forehead against mine. "Fuck. I guess we better face the music."

I nodded as I giggled and buried my face in his chest. I kissed his pec before stepping away from him. "You go first. I really do need to clean up a bit. And get dressed."

He gave me one last lingering look before snagging a towel to sling around his hips before slipping out of the bathroom. I heard muffled voices as I quickly used the facilities before splashing water on my face.

There was a soft knock on the door before Gunnar handed me an overnight bag. "Take your time, honey. There's clothes and a new toothbrush as well as a few other things."

"Do me a solid and don't get killed?"

He barked out a laugh. "Yeah. That's at the top of my list." He leaned in to kiss my forehead, then left, shutting the door behind him. I heard muffled voices from the other side of the door but not raised and angry like before.

Before I dressed, I took another healthy swig of coffee. Yeah, it probably blistered my throat on the way down, but it was fucking delicious.

With a sigh, I set down the coffee cup to open the toothbrush and toothpaste I found in the bag and brush my teeth. Dressing hastily, I looked longingly at the half-empty cup. Leaving a whole half cup was just sacrilegious. So I picked it up and drank the rest. Black coffee wasn't my preference, but it was still delicious.

I opened the door and peeked outside. Gunnar had slung on some jeans and had a T-shirt hanging from one fist while and Knuckles was up in his face, pointing a finger. I'd only met my father once years ago, but I was sure the big man was Knuckles. They were on the other side of the big open space so I couldn't hear what they were saying clearly, but the body language was pretty obvious.

"What's going on?" I demanded as I hurried to Gunnar's side. I started to get between the two men, but Gunnar shoved his arm out to prevent me from passing him.

"Do not!" he snapped. "Stay behind me."

"I'm not letting him get in your face like that." I tried to duck under Gunnar's arm, but he snagged me by my shirt collar and tugged me back, side-stepping so I was solidly behind him and Knuckles. Which is when I got a really good look at the man.

Knuckles was fucking *huge*. He looked like a giant next to Gunnar and the other man -- likely Cain, since Gunnar said it was our dads here. He was covered in tattoos over every inch of skin I could see, other than his face and neck. He wore a sleeveless black tank revealing muscled, vein-roped arms. I met his dark gaze and thought better of trying to get around Gunnar again. Instead, I fisted my hand in the back of Gunnar's shirt and took a half step back to give Gunnar room if he needed to fight.

"I ain't gonna hurt you," Knuckles grunted. The expression on his face transformed from anger to contrition. His voice was still gruff, but he looked genuinely distressed. "Sorry."

Gunnar relaxed slightly but kept me behind him. "It's all right, Pippa. Your dad just got a little... overexcited."

"Why?" I couldn't help the demanding bite to my tone. "He's the one who told you to make me your old lady. Right?"

Gunnar shrugged but didn't take his eyes from Knuckles. "Yep."

I glared at Knuckles. "Then what's all the fuss?"

"He was on top of you! In fucking bed!" Knuckles lost his cool for about a second before he closed his eyes and took a deep breath. I could tell he was inhaling for patience. "He's not supposed to be in bed with you," he grumbled. "S'not right."

"What's not right? That I shouldn't have sex with the man who's making me his old lady? Because if I'm not supposed to have sex with him, who am I supposed to have sex with?"

Gunnar growled as he glanced down at me. "Me. You're supposed to have sex with me."

Now it was Knuckles' turn to growl.

"Sounds like fucking Captain Caveman around here," I grumbled. "Well?" I looked over at Cain who sat on the couch, sprawled out like he owned the place. "Are you gonna do something?"

"What do you want me to do, honey? I'm an old man. These guys are way tougher than me." The shit-eating grin on his face said he was enjoying himself.

"You know, I really like Angel. Your wife is a sweetheart. Your daughter, Hannah, too. You? Not so much."

Cain shrugged. "I always say let boys be boys. They'll work it out on their own."

I blew a curl out of my face in exasperation, then turned my attention back to Gunnar and Knuckles. Heaving out a sigh, I focused on Knuckles. It was past time for this meeting. "You're my dad. Right?"

Knuckles nodded, his expression softening when he looked like it had been carved from granite moments before. "Yeah, sweetheart. I'm your old man."

"Then why are you fighting with Gunnar?" I frowned, trying my best to adopt a scolding tone when I was angry as fuck. "You punched him in the face! He saved me. Just like you told him to. He's been nothing but good to me since he found me."

Knuckles ran a hand over his face and sighed heavily. "I know, I know. I just… seeing him… uh… you know… like that…"

"You want to prevent that in the future?" I raised my eyebrows, putting my hands on my hips, refusing to back down an inch from the big man.

"It would be my sincerest wish."

"Great! Next time you come for a visit, *you will knock on the fucking door*!" I gave him a bright smile and threw my hands up like "DUH!" "Problem fucking solved."

"Also," Gunnar added, putting his arm around me and pulling me close. "Aren't you supposed to be in prison?"

The two men stared at each other for several seconds before a grin split Knuckles's face. "It's damned good to see you, boy." Knuckles pulled Gunnar into a tight embrace as both men clapped each other on the back several times. Hard. I thought I saw Gunnar wince, but I'd never say a word. I would never understand male bonding.

Chapter Ten

Gunnar

Once Knuckles let me go, there was my father to deal with. I'd rather continue to let Knuckles beat the fuck outta me than face my father, but I was no coward.

"Sir." I addressed him as a superior out of respect. If he wanted to be my dad, that was up to him. Still, it made my chest ache to think my father would be so disappointed in me he'd reject me.

Cain scowled. "Sir," he spat out. "Fuckin' sir." He stood abruptly and stalked toward me. Pippa stiffened, but I set her away from me, moving her toward Knuckles. Cain rolled his eyes. "And now you're protectin' your woman from me?"

"Well, you look a little like you're about to kick my ass, and I don't want Pippa gettin' in the way." I gave him a wary look, but didn't take up a defensive stance. Mainly because I knew anything he dished out I deserved.

"Little punk," he muttered at me before lunging at me to pull me into a tight embrace. Thankfully, he didn't whale on my back like Knuckles had. I wasn't sure I could take much more. Felt like Knuckles had given me the beating he was afraid to while Pippa was watching. "Your mother missed you."

"Yeah. She told me."

"Hannah, too."

"Her too."

Dad held me close for several minutes before he pulled back, blinking rapidly. "Gonna have to have a talk with Torpedo about makin' sure he gives you a better room. This one has too much dust."

"Yeah. Makes my eyes water too sometimes." I

grinned at my dad.

"Now. Introduce me to your woman proper-like."

Things were better after that. Dad told me how he'd initially been disappointed in me for not bringing the situation to him or my brothers. Or anyone in Bones MC. Every time he looked at Pippa, though, he averted his gaze. Every time he did, I saw the smile on his lips.

Finally, I couldn't take it anymore. I had to know. "OK. What's so funny?"

"Hum?" Dad looked all innocent and shit. Like he had no clue what I was whining about.

"Every time you look at Pippa, you smile. Why?"

Cain stopped trying to hold back then and chuckled, shaking his head and wiping at his eyes. "I'm sorry. And it's not you, Pippa. I was remembering when I barged in on Stunner and Suzie in a similar situation."

"Suzie?" Pippa looked confused but smiled.

"My sister. Mom and Dad adopted her and my two bonehead brothers when they were little more than teenagers. At least Cliff and Dan were. Suzie was about nine or ten, I think." I took Pippa's hand in mine and tugged her to the couch. "Didn't expect you here, Dad. We stayed long enough at Bones, I really thought you'd get there before we left."

"Well, aren't you lucky I happen to be on great terms with the president and vice president of Kiss of Death."

"Torpedo and Bohannon ratted me out." I shook my head.

"I wasn't sure I could make it to Kentucky before you left, so I went to your ultimate destination. Also, I knew where you were the second you got out of prison, I knew what you were tasked with, and I knew that motherfucker was gonna try to force you and his daughter together."

"I thought you said you didn't know my dad, Knuckles."

"Said I hadn't met him. Cain and I have worked on different sides of the table a few times." Knuckles gave Cain a level look.

"Someone has to nudge people in the right direction when they're being dumbasses." The two men chuckled before clasping hands in a firm shake. "Good to finally meet you."

"Likewise."

"Fuck me," I bit out.

Pippa narrowed her eyes at Knuckles, then shifted her focus to Cain. "Did you set all this up?"

"Does Mom know about this?"

Cain and Knuckles exchanged a look. "Well." Cain scrubbed his hand through his beard. "I mean, you wouldn't let me keep you out of prison. The only other option I had was to make sure you had help on the inside."

"Son of a bitch." I shook my head, but I could totally see the beauty of it. "You're a sneaky bastard."

"No sneakier than you."

"Did you know what really happened?" I knew Dad would know what I was talking about. God knew it had been a topic of conversation every fucking week I saw him in prison.

"Of course, I knew what fuckin' happened. I know you're all adults, but I know everything about all of you. I've made it my business to know so I could make sure you always had someone at your back. No matter where you are."

There was a beat of silence before Pippa piped

up cheerfully, "Well, that's not creepy or anything. But just so we're clear, you ever barge in our personal space like you did again, you deserve every fucking thing you see. And I'll bring it up at family reunions and Christmas dinners. You'll never hear the end of it. I'll be a scourge on your sanity --"

"OK. OK. I get the message. Knock."

"What exactly was the deal you made with Knuckles?" I had to know what had happened and how Dad intended this to end for me.

"Just a favor. A big one." Dad sat back and crossed one ankle over the opposite knee. "Knuckles was in prison for killin' men who raped and murdered his sister. You know that. But what I doubt Knuckles told you was that, about the time of the killin', his cover with the CIA was about to be compromised. He could have stayed out of prison, but he and his entire team would have been outed. It would have been a death sentence for all of them."

"How does that play with him going to prison?" I turned to Knuckles, wanting an explanation.

"The reason my sister was… hurt, was to get me in a compromising situation. They never factored in that I'd kill the men they'd hired. They'd hoped to maybe get me on video beatin' the piss outta the bastards. What they got was way the fuck more. And by 'they' I mean one of the groups I'd infiltrated and was steering negotiations from behind the scenes. It's what I do. I'm paid by someone to help get the outcome they want out of these deals. I infiltrate a group, gain their trust, and offer advice. I'd been in with that particular group, deep, for several years. I'd done enough to put the right people in place that, as long as I was in their sphere of influence, he'd never have full control over his military again. He couldn't kill me because he wasn't sure what my death or disappearance would do with his relations with the U.S. agencies he was working with. Since he couldn't afford to lose those agencies' support or business, he set me up to go to prison." Knuckles shook his head slightly before continuing, as if remembering the moment he was describing. "When they filmed me killing those bastards, I was given the choice to plead guilty and it would be assured I wouldn't get the death penalty. But I'd be in prison for the rest of my life. In return, my team got to live."

"You sacrificed yourself for your team?" Pippa's eyes shimmered, the story obviously striking a chord with her.

"Honey, if you think that's big, you have no idea what I'd sacrifice for you. You're the most important person in my life. Ever. But yeah. I went to prison to save the lives of my team and I don't regret it. Though, I'll admit, had I known it was all a setup, I'd have been more careful in the killing, then I'd have gone after that bastard, El Diablo, himself."

A chill went up my spine and my gaze snapped to my father's. Cain's mien hardened, and he was laser-focused on Knuckles. I tightened my grip on Pippa's hand, not daring to say anything. If Knuckles was fishing, I wasn't giving him anything other than the unavoidable initial reaction.

"What dealings did you have with El Diablo?" Cain was all business now, the cunning warrior of his well-earned reputation.

"Enough to know everything he does is for a reason. He wanted me in prison for a specific purpose."

"It sounds like you're saying he deliberately set your sister up for rape and murder." Cain kept his statement neutral when I knew his insides were roiling. Because mine were too.

"Oh, he set her up to be murdered, sure. But not the rape. I think the rape, when he'd specifically told his men they were to make it a clean kill, was why he let me kill them the way I did."

"You're accusing him of killing an innocent, Knuckles. That's a hell of a thing."

Knuckles snorted. "I never said my sister was innocent. She deserved the killin'. She was working directly against El Diablo at the time. I tried to warn her, but she thought she could best him."

"You still got an ax to grind with him?" Cain's question was more of a demand. I knew that tone of voice often made grown badass Marines piss themselves. I also knew Knuckles wouldn't be one of them.

"Nah. El Diablo's a bastard -- and yes, I know your connection to him -- but he's not evil. Kind of a darker shade of gray, but not evil."

"So he threatened your team if you didn't do what he wanted."

"Yep. Was a stroke of genius, if you ask me. It also put me in a much better position to get revenge with the perfect alibi. Because El Diablo wasn't the real threat. He was just doing a job he was paid to do. After his contract was up and El Diablo fulfilled his end, he came back to me and we took down the motherfucker in spectacular fashion. Took a few years, but it was worth it.

"While I was in a forced relationship with El Diablo, was when that bastard, Slash and his minions took over Kiss of Death. They killed Dart, our president, and Slash and Rat Man turned my club into a fuckin' snake pit."

"If it makes you feel better, we got most of the bastards. Bones and Salvation's Bane." Cain rubbed a finger over his lower lip. "Couple of 'em died pretty hard."

"I'd hoped you would. Did my best to put 'em in your path."

Cain snorted. "Always gotta one-up, huh?"

Knuckles shrugged. "Just keepin' you on your toes, old man."

"Was there a point to this fuckin' story, Knuckles? If not, you're borin' me to tears." Dad wasn't a good loser even with us kids. Thinking Knuckles had gotten one over on him fared about as well as it would have for one of us.

"Yeah. The point is, all this shit with Gunnar went down just as El Diablo was gettin' ready to get me out of prison. He knew me and you had a connection, so he told me what was going on and that the youngster over there was forcin' the issue and pleading guilty. It was mostly done before he could do anything about it. Wrath hadn't yet joined him, and El Diablo hadn't had enough of a warnin' to head things off."

"What?" I was starting to feel more than a bit betrayed, which pissed me the fuck off. Pippa patted my knee, and her touch helped to ground me.

"El Diablo agreed to get you sent to Terre Haute if I could get you housed with me. I was supposed to teach you how to survive and keep you alive."

"In return for what?" I bit the question out between clenched teeth. "I don't like being manipulated, Knuckles. What the fuck?"

"Calm your tits, kid. Your old man saved my life on more than one occasion. I thought for the most part we were even, but you're his kid. I did what I promised and got you housed with me. I tried to teach you how to not only survive but thrive, and I think you did."

"And Pippa?"

"What about her? You went after her on your own. Ain't gonna lie and say I didn't push you toward her from the moment I realized her mother wasn't all she claimed to be. I did. That's when I started showin' you pictures. It's why I told you about her when I figured out Beth was the bitch she is."

"My mom terrified me with stories of you." Pippa spoke softly. "The only reason I didn't run screaming from Gunnar when he told me you'd sent him is because I couldn't. I think the two things that let me accept him as easy as I did were his treatment of me, and the fact my mother was a monster."

"Honey, trust me when I tell you, she's gettin' hers."

"Was she the reason I got taken?"

Everything in me rebelled at that question. I grunted and pulled Pippa into my arms. "Shut up, Knuckles. Not another word."

"She asked the question, boy. She has the right to know."

"I have the right as her man to keep shit from her that will give her nightmares, Knuckles."

"No, Gunnar. I need to know."

"Pippa --"

She leaned in and pressed her lips to mine for a long moment. "You'll be here with me. You'll keep the nightmares away, but I have to know for sure."

I tilted my head at her, narrowing my gaze. "You suspected?"

"She was my mother in name only, Gunnar. I knew from a young age something wasn't right. She made it clear I was a nuisance."

"You didn't seem unhappy when she introduced us." Knuckles leaned forward, bracing his forearms on his knees.

"That's because it didn't start in earnest until after that visit. Like she did what she had to until you met me, then she didn't give a shit."

Knuckles clenched his fists. "Yeah, honey. She had everything to do with why you got taken. The whole reason she had a thing with me was to get pregnant with my kid."

"Why?" Pippa trembled in my arms, but she didn't back down. While I didn't like it, I certainly respected it.

"Leverage. Money. I have control over eighty percent of certain goods in the South Central and Southeastern U.S. She had interest in some of those goods." I knew Knuckles was being deliberately vague, but he got his message across. "So she played the long con. And used a child to do it. Woulda worked too. If it hadn't been for Gunnar."

"You said that day you knew I'd help you."

"I did. That's who you are, boy. You consider me family as much as I consider you family, and you'd do anything to help your family. It's how you ended up in my tender care in the first Goddamned place."

"So what happens now?" I needed to know what he expected my part going forward to be, because I had no doubt Knuckles had a longer plan than simply me rescuing the girl and living happily ever after.

"Now, I go huntin'. I'm gonna find that bitch, and I'm going to end her."

Pippa gasped and sat up straighter. "You can't."

"I can, Pippa. And I am. I'm sorry if it hurts you, but I can't let her live. Any woman who would do what she had done to you -- for any reason -- doesn't deserve to live."

"Surely she hadn't meant for them to actually sell me." She shivered and clung to me tighter.

"Baby, I wish I could say she didn't, but I've seen the proof myself."

"What do you need from me? Pippa is safe in this compound if you need my help."

"Nope. Your only job from this point forward is to take care of Pippa and any rug rats you have. Find your place here. Learn how to function on the outside. Learn to share your life with Pippa because it's not gonna be as easy as it seems right now. Once I get back, we'll see where you're gonna be the best asset for Kiss of Death."

"Christ," Cain interrupted. He sounded more amused than irritated or angry. Like this was all something he'd foreseen but hadn't wanted to admit. "Surely to God Torpedo ain't makin' you vice president again."

"Nope. He's makin' me sergeant at arms. At least until he decides he's got Kiss of Death established and remade the way he wants it. This is my club. Always was. Torpedo respects that."

"Can't say I'm surprised. Or that you're not the right person to lead this ragtag bunch."

"'Course I am. Though, I have to admit, from what I've seen of your guys, Torpedo and Bohannon have done better than I could have with everything that happened before. The club needed the break. Just wish it hadn't been seventeen fuckin' years."

"Anything else we need to clear the air on?" Cain sat back in the familiar relaxed posture I'd always associated with my dad.

Knuckles shook his head. "Can't think of

anything."

"So you're out for good, then?" The thought of my friend being out of that hellhole made me happy. And I wasn't too proud to admit I was glad I'd get to see him, if not every day, most days.

"I am." He grinned. "I'll still be with you to keep you in line." He winked at Pippa. "I'll make sure he always treats you right."

"You don't have to worry about him being good to me." She looked up at me and gave me a watery smile. "He's treated me better in the last couple of days than I've ever been treated. I'm glad you chose him for me." Christ, I loved the way she phrased that. I'd been chosen. For her protector. To be the man who loved her for the rest of her life.

"Good, then." Knuckles stood. "I'm going to have a word with Torpedo, and I imagine Cain wants to be in on it."

"Damned fuckin' straight." Dad stood. When he stood in front of us, he leaned down and kissed the top of Pippa's head. "You let me know if you need anything, honey. You're my daughter now, too."

"Just... accept Gunnar for the man he is. I know he can't do the things with your company his brothers can because of his background. But he's a good man who would literally give everything to protect his family."

"I know, honey. I've always been proud of Gunnar. All my boys turned out to be great men, but Gunnar is ruthless in a way the others never could be. Pops was right. It was best you got away from me during the years when a boy becomes a man. We'd have been at each other's throats constantly, and your mother would have divorced me."

"Yeah, well, the Marines would have been a

preferred choice."

"While I'd have preferred the military to have been in your future instead of prison, I can't regret what you did or condemn you for it. You protected your sister with everything you had. You did what you thought was the best thing for her in a very fuckin' bad situation." He grinned. "I look at it this way. You went to prison and came out a better man for it. That's something very difficult to accomplish."

"Don't know about better, but I'm pretty sure I'm meaner."

"Christ, I've missed you, son." Cain cleared his throat. Yeah. I got it.

"Damned dust. I'm definitely gonna have to have a word with Torpedo."

Chapter Eleven

Pippa

When Gunnar and I were finally alone, I had a good cry. And really. It had been a long time coming. Had it only been two days since Gunnar had rescued me? It felt like a lifetime ago. Part of me was afraid this was all a dream. An illusion I'd convinced myself was real to escape the hell I'd been thrust into. But every time I went to sleep, I woke up with Gunnar wrapped around me. He had barely left my side, and only when I had to go to the bathroom. It should have felt smothering. Instead, it felt right. Like this was how my life was supposed to be. It was definitely how I wanted it to be from now on.

"Whatcha doin', babe?" Gunnar came up behind me, wrapping his arms around my waist and kissing my neck. His beard tickled that sensitive spot and I giggled.

"Waiting on you. I thought we'd spend the night at home." We'd been given indefinite use of the warehouse flat and I was growing to love the wide-open spaces. The place really was fantastic. And so not what I expected from a motorcycle club. Probably why stereotypes weren't all they were cracked up to be.

"Stay home? You don't want to go to a wild party?" He grinned against my neck sending shivers through my body.

"Didn't say that." I reached behind me and between us to cup the front of his jeans. His cock was rapidly hardening, which was exactly what I wanted.

"Oh? So, you *do* want to have a wild party." He grinned down at me.

"Absolutely. Pretty sure we can have as wild a party as you want right here."

Gunnar growled low in his throat, his hands tightening on my hips. "You're playing with fire, little girl."

I turned in his arms to face him, pressing my body flush against his. "Maybe I want to get burned."

His eyes darkened with lust as he gazed down at me. Without warning, he scooped me up and tossed me over his shoulder, striding purposefully toward the bed in the far corner of the big flat. I squealed in delight, playfully smacking his firm ass.

"Oh, you're in for it now," he rumbled.

He tossed me onto the bed and crawled over me, caging me in with his muscular arms. Gunnar lowered his face to mine, taking my lips in a searing kiss that left me breathless. I tangled my fingers in his hair, pulling him closer as our tongues danced.

"Gonna fuck you in a bit. When I do, you're gonna scream my name at the top of your lungs. Everybody in the whole Goddamned compound is gonna know who you belong to, woman."

"Oh, God, yes," I moaned, arching up against him. "Fuck me!"

He growled low in his throat and captured my lips in another scorching kiss. His hands roamed over my body, leaving trails of fire in their wake. I tugged impatiently at his shirt, needing to feel his bare skin against mine.

Gunnar sat back on his heels and yanked his shirt off over his head, tossing it carelessly aside. I raked my gaze hungrily over his tattooed, muscular torso. I reached out to trace the intricate designs inked on his skin, marveling at the contrast between the hard planes of muscle and the softer dusting of hair.

"Like what you see?" he asked with a cocky grin.

"You know I do," I replied breathlessly.

In response, he gripped the hem of my shirt and shoved it over my head before shedding my bra as well. "So fuckin' beautiful," he murmured, palming a breast in each hand. I gasped as he lowered his mouth to one stiff peak and sucked.

"Gunnar, please," I whimpered. "I need you."

He lifted his head, his dark eyes burning with desire. "Tell me what you need, baby. What do you want?"

"I need you inside me. Fuck me! Please!" I reached between us to fumble with his belt buckle. He sat up and helped me shove his jeans and boxers down his hips so his cock sprang free, pointing due north.

"Fuck," he bit out as he fisted his cock. The head was an angry purple while pearly pre-come seeped from the tip. "We're gonna have to do a lot of this so I can get used to you. Otherwise, I'm never gonna last more than a hot second."

I would have laughed if I'd been capable of it, but the more he touched me, talked dirty to me, encouraged me to talk dirty to him… Yeah. I was in a bad way.

He positioned himself at my entrance and slowly pressed into me, groaning as I stretched around his thick girth. I whimpered, but desperately needed more. The burn hurt, but in a good way. The feeling of fullness and submission caused my inner muscles to clench around him, holding him inside me.

"Fuckin' heaven," Gunnar muttered. "You're so fuckin' tight," he growled, beginning a steady rhythm that had him plunging deep and withdrawing slowly. "Tell me you like this, Pippa. Tell me!"

"Oh fuck! Yes," I moaned, lifting my hips to meet his thrusts. "Harder! Harder!" My pleas sounded as desperate as I felt. I thought I might explode at any moment, and I wasn't certain I'd survive the detonation. And God! I loved a good metaphor!

Gunnar obeyed, slamming into me with enough force to jostle the bed. I cried out his name and arched my back, loving the feeling of him plowing into me over and over again. My nails raked down his back, leaving furrows in the skin there. He caught my hands in his and held them above my head.

"Mine," he growled against my neck, nipping at the sensitive skin there. "You're fucking mine."

"Yes," I gasped. "Yours. I'm yours!"

Gunnar moved his hand between us, finding my clit and rubbing it with rough brushes and pinches with his fingers. I screamed his name as an orgasm rocketed through my body, clenching tight around him with each wave of pleasure until he followed suit with a shout of his own. His hips pistoned harder, driving deeper as he emptied himself inside me.

Gunnar collapsed on top of me, his weight a comforting anchor as we both caught our breath. I reveled in the feeling of his body pressed against mine, his skin slick with sweat. I traced lazy patterns on his back with my fingers. I could feel his heart hammering against my chest where he was pressed so close to me. Then his heart rate slowed, and it was like he was taking me with him. My heart wanted to follow the beat of his and it wasn't long before we both finally settled.

After a few minutes, Gunnar lifted his head to look at me, his dark eyes soft with emotion. "You OK, baby?" he asked, brushing a strand of hair from my face. Gunnar leaned forward to capture my lips in a long, slow kiss that tasted like victory and love and belonging all rolled into one.

When he ended the kiss, I smiled up at him. "I

couldn't be more perfect. You're amazing."

He grinned, looking pleased with himself. "Glad you enjoyed it. I aim to please."

"Oh, you definitely pleased," I assured him with a giggle.

Gunnar rolled to the side, pulling me with him so I was draped across his chest. His arms wrapped around me. "We're gonna make a go of this, Pippa. And I swear to you, I'll be everything you need."

"It goes both ways. I'll be what you need too."

When he smiled up at me, I thought I'd never seen him look more carefree. Or more contented. "Honey, you already are."

Who can possibly know they're in love with someone in a mere couple of days? Impossible, right? No. It wasn't impossible.

"I love you, Gunnar. I don't care if it's only been a couple of days. I know with everything I am that I love you."

He kissed me again. "I love you too. I know what love looks like because I saw it in my mom and dad every day when I was growing up. I understand the looks he used to give her when she wasn't looking now. My dad, Cain Gill, the man everyone who knows him is afraid of, would look at my mom like she hung the moon. Like his next breath depended on whether or not she noticed and approved of him. Dad is so in love with my mom it hurts to watch them together sometimes. That's how I feel when I look at you."

"I never thought I'd have this," I admitted softly. "I'm not even sure I truly believed love like what you described existed. Now I know it does."

"I never thought I'd have this either," he admitted softly. "After prison and shit, I figured I'd probably end up alone or dead. But now I've got you, and I ain't ever letting go."

I snuggled into his warmth, feeling safe and cherished. "Promise?"

"I swear it," he said fiercely. "You're mine now, Pippa."

Gunnar reached for the blanket beside us and tossed it over my body. He rested one hand possessively on my ass, rubbing gently. The steady beat of his heart and the soothing feel of his hands on my skin had my eyelids growing heavier and heavier as each second passed.

I couldn't help but wonder what the future held for us. Somehow, I thought this might be the start of a grand adventure. I was definitely looking forward to what was headed our way. I knew there would be trials ahead, and I'd be lying if I said the thought of Knuckles going after and killing my mother wasn't more than a little disconcerting, but I knew I could handle it. Gunnar would see to it.

And somehow, some way, we really would live happily ever after.

Knuckles (Kiss of Death MC 2)
A Bones MC Romance
Marteeka Karland

Hannah's stubborn, abrasive, and vicious. She's also mine.

Hannah: My life as I knew it ended the night my boyfriend tried to rape me. I killed the swine, and I'm not sorry. After that night, it became my mission to rid the world of as many predators as I could. If that meant I got slapped around a little, I'd sacrifice for the cause. What I didn't count on was my brother's best friend coming to my rescue. That dangerous vibe he's giving off is making me feel things I never expected. Knuckles fought for me. Protected me. Now he's using words like "claim" and "old lady," but I'm not sure I want to be anyone's property. Not unless it means he's my property too.

Knuckles: I came to *Afternoon Delytes* to get the information I needed to destroy a woman who'd betrayed me. I never expected to see my best friend's sister take a backhand to the face. She has the biggest heart of anyone I've ever met. She's also vicious. And *mine.*

Chapter One

Knuckles

"You tell that bitch I'm comin' for her. She has a week at most to make her peace." I'd never meant a statement more in my fucking life.

"I'm just puttin' you in touch with her, Knuckles. Ain't your errand boy. You want to negotiate, you go through her people."

"Nothin' to negotiate. When you confirm your job's done, you tell her the only thing I want from her is her fuckin' head on a pike."

"You're not gettin' your daughter back until you talk with her, man. She made that very clear."

"Too bad for her I already have my daughter."

Finally, I got a reaction out of Wild Bill. Only a raised eyebrow, but way more than the man normally showed. He wasn't a man I trusted exactly, but he held to a code and I respected that. "OK… That's news."

"Is it." I didn't phrase my words as a question.

"How long have you had her?"

"Since before they managed to sell Pippa," I snapped. "I know Beth wants my supplier, and I know she worked for several months to undercut me, so I was prepared for somethin'. It never occurred to me she'd sell her own daughter for a drug deal, but it should have. I knew years ago there was somethin' not right with Beth. Even before she brought Pippa to see me. I knew there was another shoe to drop but wasn't expectin' her to actually sell our daughter to get even with me."

"Look. I got in touch with you as a favor to her. I can see I made an error in judgment." Yeah, Wild Bill could see how pissed I was. "I'll deliver your message to the bitch and go one better. I'll give you a heads-up before she does anythin' else to piss you off."

"Now, why would you do that, Wild Bill?" I drawled out the question as I leaned against the bar and took a sip of my coffee. Wild Bill had met me just outside the Kiss of Death compound in Nashville. The area we'd purchased and walled off sat in the industrial outskirts of the city, but there were still a couple bars and a strip club in the area, which was where we were currently. Little club called *Afternoon Delytes*. The music was loud, the girls had big tits, and the alcohol wasn't watered down. A good place for an enemy to be distracted if he wasn't cautious. Which was why I liked to meet here with men I didn't fully trust.

"I know I live by a code, Knuckles. A line I won't cross. If what you told me is true -- and your reputation says you know your shit before you speak -- that bitch obliterated my line. I ain't above pimpin' out girls willin' to split the profits, but I don't force women. For any reason. And I absolutely do not traffic. Beth broke both those hard and fast rules for me. I agreed to this in good faith with her mostly because I respect you. If it were my daughter, I'd kill anyone who knew what was goin' on and didn't tell me. But, honest to God, I thought Beth had the girl. Maybe in a gilded cage, or maybe it was an empty threat to you and there was no danger to your daughter at all."

"I could be lying."

Wild Bill shook his head. "Nope. That's not your style. You've always given it to me straight. Whether or not it's what I wanted to hear." I had to admit, the man might have gone up a little in my estimation. I'd still verify any information he shared with me before acting on it. It might not tell the tale, but I'd be able to better see if Wild Bill subscribed to the "honor among thieves" mentality, or if it was every man for himself.

"You know where Beth is?" Even if he was lying, I wanted any information he doled out. If it was bogus, I'd act accordingly. Which would not end well for Wild Bill.

"Yep." He took out an envelope. "I've had a guy on her for a couple months. She's at the same place she's always been. Way too rich for a nurse's salary." He handed me the envelope and I took it.

I stared at him a long time. Wild Bill held my gaze without flinching. "Few men surprise me, so I'm going to give you this one time to tell me your agenda. I won't consider you an enemy and I'll respect your territory, but only if you come clean now."

"No agenda, Knuckles. No repayment expected. No favors later. This is because I agreed to help your ex without investigatin' beyond the surface. Knowin' the girl was her daughter? Yeah. Wasn't expectin' her to hurt her own kid." He shook his head like he knew he'd fucked up royally. "I don't question things beyond the job because the job speaks for itself, but with somethin' like this, I should have dug a little deeper. Ain't too proud to admit when I'm wrong." The corner of his lips curled up in a self-deprecating smile. "I'd also prefer it if you didn't see this as a betrayal of the fragile alliance we have."

"OK, now *that* I believe." I took a sip of coffee, never taking my eyes from Wild Bill.

"How'd you get out of a life sentence anyway?" Wild Bill took a healthy pull of his beer before signaling the bartender for another.

"Friends in high places." I continued to study the other man. "I'd've been out years ago except I had to help a guy out."

Wild Bill snorted. "Right. You went in on a triple

murder the way I heard it. That ain't somethin' you get out of that easy."

"I did confess to a triple murder. Yes." The smile I gave him wasn't genuine.

Wild Bill looked like he wasn't sure whether or not to believe me. "Must have been some long, hard dick you sucked to get out of that kind of rap."

"All you need to know is it's none of your Goddamned business." This was getting tiresome. "You can spread the word to anyone you want to live that I'm back."

"Hear things are different around the club." The little bastard just didn't know when to shut up. He also knew how to stroke someone's ego with all this shit about how he respected me. He was trying to get out of the shit he stepped in with his big fucking mouth. Except his big fucking mouth kept moving.

"They are." He was fishing for news about the new president of Kiss of Death, and I wasn't biting.

We stared at each other a long time. Wild Bill probably expected me to expound, spill all my secrets, or bitch and moan about my club being under new rule, but I meant it when I told him it wasn't any of his Goddamned business.

Finally, Wild Bill raised his hands in surrender. "All right. Keep your secrets."

"No secrets to keep."

"Your club goes rogue while you're in prison, traffickin' women and children. They piss off the wrong people in Kentucky and Florida and get themselves annihilated. Then you come back, but not as president?" He snorted. "Right. Nothin' to see here."

With a low growl, I darted my hand out and grabbed Wild Bill by the throat, squeezing enough he got the message. His hands went immediately to my wrist. No doubt if I hadn't had two of my men search him before he approached me he'd have gutted me. Betting he was playing my death over in his head a hundred different ways while I held his gaze with a steely one of my own.

"Kiss of Death is my club. Nothing happens there unless I allow it. Prison or not. True, Dart got things in a bad way before Slash forced his way to the top, but I made sure the kids were either returned to their families or placed with people who would protect them. I made sure as many of the women as I could had someplace safe to go." I turned and spat; the disgust of those tasks still left a bad taste in my mouth. "I'd love to say Slash and Gremlin were necessary collateral damage, but they were both dead the moment they laid their hands on innocents and used my club to hurt them."

"Man, you ain't gotta explain yourself to me." Wild Bill's voice was tight where I was a hair's breadth from cutting off his air.

"Yet, you made a point to question me."

"No offense, man. I get it. I get it."

I squeezed a little bit more. My men stood between us and everyone else in the club, and the employees here wouldn't interfere in my business. The only thing the owner requested of me was that we not kill anyone inside her club. Wild Bill didn't know that, though.

"You get to live because I promised Medusa no killin' in her club. If the information you gave me regarding Beth proves accurate, I'll forget you were tryin' to nose in my fuckin' business. If you're playin' me, I'll make an example of you for the whole fuckin' city underground. I don't do subtle." I gave Wild Bill a hard shove.

The younger man stumbled back but kept his feet. He raised his hands again and took another step backward before he stopped. "It's accurate, Knuckles. I ain't no diplomat. Don't believe in sugar coatin' anythin'. So even though I wasn't tryin' to give you shit, I ain't the only one wonderin' if you let the reins slip, or if you were behind the shit Kiss of Death got into. Either way, you look bad."

"I make no secret things went to shit when I went to prison. I didn't have measures in place to control the police and the DA, but I wasn't lettin' the men who raped and murdered my sister live even one more day. Took me a while to get things in play, but I managed. I'll be back in charge soon enough. It's already been worked out."

"Then why the fuck ain't you taken over in name? Those pricks from Somerset are too goody-two-shoes to be fuckin' bikers."

I inhaled for patience. *You cannot kill in Medusa's club. You cannot kill in Medusa's club...*

"Christ. You really are a dumb shit." I grabbed the guy by the back of the head and slammed his face on the bar. Blood squirted with a sickening squish. The bartender danced back, narrowly avoiding getting splattered. He wisely didn't say anything, bringing out a bottle of disinfectant cleaner and taking care of the mess.

Wild Bill staggered backward, one hand over his nose, the other reaching for the gun at his back. "Motherfucker! You broke my fuckin' nose!"

"Learn when to shut the fuck up, Wild Bill. You'll thank me later."

I could see in his eyes Wild Bill was gonna pull his weapon and shoot me. That was his intent at that moment. Which was when Knight, one of my men, slid his arm around Wild Bill's neck from behind, lifted his chin, and stuck the tip of his knife against the younger man's neck. "This is the part where you take your spankin' like a man, say 'Thank you, sir', and go on your merry fuckin' way."

"You're rapidly approaching the point of no return, kid. My gratitude only goes so far." I was done with this shit.

I saw the moment he realized what just happened. Yeah. Figured as much. Kid let his anger get the better of him. I nearly smiled as I remembered another man who'd had to learn to control his temper. Gunnar had turned out fine. Wild Bill had potential, but he needed a mentor and nothing short of forced confinement would make this man agree to having a fucking mentor. Kind of like Gunnar.

"Uh, yeah. I, uh…" He cleared his throat. "Sorry, man. I-I didn't mean…"

I nodded at Knight, who kept his knife on Wild Bill but used his other hand to snag the gun at the younger man's back. "You don't play nice with others, do you, son?" Knight handed the gun to another one of my men, Hawk, who tucked it in the back of his jeans under his cut. "Learn to behave and you'll get your toy back."

If the little prick hadn't pissed me off, I'd have told Knight not to disarm him and keep it polite. I didn't want to antagonize Wild Bill. People tended to be more inclined to lash out when you were unnecessarily cruel. I wanted a fearful respect from the people I dealt with in and around Nashville. Business went smoother that way. I wanted them to respect me enough to not want to cross me, while being afraid enough to know if they did, I'd fuck them all the way up. But this little shit had gotten on my last fucking nerve and I was done.

"You had my respect for a hot second, Wild Bill. I thought you were the kind of man I could build an understanding with."

"Knuckles…" Wild Bill had a couple of bar napkins he'd snagged and held them to his nose to stem the flow of blood. It wasn't much, but he'd have a couple black eyes in the morning. Good enough for the fucker.

"You learn to control your temper, then we'll talk. I don't think you're a bad guy. I think you have lofty aspirations, which I respect. Just don't forget who you're dealing with. Be it me or anyone else. You're walkin' away this time. Next time, you might not be so fuckin' lucky."

Wild Bill gave me a couple nods of understanding. "Yeah. I hear you."

"Good." I stuck out my hand to the kid, forcing the issue of a handshake, but I was making a point. "No hard feelings." This time.

Wild Bill hesitated a moment, then took my hand. "Yeah, man. No hard feelings."

As Wild Bill walked away, Hawk laid the gun on the bar, along with the clip and the bullet in the chamber and motioned to the bartender. The guy had been hanging out in the background and was ready. "If he comes back, make sure he gets his weapon."

"You sure Torpedo and Bohannon are on board with this?" Hawk gave me a hard look. "'Cause, I gotta tell you, they saved this club from going down the fuckin' toilet. I'm solidly in your favor for president, but I can't in good conscience go against either of those men."

"You won't have to." I took another gulp of my coffee. I really wanted a fuckin' beer, but I hadn't had one since before I went to prison and couldn't take the chance of dulling my senses because I couldn't handle my alcohol. "Took me a long fuckin' time to get those guys here, and they only agreed to stay until I acclimated to life on the outside."

"You?" Knight leaned against the bar, taking a pull from his beer. "You brought Bones to Kiss of Death?"

"I did. And you have no idea how many strings I had to pull to make it happen. So I will give Torpedo all the time he needs to be satisfied I'm fit to lead this club again. The last thing either him or Bohannon are going to allow is for us to fall back to the way it was before they got here."

"It's not like Bones and Salvation's Bane left much when they cleaned house." Hawk's gaze tracked around the room. He'd been my sergeant at arms before I'd gone to prison. He and Knight had gone into hiding along with a few others of my inner circle when Dart had staged a violent takeover. I hadn't been able to help. It had taken several years for me to establish connections on the outside that filtered inside the prison. Avenging my sister had been the most important thing at the time, and the consequences took me nearly a decade to overcome. When I did, it took nearly the same amount of time for me to guide Kiss of Death into the paths of Bones, Salvation's Bane, and Black Reign MCs. The price was high, but worth it. And, if I were honest, I had no problem with being affiliated with Bones MC or any splinter club.

"Doesn't matter. That shit Dart, then Slash, did in the club's name hurt us. I was negligent in getting myself put in prison without a plan in place for the club."

"I heard the former president of Bones actually

married one of Slash's victims."

"Yeah. Cain took a woman, Angel, as his old lady. Raised three of the kids there too."

"Ice and Cyclone." Hawk gave me a nod. "I met Cyclone once. Didn't the girl end up with another of Bones's members?"

"Yeah." Something caught my eye as I continued to converse with Hawk and Knight. A woman I thought I recognized. I couldn't place her immediately, but I couldn't pull my gaze away from her. "She's married to the guy who took Bohannon's place at Bones. Name's Stunner."

"I've heard he runs a tight ship at Bones as their enforcer." Knight stroked his beard lazily. "Ice and Cyclone were promoted to president and vice president. What do Torpedo and Bohannon plan on doing when you take over again?"

"Not my business," I answered absently. The woman was with a large man. He towered over her, but he wasn't as big as me. I could tell by the way he carried himself he was a little high strung. "It'll be a while before…" I trailed off as I watched the woman speak to the bartender. She and the man she was with were on the other end of the bar. She turned around and I got my first good look at her. At the same time, the guy she was with backhanded her so hard she spun around and fell to the floor of the bar.

Before I could register what was happening, a ferocious, angry roar exploded from me. Because I recognized the woman. And some motherfucker was about to fucking die.

Chapter Two

Hannah

This was it. This was where I died. On a bar floor smelling of beer and piss and vomit… And it's no more than I fucking deserved.

I smacked my head on the floor when I fell because Dillon hit me so hard it knocked me silly, and I couldn't protect myself. There was a horrible noise like an angry wild animal, but I couldn't figure out where it was coming from or what exactly the threat was. Then Dillon's fist came at me again. I had time to suck in a breath just before the blow landed across my temple and my world tilted sharply as pain exploded through my head again.

I thought I might pass out -- prayed to pass out so the beating would be over when I woke up. Instead, something inside me refused to go down. Even for a minute.

Then Dillon was gone. I whimpered, not sure if I'd been given a reprieve or if he was simply getting rid of someone trying to pull him off me. It had happened more than once in this same club. It was why he brought me here. If he got drunk and hit me, no one would do much. Occasionally someone would try to defend me, but Dillon was a huge man. If he didn't want to do something, it took some force to make him. We'd both learned that when faced with an enraged giant, most people stayed clear. Oh, they might take out their phones and record the beating, but that was as far as it went. Which rarely helped me.

Closing my eyes, I reached for oblivion with all my heart but I just couldn't go under. There was a fight going on. I could hear the familiar sound of flesh hitting flesh. Grunts and sickening squishes. My stomach rebelled. I wasn't sure if it was the smells, the sounds, or the injury to my head, but I was going to hurl and there was no way I could get to the bathroom.

Somehow, I managed to roll over on my stomach and push myself at least part way off the floor. Sure enough, I vomited in an explosive rush. A whimper escaped me when the very last thing I wanted to do was show weakness to not only Dillon, but every motherfucker in this stupid club. I might die right here on this funky-ass floor, but I would do it in silence. Well, except for the retching.

The noise around me was gradually drowned out by the roaring in my ears as I vomited again. Just as I was about to collapse in my own puke, someone wrapped a beefy arm around my waist and pulled me off the floor to my knees.

"Easy there, girl. You're OK."

"Get… off… me." I could barely gasp my words, but I didn't want anyone touching me.

"I ain't gonna hurt you, honey. Just tryin' to get you off the floor." The guy's voice was deep and gruff. Not like Dillon's. And shockingly familiar. I was afraid to look up at him out of fear I was right, and I knew who this guy was. I was also afraid maybe I was dreaming, and it was Dillon. And he was going to finally beat me to death.

"I'll call Pain and tell him we'll meet him in the infirmary," a second man said. I couldn't get a good look at any of them because my eyes were blurry from the blow to my head and the tears streaming from them after puking my guts up.

"Knight gettin' the cage?"

"Yeah. Glad you decided not to ride to this meeting."

"Something felt off from the start. Still feels off. I

thought we might need the extra cover if there was too much trouble. Wasn't plannin' on this kind a' trouble, though."

I turned my head to look up at the guy. Again, he was sickeningly familiar, but my eyes refused to focus on the large blob looking back at me. And honestly, I didn't want to confirm what I knew in my heart was true. The man who'd come to my rescue was fucking Knuckles. "Don't want to be no one's trouble." It was embarrassing how sulky I sounded. And how hurt.

"Poor choice of words, honey. I'm glad I was prepared 'cause you ain't in no shape to ride a bike, and no way in hell I'm leavin' you here for any fuckin' reason."

"If you could just help me home, I promise I won't be any more of a bother."

"Like fuck." Knuckles scooped me up in his arms. The guy was freakishly strong, because he picked me up in a deadlift before settling me against his chest with one arm around my back and the other under my legs. He might have been picking up a gallon of milk for all the effort it took him. "I'm takin' you home with me. Pain'll take a look at you. You might be hurt worse than you realize."

"Where's Dillon?" I couldn't help the question.

I realized it was a mistake to say Dillon's name when Knuckles stiffened around me. "Dillon." He spat out the name like it left a bad taste in his mouth. "I hope you're talkin' 'bout your pet chihuahua and not the motherfucker who hit you."

I sighed. "Look," I said in a soft voice for Knuckle's ears alone. "You know as well as I do, you can't disappear him now. Too many people saw the fight."

He took me out of the club in long, confident

strides. I clung to him, ducking my head but resisting the temptation to bury my face in his chest. That would be too embarrassing for words. Especially when he was my twin's best friend.

"Fully aware of how to carry out a hit, sweetheart." His voice was as soft as mine had been when he spoke to me. "You know he's gonna die. If not by my hand, by Gunnar's."

"No!" My heart pounded at the thought of Gunnar killing to protect me. "Not again." The last two words were said in a whimper. I struggled to get out of Knuckles's hold, but I might as well not have tried. I wasn't going anywhere Knuckles didn't want me going.

"Trust me to know what I'm doin', Hannah. Ain't no one goin' back to prison. I made a promise to myself after I killed the motherfuckers who hurt my sister, I wouldn't do anything like that without a plan ever again. Not because I regret what I did, but because I took action without a plan firmly in place to buffer the fallout." He met my gaze with a steady one of his own. "Make no mistake, baby, Dillon's gonna die. But not before I'm ready."

Knuckles slid into the back seat of some kind of SUV. My vision still wasn't right. Probably because one eye was starting to swell where Dillon had backhanded me with the first blow. The car door shut, then a few moments later, we sped off.

"Wait." I tried to sit up but couldn't manage to do more than push away from Knuckles's chest slightly. My head pounded and I couldn't focus properly, but I was becoming more aware -- of way more than was good for me. "Where are we going?"

"To the compound. Pain's gonna check you over. Remember?"

"No, Knuckles. I want to go home."

"Honey, Kiss of Death is your home. Gunnar is gonna be pissed as shit when he finds this out. What the fuck, Hannah?"

"Stop the truck." I pushed away from Knuckles with more effort this time. "I'm not going back to the compound. And you're not saying shit to Gunnar."

"Stop it! Hold still. You'll make yourself sick."

"Stop the fucking truck. I want out." I continued to struggle. It didn't take much for Knuckles to hold me still. I could tell he was trying to be careful not to hurt me or let me hurt myself, but I was not going to that compound. I wasn't getting anywhere near Gunnar until any damage Dillon had done was healed. If that meant I took a vacation for a couple weeks, I'd get out of town.

"Christ, Hannah." Knuckles sounded alarmed but irritated. "Quit squirmin'. You can't get up with the truck movin'."

"I told you to stop the vehicle, Knuckles. Either let me out or take me to my house. I'm not going to Kiss of Death." Thankfully, the vehicle slowed and we pulled off on the side of the road. Knuckles was right. Moving so much, struggling after being knocked silly while in a moving vehicle made me nauseous as hell.

"She OK?" The man driving spoke softly, as if he knew my head was hurting and was trying to keep it down.

"I'm fine. I just want to go home."

"If you don't want to go to Gunnar, that's fine. I'll take you to mine."

"Either take me to my house or let me out of the fucking truck, Knuckles." I put every ounce of demand in my voice I could. I still sounded weak, but I thought I finally got my point across to him.

"Fine. But just so you understand, there is no version of events where I leave you alone tonight. Understand?"

"Probably the best I'm gonna get," I muttered. "Fine. Take me home." My stomach chose that moment to rebel. I reached for the door handle. "Right after I throw up." I fumbled until I managed to get the door open, and tumbled out onto the pavement on the shoulder of the road.

"Christ, Hannah! Be careful!"

I heaved and heaved. I wouldn't have been surprised if I'd thrown up my shoes. When I finished, I fell back on my ass against a solid body. I was pinned in the V of his thighs as he supported me. Thank God too, because I'd have fallen in my own puke if he hadn't.

"She's gonna have to have medical care, Knuckles. If she's hurt bad, Gunnar's gonna go nuclear even more than he's already gonna."

"You're such a dumb shit, Knight. And I'm tellin' Gunnar you said that." Hawk, one of the guys with Knuckles smacked the other man in the back of the head.

"What? I mean, I'd want to get her help even if it wouldn't throw Gunnar into a homicidal rage." Knight shrugged. "No offense." If I hadn't been so sick and in pain, I might have laughed. I'd liked Knight from the first moment I met him. He was like that annoying younger brother you wanted to grab by the ear and drag around just because you could. But that wasn't the takeaway from the exchange. It would be much easier for me to go to Pain, Kiss of Death's club safety officer, than for him to come to me.

"I'm not… going to… the compound." I was still nauseous as fuck, but the vomiting seemed to have stopped for the moment.

"Fuck." Knuckles held me for several moments, letting me catch my breath. "Get her a bottle of water." He didn't address my concerns, and I knew he'd do everything he could to bully me into doing what he wanted.

"Look. I'll let Pain look me over, but he has to come to my house. I'm not going back to the club for a while."

"Gunnar's gonna want to know why."

"I'm a grown-ass woman, Knuckles. I can go where I want, when I want."

He helped me to my feet, keeping an arm around me. I wasn't too ashamed to admit I needed his help staying on my feet. My knees felt like Jell-O. "Yeah, honey. You can. But I don't keep secrets from Gunnar. Not about you."

"Then make yourself be where he's not. Don't be around him for a few days."

"Not splittin' hairs with you, Hannah. I'll take you home to your house and get Pain to meet us there. I'll stay with you tonight but tomorrow, I'm telling Gunnar."

"But --"

"Be grateful I'm giving you as much as I am. I might have been the one to keep Gunnar alive when he first went on the inside, but make no mistake, I have his back as much as he has mine. Let it go."

I sighed but nodded. "Fine."

"Good. Now, let's get you back in the truck and get you home."

Chapter Three

Knuckles

There was a pressing need deep inside my soul for me to go hunting. I hadn't been prepared for this. Not in any way imaginable. And it wasn't just needing to hunt prey and not being able to. It was Hannah Gill. My best friend's sister. The daughter of a man I deeply respected. She was thirty-two to my forty-five, numbers I had to remind myself of every fucking time I saw her. I knew she was trouble the second I laid eyes on her, but I hadn't expected to watch that trouble play out in real time. I also hadn't expected the beast inside me to rise so forcefully and violently as it had when I saw that motherfucker hit Hannah. What concerned me most was how the desire to hunt and kill the motherfucker who hit her was stunted by the overwhelming *need* to see exactly how badly Hannah was hurt, to do everything in my power to make it better, and to soothe and calm her fears. Then make sure no one ever fucking touched her again.

The ride to her house on a little farm outside Nashville didn't take too long. I thought Hannah had fallen asleep but the second the truck stopped, she opened her door and stumbled out onto her driveway and toward the house.

"Hannah, wait up!" I should have known she wasn't going to obey me. Made my hand itch to spank her ass until she did what I told her. Unfortunately, spanking her pert ass wasn't ever going to be an option. Just meant I'd have to get creative. "Hannah!" The infuriating woman slammed the door shut just before I reached it. I heard the locks click, then her retreating footsteps. "Hannah!" I banged a fist against the door several times.

"Go away, Knuckles!" At least she was answering. The relief in my chest did nothing to ease the alarm in my brain. This wasn't good. So fucking not good...

"Already told you I ain't leavin' you alone. Open up or I break the door down. Simple as that."

There was a hesitation, and I could practically see her weighing her options. "I could call the cops."

"Yep. You could. And when they let me out of holding later tonight, I'll find you and handcuff you to me. Good luck shuttin' me out then."

As I hoped, the door opened, Hannah on the other side huffing out an irritated breath. "Fine. But don't touch anything. And you're sleeping on the couch."

"My, you're a regular little ray of sunshine now that you're gettin' your wits about you." I gave her a smirk to which she responded with a scowl.

"And you're an asshole!"

Instantly, the good humor I was trying my damndest to project snapped like too much tension on a rubber band. "This asshole saved you from a beatin' of epic proportions, Hannah!"

She gasped and took a step back before lifting her chin and putting her shoulders back. "I would have handled it." Her voice was tight with emotion. Mostly anger.

There was something in the back of my mind, some little voice inside my head telling me I needed to take a step back and regroup. Unfortunately, my fucking mouth didn't get the message in time. "Looked to me like you were already trying to handle it. And failing miserably. Do you think anyone in the fuckin' club would've come to your rescue?"

"Clearly, someone did." She raised an eyebrow

at me.

There was a full beat of silence before I exploded. With a ferocious roar, I pivoted and threw a haymaker at the wall, putting my fist through the drywall. "Fuckin' hell! Have you not looked in the mirror, Hannah? That motherfucker hit you! Repeatedly! *In a fuckin' public place!*" The more I yelled at her, the more out of control I was getting. None of this was her fault. None of it! Why was I taking my anger out on her? The answer was clear. Because I knew, in my fuckin' shriveled up heart, this wasn't the first time she'd been hit by that bastard. "If he'll hit you so casually and viciously where others are watching and had no fear of someone callin' the cops, where do you think he'll stop when you're in private? Huh? You think he'll stop beatin' you after you pass out? Will it be too late when he does?"

"I know exactly what he'll do in private, Knuckles! I know *exactly*! And I forced the whole situation where I knew he would hit me in public!"

Had she shot me in the face, I'm not sure I could have been more surprised at Hannah's response. I took a step backward, shaking my head in disbelief and a gut wrenching horror. "You what?" The words were little more than a whisper. I knew I was going to lose my everloving shit. Like explode like a fucking nuclear bomb.

"None of your business." She wrapped her arms around herself and looked away. "Just know I had a plan and a goal. Nothing else matters."

"Like fuckin' hell!" I crossed the space separating us and pulled her against me, wrapping my hand around her throat and tilting her chin up so she had no choice but to look up at me. "You will fuckin' tell me every fuckin' thing, Hannah." My voice sounded grim and deadly, on the edge of violence. I didn't even try to check my reaction. She needed to see this side of me because I had the sickening feeling this woman was going to be seeing a lot of me. Way more than either of us would be comfortable with.

Her eyes widened and she paled, sweat erupting over the skin of her brow and upper lip. A visceral reaction. To me? My anger? Instantly, I let her go, nearly stumbling backward in my haste to put distance between us. Nausea bubbled in my stomach, and I had to concentrate on breathing to keep from puking.

We both stood there for long, long minutes. I'm not sure Hannah moved at all. I knew I was afraid to move a muscle other than to breathe. If she ran from me, I knew I'd burn the world down to get her to come back. Given what she'd been through, the situation she'd intentionally put herself into, I was guessing she'd been hit more than just what I witnessed tonight.

"I'm sorry, Hannah," I whispered. "I'd never hurt you. Ever."

"I know." Though her reply was soft, I could see in her eyes she was telling the truth. "You were trying to make an impression."

"No, Hannah. I'm fuckin' pissed as hell and wanted you to see it. I'm not sure what pisses me off more. The fact you're admittin' you expected the assault, or the thought you might have somethin' planned you're not lettin' anyone know about."

She shrugged, trying to look nonchalant. Which meant I totally had her pegged. "I mean, take your pick. Plenty to be pissed at me about, I guess."

OK, I didn't like the sound of that. "Not sure what you mean, but I'm fairly certain I ain't gonna enjoy it."

"Look, Knuckles. I've had a long couple of days.

I want to take a shower and put some ice on my face. Maybe take an aspirin or something. Give me a minute and I'll bring you a pillow and some bedding for the couch. Then I need to be alone, please."

I grunted, not wanting to maintain the distance she was so skillfully putting between us. "I'll respect your wishes. But you will respect mine too." When she lifted her chin again, I continued. "No locked doors between us. If you need me, I will absolutely break down the door to get to you."

"You're not responsible for me."

"Nope. But this is still happenin'."

She let out a frustrated snarl. "Why are you so annoying? Why can't you just let me be alone for a while?"

"Because like it or not, you've had head trauma tonight. You don't need to be alone. Beyond that…" I shrugged, not willing to admit to her what I knew in my heart was gonna happen to us both. "I'll let you know." She rolled her eyes but pivoted and stomped down the short hallway to what I assumed was her bedroom. "And don't worry about bedding," I called to her. "Just take a soak or whatever and relax. I'll check on you in half an hour." My orders were met with a slammed door and the *snick* of the lock clicking. "All right," I muttered. "Game on, little girl."

Chapter Four

Hannah

I knew I was on borrowed time. Pain would be here soon to look me over, but one thing I'd learned about Knuckles since I'd met him a few weeks ago was that he absolutely would not let something go if he thought it was important. Knuckles was exactly like my father. Dad always knew what was going on in our lives no matter how hard we tried to keep it secret. He even knew I'd been the one to kill my boyfriend, Robert, instead of Gunnar. Dad had tried to get me to confide in him, to let him handle Robert's death and Gunnar's situation the way it needed to be handled, but I'd made a promise to Gunnar. Knuckles was just as perceptive.

True to his word, thirty minutes later, there was a knock at my door. "Hannah?"

"Is Pain here?" I didn't open the door. It was childish but I wanted to keep him waiting just because I could.

"Yep. And he's grumpy."

"I didn't tell you to call him. If he's gonna be a grouch, I'll just stay in here and lie down. I'm tired. It's been a long fucking day."

"Hannah." There was a warning in his voice. "Out here. Now."

Before I could stop myself I muttered, "You ain't the boss of me."

"Not yet." I shivered at the promise in his voice and wasn't sure if it was from fear or something else entirely. "Give it time."

"I've never wanted to punch someone in the balls more in my life." That wasn't true. I'd wanted to punch Dillon in the balls way the fuck more, but for a myriad of other reasons. And I would. Once everything died down.

More banging. "Hannah!"

"I'm coming! Christ! It's like a sickness with you!" I'd just finished dressing in the yoga pants and tank top someone had left for me. My money was on Gunnar's woman, Pippa. She was exactly what my brother needed, and I was so grateful she had his back. As for Knuckles... I had the feeling this man was going to be the biggest, prickliest thorn in my side ever imagined. And, Christ, it didn't help he was the hottest man I'd ever seen in my life. I jerked open the door and glared up at him. "You happy now?"

"Not in the least. Get your ass in here to Pain so he can check you over, then me and you are havin' a come to Jesus meetin'."

"Knuckles. Cool it." I'd only met Pain once since coming to Nashville to be closer to my brother. Now that I had him back, I didn't want to let Gunnar out of my sight. I couldn't stay in the big industrial complex they called a compound. I needed freedom to move around without the scrutiny of the men in the club. Despite his name, Pain was one of the most naturally empathetic people I'd ever met. He wasn't a doctor, but he had a natural gift for helping people.

"Not until I find out what the fuck's goin' on." Knuckles crossed his massive arms over an equally muscled and impressive chest. Honestly, how did the man get so big? He was well over six feet tall and he had to weigh at least three hundred pounds. All of it solid-as-fuck muscle.

"You saw what was goin' on, Knuckles." Pain didn't raise his voice or look at the big man. Instead, he handed me an ice pack and set about looking in my eyes and shit. "Now, if you can't be civil get the fuck outside until I'm done."

"Or you could not come back at all." I tried to give him a bright smile but couldn't quite manage.

"You take a good look at her, Pain. Really see her injuries. All of them." Knuckles looked straight at me.

"Trust me," Pain answered in a tight voice, glancing up at me. "I see them."

"How long, Hannah?" Knuckles simply to God wasn't going to let this go.

"How long what? Is your dick? From what I hear, not very."

Pain snorted before attempting to cover it with a cough. "Hold this ice pack to your face, honey. It'll help with the swelling. I've got a little something for pain too."

"I don't need anything other than maybe some acetaminophen and ibuprofen. The ice pack'll help."

"Cut the crap, you two." Knuckles snapped his fingers to bring our attention back to him. "This isn't the first time he's hit you. Why didn't you come to your brother?"

"You Goddamned well know why." My voice was barely above a whisper. "And if you tell Gunnar, I will kill you, Knuckles. Slowly and painfully."

We faced off and I knew he could see how angry I was, even with one side of my face swelling pretty badly now. He could see my fury.

His gaze narrowed and he tilted his head to the side, like he was studying an insect. It was the first time since I'd started my… work, where I thought someone saw straight through me. "Yeah," he said slowly. "I believe you fuckin' would." His voice was a rough growl, his gaze penetrating, digging for the secrets I'd buried from everyone.

Pain looked from one of us to the other and stood

slowly, inserting himself between me and Knuckles. "Maybe you need to take a step back here."

Knuckles shrugged. "No need. I see her now."

"I seriously doubt that." Yeah, I was good and pissed now that I'd had time to shake off the beating. I was bruised and battered, but I was pretty sure there wasn't anything seriously hurt. I suppose Pain would be the final judge, though.

"Oh, baby girl, I see way the fuck more than you want me to see." I had to force myself not to swallow nervously at his words. Because I was pretty sure he was close to figuring me out. Maybe not all the way, but he suspected there was more going on than I wanted anyone to know. Any show of nerves on my part would be like blood in the water and Knuckles was a great white shark. *The* apex predator in my world.

"Probably," I conceded. "But don't pretend to know me or what I do. You just met me."

"Yeah. But I know your twin pretty Goddamned well. I see the same core of strength in you." He snorted at me. "You ain't no wiltin' flower, pinin' away for the brother she condemned to prison."

"Never said I was." I was gonna fuckin' kill this son of a bitch. Gunnar would just have to live with it.

"No, but you have everyone else believin' it."

"All right, Knuckles." Pain pointed to the door. "Out. Now."

"Not on your life, Pain. I'm sittin' right here where I can keep an eye on this little hellion. She's not leavin' this house unless I'm with her."

"You can try to keep me prisoner here, but I promise you, it won't work out well for you."

"Oh, baby girl. That's exactly what I'm countin' on." That evil, predator smile was my last straw.

Without so much as a sound, I launched myself around Pain to drive my shoulder into Knuckles's solar plexus. He grunted but barely moved backward against the force of my body hitting him. I was short and slight, but I had a leanly muscled body, so I was strong. I was light on my feet, even after the hits I'd taken earlier. Even though Knuckles seemed to barely notice the hit he'd taken, I'd put myself in the dominant position, getting the upper hand.

When he would have wrapped his arms around my waist, I dropped, sliding under his legs. Coming to my feet, I kicked out and punted him behind the knee. That got a startled yell from him.

"Hannah!" He roared my name as he spun around only to meet my foot with the side of his neck. I was aiming for his jaw, but he was just that little bit too tall, and I was just that little bit too short. He caught my ankle and lifted me up in the air with one big, meaty hand. I let out a girly squeal I was sure I'd be embarrassed about later. My free leg flailed as I tried to get my bearings and fight my way free. "Calm the fuck down, little hellion!"

"Put me down!"

"Christ, Knuckles! What the fuck 'er you doin'?" Pain had a hold of Knuckles's wrist, trying to pull his arm down.

"Not until she promises to sit down and behave."

"Knuckles, she just had the shit beat outta her! Stop it right now!"

"All right." He still didn't put me down. That stubborn look on his face said he had a problem with me, and we were hashing it out right now. "How about this? Tell me you didn't let that bastard hit you. As in, convince me, after how you just attacked me, why you didn't lift a fuckin' finger to protect yourself when he came at you. You do that, then I'll fuckin' leave and you'll never hear another fuckin' word from me."

"And you'll keep your mouth shut about this to Gunnar." I had to look up at him from where I still dangled from his hand by my foot. And yeah, I hoped I was getting too heavy for him, but from the way he hadn't even broken a sweat, I didn't hold out much hope.

He snorted. "Nope. That's not a promise I can make. I'm not keeping this from Gunnar because you're his twin and he loves you." When I didn't respond, Knuckles grinned. "What? No snappy comeback?"

Pain scooped me up, taking my weight from Knuckles. If I thought he'd let Pain take me back to the couch or even to bed so I could rest, I'd have been wrong. Pain set me on my feet and Knuckles wrapped one big arm around me before lifting me to cradle me in his arms.

Knuckles settled me close to his chest and I had no way of not snuggling next to him. He smelled so fucking good! The steady beat of his heart under my ear, even for a brief moment, was almost lulling. I knew if I had a full minute to do nothing but snuggle against his wide chest while listening to his heartbeat and the breath moving in and out of his lungs, I'd be out like a light.

From the first time I ever saw him, Knuckles called to me. Tall, dark, and tortured, to say nothing of the thick muscle sculpting his body -- the very embodiment of strength in its most primal form. Colorful tattoos ran from shoulder to wrist, creeping up the side of his neck. Though he was older than me by over a decade, the added age only bolstered his appeal. It was because of how much larger than life

Knuckles was that I knew I could never let him know how he affected me. Unfortunately, I was pretty sure I'd blown that pipe dream right out of the water.

Pain gave an exasperated grunt before picking up the ice pack I'd dropped and handing it to me again. "Put this back on your face, honey. You might be a badass, but you're not indestructible." He gave Knuckles a hard look. "Pull a stunt like that again, she won't have to kill you." He shut the door softly behind him as he left.

I thought Knuckles would put me down. Set me on the couch or something. Instead, very slowly, never taking his gaze from mine, he moved to a wide, overstuffed chair and sat with me now sitting on his lap. He maneuvered me so I was straddling his hips and rested his hands on my upper thighs as he gave me a level look that brooked no nonsense. "Now. Tell me what the fuck is goin' on, Hannah."

Chapter Five

Knuckles

When I saw that fucker hit Hannah at the club, leaving her on the floor barely conscious, all I could see was a tiny woman with a monster looming over her, trying to beat her into submission. *Dead fucking wrong.* Hannah was far from a helpless victim. No. So much fucking worse. I could have *rescued* a victim. I could wrap her up in Bubble Wrap and lock her away from the cruel world. I felt a migraine coming on, starting in my fuckin' dick. *She* was the predator. I knew it in my fucking soul. And I'd be a son of a bitch if the thought of her exacting vengeance on a world of monsters didn't make me hard as a motherfucker.

Hannah frowned at me, her eyes narrowing before going wide as realization hit her. She tried to get up, but I held her still. "Oh no, motherfucker! Put that thing away before you poke an eye out!"

I slid her a lascivious grin. "I mean, if you want to get close enough for me to poke your eye, I'll happily accommodate you."

"You're a cad, Knuckles." She still wiggled and squirmed, trying to get down, until my cock throbbed when she brushed over it with her pussy. She might have had on underwear and those stupid yoga pants all women seem so fond of now, but I was certain I could feel the heat coming off her. And, fuck, I desperately wanted to bury my cock so deep inside her she'd never be able to get me out.

I raised my eyebrows, a chuckle escaping my throat. "A cad, huh?"

"And a complete asshole. Bastard!"

"Admittedly, I'm probably a bastard."

"You're an asshole too." I had to fight not to

laugh at her stubborn mien. She reminded me of an angry toddler. With a definite bite.

"Probably. But you're gonna tell me everything. Every. Fuckin'. Thing."

She gave me a disgruntled sigh. "Can we not do this now, Knuckles? I'm fucking beat. Literally."

I couldn't help but wince. Even now, the bruise on her face was a darkening red. By tomorrow it'd be even darker. "Yeah, baby. You are." I looked at her for a long time. She stared at me calmly, her gaze never wavering from mine. I could see the resolve in her face. I absolutely would not get anything of substance from her tonight. "Fine. Here's the deal. You can put this off now. Get you a good night's sleep. Take time to get straight whatever lie you're going to tell me. If you do, I'm staying in your room with you. You are not leaving this place without me going with you."

"You're out of your mind!"

I shrugged. "You don't like that option? Then you spill it all. Now."

I let her look her fill, knowing she needed to push her boundaries. To know that I wasn't going to give in on this. I saw the exact moment she decided she'd rather give me something now and run when my back was turned. It was hard to keep the smile off my face, because I knew the second she opened her mouth everything she was spilling was complete and utter bullshit.

"The reason I didn't fight Dillon at the club was because I freeze up when I see him coming at me." She shrugged. "I took a couple self-defense classes and I was pretty good." She sounded reasonable. Even shivered as if remembering everything she'd gone through. "But when I see him, hear him, I can't seem to make myself do much to defend myself. Certainly not attack him."

"You did your research, I'll give you that."

Instantly, her expression changed from matter-of-factness to a deep scowl. Yeah, she didn't expect me to buy it either. "You don't know anything about what I do, Knuckles."

"Which is the whole Goddamned point. Explain it to me."

"It's none of your fucking business." Finally, she threw a serious elbow at me, catching me across the cheek hard enough to make my ears sing. I let her out of my grasp and she moved away from me a couple feet. Like that would save her if I decided to bring her back to sit on my lap. "Look, I didn't ask for your help back there. I didn't need it. Everything happened the way it was supposed to. Right up to the point where you stuck your big fat nose in where it didn't belong."

"You got hit pretty fuckin' hard there, girl. No doubt you got a concussion. How exactly did you have it handled?"

She shrugged, and I knew she was getting ready to lie. I thought it would be better than what I'd got before, but apparently Hannah couldn't lie worth a damn. "Dillon would have taken me home and I'd have slept it off." Christ! The woman was looking everywhere but at my face, biting her lip for fuck's sake. Like a little kid who knew she was in trouble, trying to make something up on the spot and failing miserably.

"You are soooo full of shit." I chuckled, think I even snorted a little. "Stick to the truth, girl. You're a horrible liar, *and* you can't tell tall tales for crap. You need to learn to think on your feet if you're gonna keep doin' this shit."

"Fuck you, Knuckles. And I'm not a little girl!

You know I'm the same age as Gunnar, right?"

"Well, considering you're his twin, I'd hope you were the same age. Also, Gunnar's a kid next to me. You're a kid next to him."

It was like I'd flipped some kind of fucking switch. Hannah's expression hardened. In the place of the vulnerable Hannah, the too innocent Hannah, and the angry spitfire Hannah, was a stone-cold killer. I knew the look intimately because I saw the same raw intent on the face I saw in the mirror every fucking morning.

"All right," I said, nodding. I stood slowly. This was the woman I wanted to bring out to play. "I think I finally hit the jackpot."

"What did you guys do with Dillon?" It was more of a demand than a question. She held herself loosely, readying herself for battle. I'd seen that look a lot too. Just before I was challenged in the yard. After that, I always pounded that same someone into the ground. Which wasn't the best option this time.

"Why do you want to know?"

"So I can finish what I started tonight."

"What's that, Hannah? What did you start?"

"He's a serial abuser, Knuckles. It's escalating. Tonight was the last test, and he passed with flying colors."

There was something in her eyes I didn't like. I wasn't sure I could put a name to it, but this was about more than punishing a piece of shit like Dillon. It was...

I cocked my head to the side in confusion. "You're not doin' this to punish Dillon." When she opened her mouth, I spoke over her. "Not *only* to punish Dillon." When she continued to stare at me, I continued. "You're punishin' yourself."

"Think what you want, Knuckles. I can deny it all I want, but you're gonna believe what you want. I have a purpose in life. A way to make the right people pay. There's no way anyone can deny what they did."

I thought for a moment about everything she'd said. And about what she hadn't. I knew she was planning on leaving the second I turned my back. I'd have to be blind not to see her intent. Or stupid. And I was neither. "Knight says Dillon went home. Been keepin' tabs on the place and he's not left since he got there."

"Good. Tell Knight thank you for me."

"You tell him yourself."

She shrugged and turned to go to her room. I knew I should follow her and demand she not lock the door. And that she stay put and rest. I also knew it wouldn't do a Goddamned bit of good. Hannah was more like Gunnar than I'd first pegged her for. It was because she was a woman. It had been a long fucking time since I'd had to read a woman in anything other than a prison environment. I had no idea how to pick up on the subtle cues from her that were imperative to staying alive where I came from. It was both unnerving and exhilarating.

It wasn't long before I heard a small *thump*. I stood and strolled to Hannah's room, opening the door she hadn't bothered to lock. She'd likely known I'd just break the door down if she did and was trying to save her house from any major damage. The window in her bedroom was open, the breeze moving the sheers in a gentle wave.

I chuckled as I took out my phone and texted Knight.

Me: *She's gone.*

Knight: *Got her. Car GPS.*

Me: *I'm headed that way. Eyes open.*

Knight: *Sending Chains and Hawk as backup.*

Me: *Tell Torpedo.*

Knight: *Tell him yourself.*

"Fucker." I couldn't help the smile as I tucked my phone in my pocket, checked my knife, then tucked it in the waistband of my pants. I'd prefer my gun, but being an ex-con makes carrying one not the best option. Next was my throat mike and earpiece. Both tested out OK with Knight, so I headed out to my bike. No need to hurry. I knew where Hannah was going, and I'd know if she got into trouble and needed help.

The ride to the little house in the suburbs was uneventful. I took my time, enjoying the ride. Knight had already tapped into the guy's security camera in case things went sideways before we got there.

"Man, I can't wait for you to see this shit." Knight's muttered comment came from my earpiece.

"She good?"

"Oh, yeah. She's good, all right. Ain't gonna be much left of her boy there when she gets done."

There was something itching between my shoulder blades. Something telling me I better get my ass in gear and get to Hannah. One thing I'd learned in prison was to trust my instincts. If something seemed off, it was.

I gave the bike more gas, speeding up and weaving my way through traffic until I pulled up at the sprawling McMansion inside a gaited property. Chains pulled up at the same time I did and was off his bike in quick, efficient movements. The gate had a keypad, and Chains had some kind of gadget he used on it. I had no idea what. Didn't fucking care. I wanted inside this property. Now.

Seconds later, the gate swung open and I rolled

through, not caring if my bike made noise. No one was around to hear anyway. There were no close neighbors. Knight had confirmed no one was in the house but Dillon and Hannah.

"Uh, guys, you might want to, uh… she's gonna kill him. Like right now."

Yeah. I thought so.

Strangely, I expected panic would hit me when it came to the physical confrontation I knew was gonna happen when Hannah got there. I had no idea exactly what was going on in her head, or what her end game was, but I was willing to let her beat on a few dipshit assholes beating up on people weaker than them. Or, at least, people smaller. And there was no doubt in my mind she could take care of herself.

Unlike Gunnar, Hannah was small. Delicate even. Until you got a good look at her. She was covered in a layer of fine muscle. I got a look at her midriff when she had on that tank top and would move a certain way. Her abs were ripped better than most men I knew. Her arms were finely muscled, so you wouldn't guess the strength in them. I saw how they stood out when we fought briefly. Also, the way she sat on my lap, the way she stood up to me and never flinched back from a fight and didn't hesitate to make her stand? Yeah. Hannah wasn't a woman who'd been beaten down by an abuser. If anything, she was ready for an abuser to fuck with her. Wanting it, even.

Which was how I ended up whistling a tune as I rode down the road even if I did crank the throttle a bit to pick up the pace. I was certain down to my bones Hannah could take care of herself, had probably even planned this very scenario with that fucker. Didn't change the fact I still need to be by her side. To be honest, I was really fucking looking forward to seeing the carnage she was unleashing at this very moment.

I pulled around to the back of the house. The attached garage was open so I pulled inside, making myself at home. Chains and Hawk followed me. We weren't quiet either. Hawk even revved his big Hog a couple times before shutting it down.

The silence after the constant rumble was deafening. There was nothing. Nothing at all.

"You think Knight was wrong? Maybe she snuck out with dickwad in tow without Knight pickin' up on it." Hawk scrubbed the back of his neck as he looked around the garage, which had one car in the three bays. The rest was spotlessly clean, with none of the suburban garage-y things inside or outside. No garden hoses. No lawn mower or weed whacker. The floor was a gleaming black-and-white check. The silence was almost eerie.

"I didn't get it wrong." Knight's voice came through my earpiece. "Second floor. There's a room on the southwest corner. That's where she's got him. Thankfully, she had the foresight to put down plastic on the carpet." There was a pause. "And the walls. I'm not sure, but there might be some plastic taped to the ceiling too."

"Jesus." Chains chuckled. "She's serious about this, huh?"

"Yep." Hawk opened the door to the back of the garage leading into the house. "Let's go see what she's up to. If we need to call in someone to clean up, I'd like to get it done sooner rather than later. Replacing ceiling stucco might take a while." We all snorted. My brothers took everything in stride. No one questioned if we were going to cover for Hannah from whatever we were getting ready to find upstairs. Didn't matter that Hannah wasn't part of our club officially. She was

Gunnar's sister, so they just assumed the club would take care of it and made plans accordingly. Torpedo and Bohannon would both be proud.

I had to stop myself from rolling my eyes at the thought of the two of them approving anything I did or didn't do. Kiss of Death was *my* club. They were just keeping an eye on it until I was ready to take over again.

"Does Gunnar know we're here and what's goin' on?" Chains moved in front of me, leading the way up the stairs. The laundry room just inside the house off the garage was empty and almost sterile in its cleanliness. The kitchen we went through to get to the main stairs was the same. Not a dish in the sink. Spotless counter tops with nothing sitting on them except one large vase of fresh flowers. The room was dimly lit with the only light being on the baseboards lining the hall. Safety lights.

There were a few small tables with more fresh flowers. Enough that the hallway reminded me of the way a funeral home smelled. There wasn't a speck of dust, cobwebs, clutter, or anything to suggest anyone actually lived in the place. From what I could tell, the whole fucking place was unnaturally tidy. There was nothing out of place anywhere I saw on the way through the house to the upstairs.

The closer we got to our destination, the more I could hear voices, one of them Hannah's. She had someone with her in the room Knight indicated, but I couldn't tell if it was a man or a woman. The sounds were pretty high-pitched. Could go either way.

I opened the door and Chains went ahead of me into the room. I followed, and Hawk brought up the rear. In the far corner of the room, the man I'd seen hit Hannah sat on a tall, white stool, his feet braced on the middle rung with his knees apart. Oddly, he was dressed in an expensive-looking suit but no socks or shoes. The whole corner was covered top to bottom in thick black plastic. Around the stool were what looked like thousands of roofing tacks covering nearly every inch of the plastic on the floor. There were also several large pieces of broken pottery scattered around the stool like they'd been dropped or thrown.

Dillon sat on that stool holding a… flower vase above his head? Like the one on the kitchen counter. And the ones on several small tables throughout the house. I stared at those flowers. Unless I was mistaken, every vase I'd seen had flowers arranged exactly the same. I'd done every mental exercise I could find in any book on psychology and improving your brain activity and all the shit in the prison library. I'd encouraged Gunnar to do the same. Both of us had practiced and practiced until we basically taught ourselves to have close to photographic memories. So, I was ninety-nine percent certain.

"Now, now, baby boy." Hannah's voice was deceptively sweet. Saccharine sweet. "No one is making you stay like this. All you have to do is get off the stool and walk away."

"You put roofing tacks everywhere, fucking bitch!" Anger bloomed over Dillon's face and he threw the vase against the nearest wall. The second he let the vase go, there was a harsh *ZAP*! and a shrill shriek erupted from his throat. "Give me another vase! Give me another vase!"

Hannah gave a sigh, like she was terribly sorry… for him. "You really should have thought your actions through, Dillon. I've already proven the pad is pressure sensitive up to three pounds." She shook her head sadly. "I'll have to go find another vase. I don't have any more in this room. Exactly two vases of fresh cut flowers per room, unless it's one of the suites like this one. Suites get three vases of fresh cut flowers. Remember, Dillon? You just broke the third vase." She sighed again, her shoulders slumping. "I don't want to break up the set in the hallway. That would make everything terribly mismatched. Like the time when you hit *her* over the head with the one on the left at the end of the hallway. She had to put Legos in her shoes while she walked to the flower store to get more, then walked home. No. I learned the lessons Carol paid for pretty well --" She was cut off with another *ZAP*! and a shrill scream from Dillon.

"Hannah! Please! Get me another vase! I don't care from where! Please!" Dillon was frantic now. He stood on the stool rungs but was too awkward to hold the position no matter which bar he put his foot on.

"I can't break up the set, Dillon." She gave him a look of sympathy so sincere I swear she actually felt sorry for the guy. "You taught me and Carol the importance of appearances. The hallway is too public an area. This house might be our private residence, but you never know when there will be guests who'll need to come down the hallway."

"Look, Hannah." The man looked desperate. Sweat glistened on his forehead, one bead trickling down his temple. "I get it. I'm sorry. I realize how silly it all was. I shouldn't have gotten angry with her all those times, or with you tonight, OK?"

Hannah's face lit up and she clasped her hands in front of her in an "oh, goodie" pose. Her soft brown curls swayed gently as she bounced up on her toes like she was excited. "Really? So when I move all those tacks and let you down from the stool, you won't be angry with me?"

"Nope." He smiled, sensing victory. I was anxious to see how this played out because there was no way Hannah was letting that bastard off the hook that easily. I knew it like I knew my own name. Of course, if I was wrong, he still wasn't getting off the hook -- the giant meat hook I'd hang his bleeding body from. "All's forgiven." I could practically see the wheels turning in his mind, the plans, all the ways he was going to hurt Hannah when he got down from the stool.

If it had been more than a step or two, the guy might have jumped down and taken the pain to one foot, but the room was rather large and she had him in the corner farthest from the door. She'd apparently removed all the furniture except for the tables where each flower vase had sat. He'd have to make at least four steps to even get off the plastic.

"OK. Let me go find something to remove --" another ZAP! and a scream from Dillon.

"Turn this motherfucking thing off, Hannah! Right fucking now!"

She smiled sweetly. "I'm sorry, Dillon. But the switch to turn it off is on an app on my phone."

"Well, get your Goddamned phone..." he trailed off, his eyes getting large and round as he seemed to remember a problem with Hannah getting her phone.

"That's right. You took my phone when I tried to call 9-1-1 after you pushed me down the stairs two days ago. I promised not to tell them what happened, that I'd only get my wrist looked at where I was certain I'd broken it, but you told me to put an Ace wrap on it and suck it up. You wouldn't let me have my phone back, would you, Dillon?" She sounded so sweet, so matter-of-fact it was hard to argue with her. "You said bitches who couldn't keep their mouths shut didn't get to have phones."

"You got it looked at later," he whined. "Anyway, I was right. It wasn't broken."

"And you still don't get it." She shook her head sadly as another *ZAP!* followed by several shrill shrieks from Dillon echoed through the room. Sitting on the pad like he was, I had to wonder if his balls were singing. No way they avoided damage. Made me smile. Again, Dillon tried to balance on the stool, keeping his ass from what was apparently a shock pad. I was betting there was some serious juice that wasn't supposed to be there. "It's not about being right, you son of a bitch." There was the Hannah I was expecting. All pretense at feeling sorry for Dillon or, more probably, pretending to be the woman Dillon wanted her to be, was gone. It was all a mind game. A way of fucking with him. "It's about not fucking torturing the woman you married, or the woman you're dating."

I sucked in a breath. "Now, wait just a Goddamned minute!" Hannah didn't even glance in my direction at my outburst, obviously already knowing I was there. God, this woman was complicated! I had no doubt in my mind now that Hannah knew her surroundings exactly. I knew she was an experienced fighter, but she was so very much more than that.

"Oh, thank God!" Dillon practically sobbed in relief. "She's crazy. You've gotta help me. Just move the tacks so I can get off the stool. I can take care of the rest."

I tilted my head, then glanced at my brothers to see their reaction. "Whadda ya think, Hawk? Should we help a brother out?"

Hawk snorted. "You know he still don't get it. Right?"

"Oh, I know he don't fuckin' get it," I bit out. "It sounded a lot like you knew his wife, Hannah."

"She's the reason I'm here." Hannah leveled her gaze on me but didn't expound. Instead, she cocked her hip, suddenly looking very bored. The bruising on her face was stark even in the shadows of the room, and I felt a smoldering rage building again. Now, I had a target for my rage right in front of me. "And you're right. He's a dumb motherfucker. I knew he'd never get it, but I really tried to give him the opportunity to at least pretend to be contrite." Hannah stood there, her lips curling into a smirk as Dillon squirmed on the stool just before the pad delivered another shock. His face contorted in pain. When he could breathe again, he screamed in pain and fury over and over.

The shocks seemed to be coming with increasing regularity. And intensity. We all stood there and watched dispassionately. I didn't know about anyone else, but I was enjoying the fuck out of the show.

"Please, Hannah," Dillon's voice cracked, eyes wide with that pleading kind of panic that always seemed just a little too late. Which, of course, he was. "I'm begging you." Tears and sweat streamed down his face. Kind of surprised me the guy hadn't tried to use his suit jacket as a way to get across the tacks, but honestly, it wouldn't have made a difference and I think he knew it.

Hannah tilted her head slightly, those brown curls swaying as if considering his words. "Begging?" she mused aloud, her tone only slightly mocking. "That's new for you."

And the shocking continued. At one point, Dillon almost toppled over. I was surprised he didn't, given how hard those shocks seemed to be getting. I wondered where the limit was, but honestly, I couldn't give a fuck. Bastard deserved this and more just for hitting Hannah at the club tonight. Judging by his other transgressions, he deserved a whole fucking lot more than what he was currently getting.

Across the room, Hawk flicked a gaze my way, an eyebrow arched. "So? We doing this, or what?"

Dillon's eyes darted between us like a cornered animal. He stammered out a pathetic half-laugh. "Yeah, c'mon guys, help me out here."

"Huh?" Hawk gave Dillon a questioning look. Then his eyes widened in understanding. "Ohhh… You thought I meant that we should help you." He grinned. "Yeah. No. I just want to get this done so I can make sure the mess is cleaned up in time for me to go to my kid's birthday party."

Another ZAP! had Dillon's body jerking violently before settling back into trembling. The motherfucker had threaded his feet through the rungs of the stool in an effort to stay on it. He was either stupid or a fucking pussy, because I was pretty sure the pain he'd get from the tacks on the floor was nothing compared to what he was feeling now.

"How many others have there been, Dillon? How many other women have you terrorized?"

"No one! I swear! No one!" He was panting now. I thought he might have pissed himself.

Hawk leaned back against the wall casually, crossing his arms over his chest with an amused snort. "Dumb bastard."

"You honestly think I didn't do my homework before I came after you?" Hannah tilted her head looking at him like the dumb shit he was. "I baited you. And you did exactly what I was told you would do. Right down to the fucking flowers in every room."

"What?" He looked so dumbstruck I had to cover

my smile with my hand. Not because I didn't want him to know exactly how big a dumb shit I thought he was, but because I knew I was gonna get to play scary monster come to eat his face pretty Goddamned soon and I wanted to get into character. Because, yeah. I was gonna enjoy the fuck outta this.

"Before Carol, there was Marissa. And before her, a woman named Geri. Pretty sure you know why I couldn't talk to her."

Dillon went white, his mouth opening and shutting before he swallowed hard. "I don't know what you're talking about."

"Doesn't matter." She smiles sweetly. "Even if you don't admit what you did to the others, I know what you did to me. So do several people in that club. I also made sure we were in the direct line of a security camera before you hit me."

"Please, Hannah." Dillon wept as he begged. "I can't take any more. Please."

"Let me ask you something." Dillon lifted his gaze to hers. "What did you do to me when I begged you to stop?"

Dillon's face crumpled, and he sobbed and sobbed. Hannah moved to the edge of the tacks on the floor and waited. The shock pad went off again and she moved forward. I glanced down at her feet to see she had on thick-soled boots at least. The second Dillon's body relaxed after the shock, she lunged forward and plunged a knife into the side of his back five times in rapid succession, going for his kidney and the renal artery. The abdominal aorta if her knife was long enough. She twisted her knife before jerking it out the final time and stepping back.

Dillon looked at her in shock as he clamped his hand over the wound. Blood poured through his fingers. "Oh, God." He gasped. "Oh, God!"

"God doesn't give a shit about you, Dillon. No one fucking does." Her words had no heat in them. She delivered them in a "so sorry for you" voice that made me smile, especially when Dillon started sobbing.

He tumbled off the stool and onto the roofing tacks with a strangled cry. He was definitely bleeding out. Just not very quickly.

Dillon rolled over with a groan and a cry, finding and clinging to my gaze, pleading with me. "Please, man. Call an… ambulance." He was already gasping for breath with the blood loss. "Don't let… me die."

"Sorry. We're ex-cons and refuse to carry cell phones so no one can track us. She's the only one with any way to call help and, if I heard correctly, you took her fuckin' phone." I shrugged. "Them's the breaks, pal." I almost thought the smartass was more fun to play than the eat-your-face-off monster. Almost.

Dillon sobbed out another breath, gasping once. Then again. Then he was still.

"Well. That was fun." Hannah's bright smile was genuine. "You guys wanna grab a beer after I clean up the mess?"

I rolled my eyes at her. "Come on, little hellion. You're in a heap o' trouble."

Chapter Six

Hannah

I knew Knuckles would follow me. I had hoped I'd be done with Dillon before he got there, but everything worked out for the best. And, as an added bonus, I didn't have to clean up the mess myself. Turned out that was a very good thing because the roofing tacks had seemed like a good idea, but they made cleanup a bitch.

"You do realize that could have gone a whole other way, right?" Knuckles. God, could the man not give me a moment's peace? And not because he was a thorn in my side, though he was. The man was sin on a way fucking off-limits stick. He kind of worked with my dad, so it would just be all kinds of yucky for me to fantasize about his big body and what he looked like under that tight T-shirt and his colors. My dad would have a fit. And not because of the ex-con part either.

Dad was kind of protective of me and Suzie. Me more than Suzie because my sister had her own protector. Her husband, Stunner. Whose ass Dad had kicked. In the literal sense. Dad was funny like that. He'd intimidated or otherwise run off every single boyfriend I'd ever had. Except for Robert. Dad had only met him once and his dislike of him was more than vehement. It bordered on outright hatred. Guess he either knew or suspected what I was too stupid to accept. So, given the fact Knuckles was a guy -- no matter how much older than me he was -- and I was dad's youngest daughter? Yeah. Nitroglycerine was less explosive than my dad faced with a man in my life.

"I had everything under control." I shrugged. "I mean, I should have reconsidered the roofing tacks, but I enjoyed the shit outta him not wanting to get away from the shocking by stabbing himself in the feet."

"Roofing tacks might have been the less painful route." Knuckles grinned and sweet God in heaven, how could a man so gruff, grizzled, and basically shit-yourself-scary look so Goddamned gorgeous when he fucking smiled?

"Dillon was all about psychological games." I turned what I knew was an evil smile on Knuckles. "I beat him at his own game."

A sharp laugh escaped Knuckles. "Yeah, baby girl, I guess you did. Now. You and I have unfinished business back at the compound." He held out a hand, fully expecting me to take it. I surprised myself when I did. "Come on."

He took me out to the garage and his bike. I knew what it meant for a biker to put a woman on the back of his bike. Most of them avoided it for any reason unless the woman was theirs. I'd seen Trucker take a cage instead of his bike when he knew there was a chance of someone having to leave with us. So when Knuckles tossed me a helmet before straddling his bike, I gave him a confused look.

"What?" I looked from the helmet to him and back.

"Put the fuckin' helmet on, Hannah. Your daddy might let you ride without one, but not me."

"I got here myself, I can get back myself."

"You got a ride here?"

I shrugged. "Don't need one."

"You do now, honey. You just killed a man in there. Yeah, we're cleanin' it up, but if we miss something, we don't want your ass on the line."

"Don't you think your big Hog there is a little noticeable?"

He grinned at me. "It might be. If anyone saw us."

"But they won't?"

"Nope. But we have to time it right. That means you come with me. Now. Helmet. Get on the bike."

I took in a nervous breath. "Alrighty then." Thankfully, Knuckles didn't say something stupid like reminding me to be careful and not touch the pipes, so he got to live. But, oh my God! Riding on the back of his bike… My thighs were practically hugging his ass. His smell permeated my every breath. Yeah. I was sporting a wettie, make no mistake about it. It was ironic that I finally had this man between my thighs and he was facing the wrong fucking way.

Fuck my life!

Once we were on the road, I lifted my face to the breeze. I could ride a bike on my own. No way I had grown up in the Bones MC compound where my dad was president and not learned how to ride a bike unless I really didn't want to. Not because my dad insisted, but because he forbade us girls from getting on a bike. Not because of some misguided, chauvinistic beliefs. Dad was terrified of anything happening to us. He was just as protective of the boys, but in different ways. Usually making them think whatever he wanted or didn't want them doing was my brother's idea to begin with. Truth was, though, I loved riding with someone instead of by myself. That way all I had to do was move with them, enjoy the scenery while the wind blew in my face, and let it take me away to a place of pure joy. Free from worries for even a little while.

We stopped at an intersection. It was one with a four-way stop sign instead of a roundabout or stop lights. I tapped Knuckles on the shoulder. He turned his head slightly to hear my request.

"Take me home." I pointed to the left. The second I spoke, I knew I'd fucked up. Or maybe this had been his plan all along. Knuckles snorted, then turned right. Toward the Kiss of Death compound. "Fucker." My muttered response got another snort out of him.

He didn't even slow down as he approached the gates to the fucked-up compound that was Kiss of Death. These guys had basically taken up four city blocks of warehouses and strung them together, walled them off, and made a small community that they kept to themselves. I can't even imagine the permits and fees it cost to do some of the integration they did -- city streets technically still ran through their territory -- but somehow they'd done it.

The streets were lined with camo canvas, masking movement from overhead. There were a few small open areas with either a park or a community pool, but that was it. Everything else was masked from overhead view.

I'd been to the compound a few times since Gunnar came home. I missed my brother. For years I'd blamed myself, and I suppose I always would to some extent. But now that I had him back, I was afraid to let him out of my sight. It's why I'd moved to my little farm outside of Nashville. I could see my brother every day if I wanted. And Pippa. I was so glad Gunnar had Pippa. It was easy to see how much she loved my brother. I felt better knowing he had someone to help him navigate life outside of prison. Especially since he'd spent fifteen years of his life behind bars for something he didn't do.

In all the times over the last couple of months I'd been to the KoD compound, I'd never been anywhere other than either the main clubhouse -- where parties and gatherings other than church were held -- and the warehouse with Gunnar and Pippa's apartment. When we sped past both, a sliver of unease tickled my spine. A couple minutes later, we pulled into an underground garage exactly like the ones in all the enormous warehouse buildings they owned.

We pulled into a parking space, and he shut the bike down. There were a few other bikes and the occasional truck or SUV in a space, but mostly the motorcycles of the men living in this building.

"Where are we?"

Knuckles didn't answer. He pressed the button on the elevator and we waited. A few seconds later he ushered me inside the elevator car and pressed the button for the top floor. The doors opened again, and he guided me out by my elbow.

"Knuckles. Ain't asking again. Where the fuck are we?"

He stopped at one of doors and unlocked it, dragging me inside with him. The apartment was a small studio. There was a stove that still had the cardboard over the burners, a sink with one basin, a fridge, and a microwave. The microwave door was open, but the inside was spotlessly clean. The whole room was.

As he closed and locked the door, he nodded to the small, square table. There were only two chairs, placed across from each other. I took one, he took the other. He laced his fingers in front of him, his forearms resting on the table.

"Now. Explain that whole torture by roofing tacks and electric shock thing."

"What? You think the guy didn't deserve it?"

"Oh, he deserved what he got and more. What I don't get is why you let him hit you, Hannah. Unless you were completely plastered, you could've fought that fucker off with your eyes closed."

"Yep." If he wasn't answering my questions, I wasn't answering his. We stared at each other for a long time. I didn't have to explain myself to him, and had no intention of doing so.

"All right." Knuckles placed his hands on the table, spreading his fingers wide. He had tattoos over most of his skin. His forearms were thickly muscled and roped with veins, his biceps stretching the T-shirt he wore. The leather vest with his name on the chest hung open. I knew on the back was the Kiss of Death emblem proclaiming them a one percenter. I'd heard the saying that ninety-nine percent of MCs were law-abiding. His patch proclaimed his club to be in the one percent of outlaw motorcycle clubs. I thought Torpedo and Bohannon would have tried to distance Kiss of Death from what the term outlaw implied, but fact was, even Bones dipped their toes on the wrong side of the law from time to time. His beard was full and long, and he looked exactly like what he was. One hundred percent outlaw biker. And, fuck me, it was a fucking great look on him. "How about you tell me how you met fucktard."

"How is any of this your business, Knuckles?" I kept my tone even, but I felt a little like a child called into her father's office to be punished.

He shrugged. "It's not, really. And it doesn't really matter, except that Gunnar is gonna kill someone when he finds out about this."

"I killed Dillon so Gunnar wouldn't," I bit out, unable to contain my anger at the image he painted. It was a simple saying, really. People dropped the phrase "I'm gonna kill" someone or something all the time. But in this case, I cringed. Gunnar taking the rap for killing someone he hadn't was what got him taken away from me in the first place. The man was my twin, for Christ's sake! Which was even worse when you factored in how I was the guilty party. I was the one who'd killed that swine, Robert. Gunnar had confessed to the murder in order to keep me safe.

Knuckles raised an eyebrow. "Oh, I'm fully aware. What I don't get is why you let things escalate as far as they did."

"It happens all the time, Knuckles. Who knows why women stay with their abusers? There are so many different reasons and all of them seem valid at the time."

"Ain't interested in other women, Hannah. And I know you weren't really with him. What I want to know is how many times you let that bastard beat on you before you took matters into your own hands tonight."

"A few. I needed him secure in what he was doing, so he'd lose his cool in public."

Knuckles jerked back like I'd struck him. "You were baiting him?"

"I guess you could say that. I already knew what he'd done to Carol. And one of the other women I mentioned? He killed her. Said it was a boating accident and she got washed overboard."

"Pretty sure we'd all agree the fucker needed to die. That's not in question. I want to know why you got involved. And I got a feeling this isn't your first time out." His hard, knowing expression let me know I was busted. I didn't care about getting caught, but I didn't want it to be Knuckles who put the pieces together. Or Gunnar. I kind of expected it would be my dad who'd figure it out.

"Again, not your business."

"Yeah?" He stood so abruptly his chair tumbled backward and skidded across the room. "I'm makin' it my fuckin' business." The hard, angry words almost made me flinch. Not out of fear, though. Knuckles was many things, a killer among them. But he'd never hurt a woman unless she needed it. Then it would be as quick and painless as he could make it. No. I wasn't afraid he'd hurt me. I was afraid of the disappointment I'd see in his gaze.

It was always hard enough to take it from Dad. But, even if I never acknowledged my feelings to myself, I'd basically had a crush on Knuckles from the first day I met him. If I looked like a fool in front of him, I wasn't sure I could bounce back. There was something about Knuckles that drew me to him. Probably his loyalty to the people he cared about.

"Sorry, Knuckles. You don't get to make that choice."

"I do when I have to watch you stand there and take a punch." His reply was clipped. Angry. He had to close his eyes and take a breath which I kind of found amusing. "You probably don't know much about me, Hannah, but I killed three men to get to go to prison. They raped and murdered my sister. So seeing someone hit my cell mate's sister is a huge fuckin' trigger for me."

"I didn't go to that club with the intention of you being there. While I respect that people have triggers, I didn't have you in mind when I went out last night."

"Didn't say you did. But I was there. And there was no way I couldn't *not* interfere. Didn't matter if it was you or someone else. I will never stand by and see someone strong hurtin' someone weaker just because they can. The fact it was you made it that much worse."

It was my turn to stand and pace away. "Christ," I muttered. "Look, if it's about this happening in your city, I get it. You don't want blowback. I only went after Dillon because Carol is my friend."

"OK. We're getting somewhere now."

I'd walked to the bar in the kitchen area. It was the only thing separating the kitchen from the living room. When I turned around, Knuckles was right behind me. I sucked in a breath as he caged me in, his hands flat on the bar on either side of me. The look he gave me was that of a man who expected to be obeyed. Unfortunately for Knuckles, my father had given me that look many times, so I was immune. No, my reaction to Knuckles was all about his close proximity and the scent of clean sweat and gasoline and the heat coming from his big body that had me weak in the knees. This was definitely a bad time for my fucking hormones to kick in.

"You afraid, little girl?"

I tried to scowl at him but wasn't sure I pulled it off. Especially since my heart was hammering in my chest so hard there was no way Knuckles would fail to notice how my pulse fluttered at my neck. "I'm not afraid of anything."

"Oh, I think you are."

"Am not." Fuck. I actually stuck my chin up. What was it about Knuckles that made me want to stand up to him like a teenager to a parent?

He slid me a grin. "Yeah?"

"Yeah."

"All right. Tell me what this is all about. You've killed before. Not only did you not flinch when you stabbed that motherfucker, you committed to the kill before you approached him."

"Why wouldn't I? He was a bastard who preyed

on the people he was supposed to love."

"I don't give a fuck about Dillon or anyone else in that situation. I care about you. So, I want to know why you're putting yourself in this kind of danger. More than once, apparently."

"It's just my thing, Knuckles. This is my contribution to society. I take scumbags off the street."

"Vigilante justice, huh."

"I suppose so."

"No." His snarl was a surprise. My gaze snapped to his where I'd been looking anywhere but at him. His closeness was distracting. Knuckles was larger than life. And I didn't mean only his size, though he was a big-ass motherfucker. Standing over me now, the man oozed sex. The carnal, nasty kind. I wanted to jump him, to make him take what his gaze was promising.

I wasn't a virgin by any stretch of the imagination. I was thirty-two years old, for Christ's sake. But I had never wanted to have sex like I wanted to have sex with Knuckles. Maybe it was the violence from earlier. Maybe it was the man himself. Or maybe, it was because this was the first time I'd ever truly wanted to have sex with a man. It wasn't happening, but that didn't mean I didn't want it to happen.

"No, what? I didn't ask a question."

"You're not settin' yourself up to be beaten and probably raped out of a sense of justice, though I'm sure that's what you tell anyone who knows about what you do."

"Isn't justice enough?" Could the man get any closer to me without touching? I really wanted to find out. Suddenly, everything I'd been doing since Gunnar went to prison seemed like a bitter victory. Sure, I'd won every battle I'd taken on. But at what cost to myself? Then the only question was if I cared about the cost. The answer was a resounding *no*.

"It goes deeper than vengeance."

"You're imagining things."

"Fine. We'll drop that topic for now." For some reason I didn't feel like I was getting a reprieve. "Are you scared of me?"

"I already told you. I'm not afraid of anything."

"Good. So If I did something you didn't much like, you'd take care of me in a permanent fashion. Yes?"

"Where you going with this, Knuckles?"

He leaned in closer, his giant frame dwarfing my more petite one. "When I count to three, I'm gonna kiss you, Hannah. If you don't give me a good hard shove or knee me in the balls, I'm gonna to kiss you until you don't know your own name. Then, if we're both feelin' it the way I think we're gonna feel it, I'm gonna strip you naked, throw you up on this fuckin' bar, and eat your pussy until you fuckin' scream my name, little girl." I gasped in a breath and would have fallen on my ass if I hadn't been holding on to the edge of the bar. "One." He started counting.

"Oh, shit," I muttered. I wasn't sure if I was scared or eager. Probably both.

"Two."

"Three." I sighed, and pulled him down by his beard and met his lips with mine.

Chapter Seven

Knuckles

I… was fucked. In the metaphorical and, I *really* hoped, the physical sense. There were so many parts of the English language where fuck would be appropriate in this very moment I'd never run out of creative ways to use it. I'd known this was a mistake. Knew it before I told her I was gonna kiss her. But my body had other ideas and little head took over big head. Or something.

I just wanted to push her a little. To see where all those looks she was throwing me were going. More than twenty years in prison made my social skills a little rusty. If I'd ever had any. Women always fell into my lap whether I wanted them or not. My rank in the most powerful club in the area made me a prime target for club whores looking to cash in. It was harder to keep the women off me than it was to keep the police in line. This woman, though…

If I never kissed another woman after this, I'd consider myself lucky to have had the chance to kiss Hannah. And if my brothers ever heard that poetic shit, I'd get laughed out of the club.

But sweet God Almighty, the woman was delicious in a way I'd never imagined. There was the bite of the warrior I'd seen mixed with a strange hesitancy that felt like anxious energy. And then it hit me. And I had my answers. I knew why Hannah did what she did, and as much as I wanted to take this kiss further, as much as I wanted to make good on my promise to spread her out and eat her pussy until she passed out, it wasn't happening tonight. At least, not until we got a few things straight.

I let her take the lead, which didn't help my resolve not to take her as far as she'd go. Once the sensations settled around her, she was more demanding, almost desperate. Hannah was punishing herself, and I was pretty sure that now was part of her self-imposed punishment. I absolutely could not let that happen. I would not let her lump me in with any other men she'd slept with because I knew that was what would happen. I also had a sickening feeling, given how hard I'd been told Hannah had taken it when Gunnar had gone to prison, she wasn't as experienced in mind as she was in body. Which I should have thought of before I kissed her, but here we were.

I pulled back, my breathing heavy, and pressed my forehead against hers. "Fuck, Hannah," I whispered her name like a prayer.

"Why'd you stop?" Hannah shuddered in my arms. I wasn't even sure when I'd wrapped myself around her, but she was solidly against me and that's where I wanted to keep her. She tried to pull me back by my beard. "Please, Knuckles."

"Much as I want your tight little pussy around my cock tonight, I can't until we have a serious conversation. The last thing in the world I want is to take advantage of you or hurt you worse than you've already been hurt." My voice was rough with need. I wanted to kick my own ass. Both for not realizing what was going on with Hannah, and for not taking what she obviously wanted to give. Because I had no doubt I could make her feel as good as she made me feel. She'd never look at me again, though. She might not do it intentionally, but taking what I wanted from her would make me just like all the other men she'd been with.

"I'm not hurt, Knuckles. And you're not taking advantage of me. I know exactly what I'm doing. Like you said, if I don't like what you're doing, I'm more than capable of handing you your ass."

"I know you are. But this conversation has to happen, one way or another, and I'm not fuckin' you until it does."

She stiffened in my arms. "What? Why the hell not? You said --"

"I know what I said." I leaned in and touched her forehead with mine, cupping the back of her head to hold her steady. "I meant every fuckin' word. You tell me you're not holdin' onto some big feelings goin' back to the night things went to shit when you and Gunnar were kids, and I'll fuck your ever-lovin' brains out. But you're gonna have to make me believe it, and we've already established you can't lie for shit."

She gave a frustrated grunt before pushing me away. I didn't let her push me far. I'd get out of her personal space, but I wasn't letting her more than an arm's length away from me. "What was the play here? You think you can get me all worked up and I'll just spill my guts?"

"No, honey. I'm a selfish bastard, though."

"No! Really?" Her mock surprise made me raise an eyebrow.

"Is that sass?"

"Nope. It's sarcasm."

I tilted my head, moving closer to her. I gripped her waist and lifted her to sit on the counter. She gasped, her hands going automatically to my shoulders. Even though it was wise to put some distance between us, I knew I couldn't give her too much. I also had this overwhelming drive to push her. Just a little. I shoved her knees apart and stepped between them, moving my hands to rest beside her hips with my palms flat on the counter.

"Here's what's gonna happen, Hannah. You're gonna tell me exactly what you've been doing since that night. And you're gonna tell me exactly what you hoped to accomplish."

She sucked in a breath. "I... what?"

"When did you start targetin' abusers?"

I didn't think she was going to answer me, but she finally gave a heavy sigh, like the weight of the world was on her shoulders, and leaned forward to rest her forehead on my chest. "I didn't set out to do this. It started when I was in college. My roommate had trouble with her boyfriend one semester. When it came time for Christmas break, I helped her make plans to get away from him. She didn't have family anywhere who could help her. He'd isolated her financially and was working on whittling away at her friends."

"Classic abuser."

"Yeah." She looked up at me, her eyes glassy and full of so much pain it nearly took my breath. "I wasn't ready for the backlash. I helped her get away, but I didn't get help covering her tracks. When he found her, she called me, screaming." Two tears overflowed Hannah's eyes and trickled down her cheeks. "I tried to get to her, but I was an hour away. I listened to him rape and beat her to death, Knuckles."

It took everything inside me to not react. I knew she needed to get this out. And, honestly, this wasn't anything I didn't expect.

She shifted her gaze, her expression hardening. "When I got there, she was already dead. Had been for at least ten minutes."

"He still alive?"

Hannah shook her head. "No. I killed him that night."

"You get help cleanin' up the mess?"

Again, she shook her head. "His parents had a log cabin way out in the middle of nowhere. It's why it took me so long to get there. It was little more than a hunting cabin, though he made it seem more grandiose. I think he was in shock he'd actually killed her when I found them." She took several deep breaths then met my gaze steadily. "I walked right up to him and stabbed him in the neck over and over until he stopped moving."

"How did you get rid of the body?" It was a long time ago, but I might need to do some clean up just in case.

"Burned the place. Took several days and I was terrified I was going to get caught, but I burned everything to ash. Including Calvin."

"Had to have taken a fuckin' hot fire. No one saw?"

"When I say this place was way out in the middle of nowhere, I mean literally that. Part of the drive there, I had to take an ATV. It was built at the edge of a clearing, but it had started to grow up. It was my good luck several days of rain followed. I remember the temperature dropping and it stayed just above freezing. I tried to burn it at night so the smoke wasn't visible. The fire probably was, but no one investigated."

"So you kept at it until everything was ash?"

"Yes. Then I buried as much of the ash as I could."

"Not very efficient, but pretty thorough."

She took another deep breath. She'd put on a good act before, so I paid close attention to her. She was a pretty good actress, but she couldn't lie for shit. Which, I admit, was a conundrum in itself. "I learned better after the first time." She finally met my gaze, her lips set in a firm line. "Took me a decade, but I finally became a pretty proficient serial killer."

I barked out a laugh. I knew she was serious. "I mean, I guess that's one way of looking at it."

"It's what it is, Knuckles. I target men who abuse women. I get them to let their guard down. I play the part of a meek, submissive woman, and when they prove they'll use force to get what they want, or their fists to take out their frustration on a convenient target, I consider them a lost cause and take care of the matter."

"How many, Hannah?"

Again, she looked away. She might be OK with what she'd done, but in the end she'd still taken lives. And despite the front she tried to put up, she couldn't fool me. Herself maybe. But not me. "Five. I take my time. I don't want to get it wrong."

"If a man'll hit a woman as hard as that motherfucker hit you and do it in front of a room full of witnesses, he's a lost cause."

"I agree," she continued. "Which is why that's usually the last test. Though, there were three of the five who didn't make it that far. They'd have killed me, and I knew they would because the suspicion was they'd already killed at least one woman."

I waited until she met my gaze once more, this time, pinning her with my stare so I could let the weight of what I was about to say settle over her as fully as it could. "Listen to me, Hannah. I mean no disrespect to you or your abilities. But you will not do this again. Not on your own. You want to continue takin' these scumbags out, great. But you do it with backup and a solid plan everyone agrees to."

"This isn't a worldwide operation, Knuckles. Just

me."

It was my turn to lift my chin. "You're part of Kiss of Death, ain't 'cha?"

"No." She chuckled. "I'm part of Bones MC. At least, that's my home."

"And your twin is part of Kiss of Death MC. That makes you ours. You want to do this, you'll have help. Help I trust."

"But --"

I cut her off with a kiss. We weren't nearly done, but she wasn't going to argue with me. If that meant I distracted her, I'd enjoy the shit outta distracting her.

My tongue tangled with hers and I loved the silky glide. The sweet taste of her mouth nearly drove me insane with want. I pulled back, my chest heaving as I struggled to maintain control. Hannah's eyes were dark with desire, her lips swollen from my kiss.

Her hands tangled in my hair, pulling me closer. When I finally broke the kiss, we were both breathing hard. Her pupils were wide, and her face flushed with desire. God, she was beautiful, even with the bruising from that bastard's fist.

"You can't just kiss me to win an argument," she whispered, but there was no conviction in her voice. In fact, she had an almost dreamy look on her face, and I began to realize I might have missed more social cues than I first thought. This woman wanted me, but it was more than simple lust. I'd had that with Beth in spades, and knew what that felt like. While there was definitely a healthy dose of lust with Hannah, I wasn't willing to settle for anything less than her being mine.

"I'm not tryin' to win," I murmured against her lips. "I'm tryin' to make you understand. You're not alone in this anymore."

She looked up at me, and I saw something crack

in her facade -- a hairline fracture in the armor she'd built around herself since she was seventeen. "I've always been alone in this."

"Not anymore." I brushed my thumb across her lower lip. "You think I'm just gonna let you keep puttin' yourself in danger without backup? Without someone watching your six? Think again, baby girl."

"I'm not your responsibility or under your control. Like I said before, you ain't the boss of me." The callback was probably supposed to be funny, but to me it sounded exactly like what it was. Hannah's attempt to justify her going it alone when she knew she was wrong.

"Nope. You're mine to protect."

That got her attention real quick. "What?" She sat up straighter and actually shoved at my chest. "I'm not yours," she said vehemently. "I'm my own person."

"Never said you weren't."

"I don't even know you. Not really. You don't know me either."

"I bet I know you better than you think. And if I'm right, you're doing everything in your power to make up for what you perceive as weakness on your part when Gunnar went to prison for killin' the man who tried to rape you."

Her tears, which had mostly dried, started again, and she let out a little sob. "He didn't even tell the cops that much. He said Robert had threatened to hurt me. If he'd said he walked in on us while I was screaming for him to stop or *anything* other than what he said, he might have gotten off. At the very least he wouldn't have been locked up as long as he was."

"He didn't want any of that to touch you any more than it already had. He thought you havin' to kill that scumbag was punishment enough. He said it gutted him to think of you havin' to go through any kind of trial, so he got through it the fastest way he could. He said you'd been through enough."

"He shouldn't have been the one to make that decision! Don't you get it? I should have told Mom and Dad at the very least!"

"Yeah," I agreed, nodding my head but still gripping her hips so she couldn't wiggle free. "You shoulda. Gunnar told me he made you promise immediately after he got there you wouldn't say a word about what happened to anyone. He said he made you promise over and over and over when he knew you were most vulnerable, because he knew you would never break a promise to him. No matter what."

"That was the one time I should have. Blind obedience is never a good thing."

"You weren't blindly obedient to your brother. You respected him enough to keep a promise, even though he'd extracted it under duress. He said you begged him several times to let you tell your parents or Mama and Pops, but he wouldn't give his blessing."

"Not even as they were leading him out of the courtroom to go to a juvenile detention center until he was eighteen. Then to a federal prison." Her gaze was unfocused, obviously remembering the moment she was describing. "I knew he was scared, but he would never give in. For the first couple of years, every time I came to visit, I pleaded with him to let me tell someone. Then I just stopped. He was getting increasingly irritated when I'd bring it up, and I didn't want him to hate me even more than he already did."

"You know he never hated you. Right?" It hurt to think Hannah was unsure of her brother's love. Gunnar adored his twin. If anything, he felt guilty for not going to their dad himself and saving Hannah the pain of him being in prison. But, live and learn. The sixteen-year-old Gunnar did what he thought was best and the thirty-two-year-old Gunnar had learned to live with his decision.

"He should have. He had every right to."

"Past time you and Gunnar sat down and had a conversation." I brushed a curl off her forehead and tucked it behind her ear. "While you're havin' that conversation, when you have him all high in his feels, I'll let him know I'm claimin' you. Maybe he'll leave my balls intact."

She gave me an exasperated look, which made me chuckle. "You're not claiming me, Knuckles."

"Tell yourself that all you want, but it's happenin'."

"We've kissed two times. One of those wasn't even a real kiss. You were just trying to shut me up." It seemed like her eyes were shooting daggers at me, but there was something else there...

Realization kicked me in the balls. I don't think I would have been more surprised if she'd really had kicked me in the balls. "Oh, that sounded suspiciously like a challenge, baby girl. Is that it?"

She bit her lip nervously and I saw the pulse at her neck speed up, fluttering under her delicate skin. "I didn't say that." There was a hint of a smile on her face, but I saw the uncertainty also.

"Not sure you had to say it. Your meaning was pretty clear." I leaned in closer, giving her plenty of time to push me away.

"You think so?"

"I know so."

"Then what are you waiting for? If you want to count a second kiss, it's gotta be a real one."

"My fuckin' pleasure."

Chapter Eight

Hannah

What was I doing? This was the worst idea in the history of ideas! Why the hell had I basically dared Knuckles to kiss me with feeling? There was no way I could handle a man like Knuckles in a sexual situation. Not like this. Not when he had me tied up in knots just being near him.

He threaded his fingers through my hair, cradling the back of my head in his big hand. A low growl from him made me shiver. There was no fear or dread, or anything other than an intense lust so strong I needed to scream.

His lips moved over mine in an aggressive glide, his tongue slipping into my mouth with a hunger I knew all too well.

My body responded instantly, heat pooling between my thighs as I wrapped my legs around his waist, drawing him closer. I needed his massive body nearer to me. Imprinting on me. I wanted to feel his heavy weight pinning me down when that was never a position I'd assumed willingly. I wanted it with this man. And I had no Goddamned idea why he appealed to me so fucking much!

I melted against him, my body responding without my permission. His taste was intoxicating -- whiskey and sin and something uniquely Knuckles. He was overwhelming in the best way possible.

I'd given myself to men who weren't nearly as big and aggressive as Knuckles. Men who were rotten to their core. For me, sex had never been about pleasure. Not since that first time, and that situation had turned from pleasant to terrifying in the space of a heartbeat. But this...

I had nothing to compare with the sensations coursing through me from this kiss. I felt like I'd been waiting for this my entire life. Maybe I had. His beard scratched against my skin as he deepened the kiss and I found myself clutching at his shoulders, digging my fingers into the solid muscles there.

When he finally pulled back, we were both breathing hard. His eyes were dark with desire, pupils blown wide.

"That real enough for you?" His voice was rough, gravelly. I expected him to smirk at me, to know how he'd affected me and make fun of my inexperience, but that wasn't the look he gave me. There was smoldering intensity. And I could most definitely feel his cock pressed against my pussy through our clothes.

I couldn't speak, could barely think. All I could do was nod, my heart hammering so hard I was sure he could hear it.

"Good," he murmured, his thumb tracing my lower lip. "Because I'm just getting started."

He lifted me off the counter in one fluid motion, my legs automatically wrapping around his waist to lock my ankles as he carried me across the small studio to the bed in the corner.

He laid me down with surprising gentleness, his large body covering mine as he settled between my thighs. The weight of him should have been terrifying, but instead it felt like an anchor, grounding me in the moment.

"Tell me to stop and I will," he whispered, his breath hot against my ear. "No questions asked."

I shivered. This time there wasn't an ounce of fear. I wanted this. Everything Knuckles was willing to give to me, I fucking wanted. "Don't stop," I managed to say, my voice barely above a whisper.

His answering smile was predatory, sending another wave of heat through me. He lowered his head, trailing kisses along my jaw, down my neck, pausing to nip at my collarbone. I gasped, arching into him.

"I've wanted this since the first time I saw you at the clubhouse," he confessed against my skin. "Knew it was wrong. Knew Gunnar would have my balls. Didn't fuckin' care. Still don't." The mattress dipped under his weight as he positioned himself above me, arms braced on either side of my head.

The intensity in his eyes made me shiver. This wasn't just about sex for him; I could see that now. There was something possessive, something primal in the way he looked at me. Like he was claiming more than just my body. His mouth crashed down on mine again, hungrier this time, more demanding.

His beard abraded my skin as he moved from my mouth to my cheeks, then down my neck to my collarbone. Then he inhaled deeply, like he was trying to take my scent deep inside him where he'd never be rid of me. I was woman enough to admit I loved that thought.

"Jesus Christ," he muttered against my skin, his voice rough with want. "I knew you'd be responsive, but this..." His hand slid under my shirt, his calloused palm hot against my stomach.

"Take it off," I demanded, surprising myself with my boldness. "I want to feel you against me."

He pulled back just enough to search my face, his eyes dark with desire but also questioning. "You sure about this, Hannah? We can go as slow as you need to."

Instead of answering, I reached for the hem of

my shirt and pulled it over my head in one fluid motion. His sharp intake of breath as he took in my simple black sports bra was all the encouragement I needed.

I'd had men look at me with lust before. But never like this. Knuckles was focused squarely on me, on the way my body responded to him. The man was on a fucking mission, and I was afraid it was to drive me out of my mind with wanting him. And goddamnit, it was working!

"Fuck," he breathed, his gaze traveling over my exposed skin with such hunger it made me shiver. "You're goddamn beautiful." He inhaled deeply again. "Smell so fuckin' good." His voice was like another hand to stroke me with.

His work-roughened hands skimmed up my sides, leaving goose bumps in their wake. When he reached my bra, he shoved it up over my breasts, drawing it slowly over my head to toss it aside.

The cool air of the room pebbled my nipples, but it only added to the sexual tension gripping my body.

"Please," I whispered, not recognizing my own voice. I'd never begged a man for anything, especially not like this. But Knuckles wasn't just any man.

As he stared at my bare breasts, his eyes darkened. The man was practically salivating as he looked his fill. I felt exposed, vulnerable, but the admiration in his gaze made me feel beautiful rather than afraid. It had been a really long time since anyone had looked at me the way Knuckles did, and it was intoxicating.

"Fuckin' perfect," he growled, lowering his head to press his lips against the swell of my breast. I gasped, arching into his touch. "Absolutely fuckin' perfect."

Knuckles's mouth closed over my nipple, and I nearly came off the bed. His tongue swirled around the sensitive peak while his hand cupped my other breast, thumb brushing back and forth. My hands fisted in his hair, holding him to me as waves of pleasure radiated through my body.

I'd never felt anything like this... this raw need coursing through me. My body was on fire, every nerve ending alive and screaming for his touch. Even through my yoga pants, I could feel the heat of his erection pressing against my pussy, and I instinctively rocked my hips against him, seeking friction.

He groaned against my breast, the vibration sending another jolt of pleasure through me. "Keep that up, and this is gonna be over before it starts," he warned, his voice rough.

"I need..." I trailed off, not even sure what I was asking for.

"I know what you fuckin' need, woman." His growl should have scared me. Or at least triggered all the shit I'd put myself through in my quest for... vengeance? Justice? Fuck if I knew anymore. Instead, the desperation in his voice only fueled my need.

Given everything I'd put myself through over the past decade, I didn't think I could get excited about sex. I'd never really had sex for the pleasure of it. Because I wanted to. There was always a goal, and I'd never relaxed. I became pretty good at faking everything. Or, I thought I had until Knuckles angled his hips to give me the perfect amount of friction on my clit. Given the intensity of the first orgasm that ripped through my body, I had been grossly underperforming. I came so hard I saw spots.

"Fuck me." The words seemed to explode from Knuckles. He shuddered around me even as I was coming down from a euphoric high. "Sweet Christ, I've never seen anything so fuckin' beautiful as you comin' your brains out." He didn't sound condescending or superior. No. This huge, alpha male sounded in awe of what he was seeing.

As my vision cleared, I met his wide-eyed gaze. The man looked like a kid who'd just discovered Santa Claus was, in fact, real. There was a mixture of awe, lust, and a look of greed so profound I knew my life was about to change forever. And those changes would have a ripple effect. Either way, I knew my hunting days were over. Not necessarily because I knew Knuckles would want that. But because there was no way I could ever allow another man to touch me after knowing what it was like to be in Knuckles's arms.

With his weight still firmly pinning me to the bed, Knuckles slid his fingers down my body, trailing fire across my skin until they reached the waistband of my pants. He paused, his eyes seeking permission.

"Yes," I whispered, lifting my hips in invitation.

With agonizing slowness, he peeled the pants over my hips. He gave a frustrated grunt when he had to sit up on his knees to pull my pants and panties down my legs. The cool air against my overheated skin made me shiver, but it was nothing compared to the tremors that ran through me when he settled back between my thighs. I whimpered when my bare pussy brushed his muscled abdomen.

He looked up at me, waiting until my gaze found his. "I told you I was gonna eat your pussy until you screamed my name," he reminded me, his voice a low rumble that vibrated through me. "And I always keep my promises."

I raised up on my elbows, my breaths coming in little pants. If he was really going to eat my pussy like he promised, I wanted with everything in me to watch him do it. Until I couldn't. Given the orgasm Knuckles had already given me, I doubted I'd be able to recognize my own name before he was done with me.

The first touch of his tongue against my clit had me arching off the bed with a strangled cry. He chuckled, the vibration sending another jolt of pleasure through me, before he gripped my hips firmly and held me in place.

"Easy, baby girl," he murmured. "We're just gettin' started."

He worked me with devastating skill, alternating between broad strokes of his tongue and focused attention on my clit until I was writhing on the bed, crying, *begging* him to finish me.

The motherfucker didn't!

Knuckles shoved away from me with a yell and pushed himself off the bed. I was about to protest -- loudly -- when he unfastened his jeans, shoved them off his lean hips, and stepped out of them. Veins roped his arms from his hands and wrists, up his forearms and biceps. Lean hips and powerful, thick thighs rounded out his perfect body. Between his legs, in a nest of dark hair, his cock stood angry and proud.

Knuckles's breath was deep and even, his unblinking gaze hard on me. I loved the way his focus was solely on me. With slow, deliberate movements, he shifted his attention to the nightstand beside the bed. He pulled out a pack of condoms and took one out.

"Ain't sure this first time's gonna last beyond the second I get inside you, but I promise you I will rebound and you *will* come." I would have chuckled at his words except I found I needed the reassurance. Somehow, this man… knew. He knew my insecurities. Did he know he'd given me the first orgasm I'd ever had by a hand other than my own?

"I don't think that's going to be an issue." I reached for him, wanting this with every fiber of my being. His powerful body was an aphrodisiac on its own. The tattoos. With him naked before me now, I noticed the shattered chain ink winding around his hip. He noticed my gaze.

"You're staring," he said, his voice rough with need as he sheathed himself.

"Can you blame me?" I whispered, my gaze roaming back up his body to meet his eyes. The intensity I found there nearly stole my breath. "You're... breathtaking."

He moved back onto the bed with predatory grace, lowering himself over me once more. Sweat slickened his skin and I knew he was as turned-on as I was. The feeling of his skin against mine, all that hard muscle and heat, made me whimper. I wrapped my legs around his waist as he lowered himself to me, bracing himself on one, powerful arm. He guided his cock to my entrance before lying fully on top of me. I squirmed, trying to impale myself on him, but he snarled at me. "Hold still," he bit out. "I'm hangin' on by a fuckin' thread here." Still, his hips snapped forward, making the head of his dick stretch my entrance but not quite penetrate. "Motherfuck." He tensed, shuddering above me. "Fuckin' embarrassin'," he muttered before shaking his head. Fine droplets of sweat flung from his shaggy hair.

"Please," I whimpered. "If it's too much, you can come in my mouth."

"Goddamnit, woman!" His eyes were wide and wild. The man looked like he was on the verge of losing his shit. "Don't say shit like that! I'm about to blow my fuckin' load before I even fuckin' get inside you!"

In answer, I wrapped my legs around his waist and arched my back, dragging him just that little bit closer. His dick pushed through my entrance, stretching me deliciously before he stopped.

Knuckles roared before shoving himself as deep as he could go inside me, and I sucked in a breath. I had a moment of panic. He stretched me almost uncomfortably, but just shy of pain. The burn added to my pleasure in a way I'd never expected. Now I was the one breaking into a sweat.

Instantly, he stilled. "Did I hurt you?"

"W-What?" I looked up at him in confusion, the haze of lust making it hard to think. "NO!" I cleared my throat and tried again. "No, Knuckles. You didn't hurt me. Not at all."

"I ain't done this in a long fuckin' time." I knew the admission wasn't something he'd wanted me to know. The fact he went outside his comfort zone and made himself vulnerable settled something inside me I didn't know was uneasy.

"I have," I said, looking up at him with what I was sure were wide, wild eyes. "And it's never felt like this."

"Christ, don't I know it." His muttered reply held a wealth of relief. The tension in his shoulders was still there, but I thought it was more from exertion than him being unsure about what we were doing. Knuckles settled his weight fully on top of me. I was surprised at how good it felt to have his big, hair-roughened body pinning me to the bed, but it was as delicious as the rest of this experience. He rested his forehead against mine with a shattered groan and shuddered above me again. "You ready?"

I couldn't help the smile even though I knew he

probably couldn't see it. "I think I've been waiting for this moment since..." I trailed off, unsure. "This is what I've always been looking for."

He kissed me gently. Then with more passion. "You sure I didn't hurt you? You're OK with me on top of you?"

"I wasn't sure how I'd like this position, but this experience is so far removed from any other situation I've ever been in, it's not even the same act." I meant every word too. Sex had never been like this. Of course, I'd used sex as a weapon. And that was never something I'd desired. Ever. This, though... "I can't imagine you taking me any other way, Knuckles." I reached up to stroke his face with my fingers before whispering, "Please don't stop."

Something flashed in his eyes -- possession, triumph, relief -- before he captured my mouth in a searing kiss and began to fuck me. For the first time in my adult life, I completely surrendered to the moment, to the feelings coursing through me. I wasn't playing a role. I wasn't setting a trap. I was just Hannah, wanting this man with an intensity that frightened me.

It took him a few seconds, but when he met my gaze again, there was a frightening intensity in his eyes. "I'm gonna make you feel so fuckin' good, Hannah. I swear it on my life. If I come in the first fifteen seconds it's gonna be fourteen seconds longer than I thought I would, but I swear to you, I will make you come so hard you see stars."

I pulled him down for another kiss, whispering against his lips. "I already did, Knuckles. Now I want more. I want you."

"Thank fuck." Then Knuckles started to... *move.*

Chapter Nine

Knuckles

Every muscle in my body strained to hold back, to not come the second I pulled out of Hannah's tight cunt and drove back inside her again. Jesus Christ, it was like nothing I'd ever felt before! Her slick walls gripped me, her legs wrapped around my waist, her soft gasps in my ear... It took everything I had not to lose my fucking mind.

I'd been with women before. Plenty of them. Even in prison I'd had more than one woman on the inside offer herself to me before Beth. But this was different. This was Hannah. I think I knew the second I saw her there would never be another woman for me, but being inside her now? Yeah. She was it. This was where I was supposed to be. Inside this beautiful, courageous, reckless woman who was all mine.

"Knuckles," she whispered, her nails digging into my shoulders. "Please move. Fuck me like you need to." She nipped my earlobe in encouragement. "I promise I won't break."

I'd been so focused on not coming like some teenage virgin that I'd forgotten to actually fuck her. I pulled back slowly again, watching her face for any sign of discomfort, then thrust forward, setting a steady rhythm that had her arching beneath me.

"Fuck," I growled, dropping my head to her shoulder. "You feel so Goddamn good."

Her pussy clenched around me with every thrust, drawing me deeper, making me want to mark her, claim her, make her mine in every way possible. The sounds she made were like a drug I needed more of. I needed to hear her like this on a constant loop, to know I was the one who made her make those sounds.

Fuck me. Fuck me. Fuck me.

The words kept repeating in my head like a goddamned mantra as I fucked Hannah. Her tight, wet heat gripped my cock like a velvet vice, threatening to undo me with each thrust. Being inside Hannah was like coming home. As I relaxed into the sensations her body created within me, I settled. Felt more… centered. Knowing she was now mine, that she was now mine to pleasure, to take pleasure from, and, most of all, to protect like a rabid dragon guarding his treasure. Because that's exactly what I was.

I tried to keep my pace steady, to make this good for her, but the way she responded to every touch, every thrust, made it difficult to maintain control. Her nails dug into my shoulders, her back arched to take me deeper, and fuck if that didn't make me even harder inside her.

"Knuckles," she gasped, my name on her lips sounding like a prayer. "I'm gonna come…"

I shifted my weight to one arm, using my free hand to slide between our bodies until I found her clit. The second my fingers made contact, she cried out, her inner walls clenching around me so tightly I had to grit my teeth to keep from following her. Her pussy milked and squeezed mercilessly, drawing me deeper inside, tempting me to dump my entire load of cum inside her. To breed her. Make as many ties to her as I possibly could so she'd never leave me.

"Fuck! Hannah!" I screamed her name as my back bowed and I bellowed to the rafters. My release hit me like a freight train, my hips jerking against hers as I emptied myself inside the condom. My entire body shuddered with the force of the orgasm that hit me. Spots danced in my vision as I collapsed on top of her, barely catching myself on my forearms to avoid crushing her.

Hannah's body trembled beneath mine, her inner walls squeezing me with aftershocks. I buried my face in her neck, inhaling her scent of sweat and sex and something uniquely Hannah.

Her body bowed off the bed, her pussy clenching rhythmically around me as she screamed, holding nothing back. The sight of her coming undone was the most beautiful thing I'd ever seen. Her lips parted, eyes unfocused, cheeks flushed... She was utterly magnificent.

For several long moments, neither of us spoke. I could feel her heart hammering against my chest, her breath coming in short gasps that matched my own. When I finally found the strength to lift my head, she was watching me with an expression I couldn't quite read. Something between wonder and fear, maybe?

"Jesus fuckin' Christ," I muttered against her skin, feeling her pulse flutter beneath my lips. "You're fuckin' amazing. You OK?"

She nodded slowly. "I'm... yeah. I'm good. Wonderful, actually." She gave me a tentative smile. "That was --"

"Fuckin' intense." I finished her sentence. Then she smiled. A wonderful, glorious, beautiful smile. And I... was... *done*. "You're so fuckin' perfect," I whispered. I hadn't meant to say the words out loud, but I would never take them back. They were the fucking truth.

She finally relaxed completely beneath me, her fingers tracing lazy patterns on my back. "Not so bad yourself -- for an old man."

I lifted my head to look at her, finding her eyes sparkling with mischief despite the exhaustion evident on her face. "Old man, huh? Give me five minutes and

I'll show you what this old man can do."

She laughed, the sound warming something deep inside me. I eased out of her carefully, dealing with the condom before pulling her against me. She came willingly, curling into my side like she belonged there. And she did.

"You know this changes things," I said after a few minutes of comfortable silence. "Between us."

"I figured as much when you started talking shit about claiming me." Her voice was light, but I could hear the uncertainty hovering.

I scowled at her. "That ain't just talk, woman. You're mine and I'll kill any motherfucker who says otherwise." Her expression shifted, then. She closed part of herself off from me, and everything inside me rebelled. I never wanted secrets between us. Nothing. But especially not her feelings. "Hannah?" I tilted my head, giving her my best "don't fuck with me" expression. "Don't shut me out. I'm an idiot when it comes to women and feelings and shit, but I never want to hurt you in any way, so you're gonna have to tell me what's goin' on in the beautiful head of yours."

She glanced away. Her throat worked as she swallowed several times. "This whole 'claiming me' bit." She cleared her throat but didn't continue.

"Honey, say what you gotta say." I stroked damp hair away from her face. My hands were scarred, tattooed and rough. Her skin was... not. She was so soft and delicate, yet the fine muscles in her body spoke of her strength. The fact she'd hunted men who hurt women, deliberately putting herself in a position to be hurt, knowing from the beginning she *intended* to get hurt, told me all I needed to know about her core strength. Hannah was the perfect old lady for an ex-con biker like me. She'd need every ounce of that strength to be by my side.

Hannah bit her lip, then met my gaze. "I need to know if this 'claiming' business is just some kind of possessive biker thing like it is at home, or if there's more to it. I'll wear a property patch because I know it's as much for my protection as it is to let the world know I'm yours. But I'm not interested in *being* anyone's property." She looked away as if she thought this was a deal breaker. Almost as if she expected me to be a bastard. I'll admit, before I met Hannah, the only reason I'd have taken an old lady would have been to seal an alliance I desperately needed. *Before.* Now? I didn't care if my whole club burnt down around me. I would protect Hannah with my Goddamned life and consider death my ultimate service to her. "I've spent too long fighting for others to let myself be owned."

I cupped her face, my thumb tracing her cheekbone. "Baby girl, I don't want to own you. I want to belong to you as much as I want you to belong to me. I want you by my side. It means I got your back, always, the same way I expect you to have mine. It means I'm yours and you're mine, and we protect what's ours." I held her gaze steadily. "It ain't about possession. It's about partnership."

"You promise." She made it a demand. "Because I will go my own way when I don't agree with you. I didn't go against Gunnar when I knew he was making the wrong decision, and I will never put myself or anyone I love in that position again. I understand why he felt he needed to protect me, and I'm more grateful than I could ever express to him. But I'm never doing that again, Knuckles. I don't care how angry you get."

"Honey, our dynamic is different. You know that. Like I said, we're partners."

"Partners," she echoed, testing the word.

"Yeah. And there's trust. I trust you with my life, Hannah. I want to be the person you trust with yours." I pulled her to me for a soft kiss, sealing the deal. "Anything else you have reservations about or need clarification for?"

"I don't want to be one woman in a revolving door of club whores." She stuck her chin up as if she expected pushback on this. I just smiled. God, this woman was fierce. So fucking perfect for me it was scary. I had to chuckle, which got her back up. When I didn't immediately respond she narrowed her eyes and snapped, "What?" I loved the bite of demand in her voice, in the scowl on her face. "There's nothing Goddamned funny about it!"

"Honey…" I continued to grin at her. I knew I was about to get into trouble, but I couldn't seem to help myself. "How do you expect the club whores to just walk away from this total package?" I gestured to my body, then to my cock which gave an interested jerk. Not at the thought of the club whores, though. I found myself holding my breath, waiting for the explosion that was about to hit me. This was going to be epic. I was a sadistic bastard for looking forward to the fireworks.

Her eyes narrowed dangerously, her jaw clenching so hard I thought she might crack a tooth. For a split second, I thought she might hit me, and part of me was looking forward to it. As evidenced by the excited jerk of my cock once again, the bastard.

"You think this is funny?" Hannah's voice was deadly quiet as she leaned up, the sheet falling away from her naked body. If looks could kill, I'd be a dead motherfucker right now. "You arrogant, self-important asshole!" She shoved at my chest hard enough that I had trouble holding on to her. "Is this a fucking joke to you? Because I'm not laughing! You think I'm gonna sit by while you fuck everything in sight?"

I shrugged, knowing I was gonna pay for this later. "I mean, I've been in prison more than twenty years. I'm kinda hard up."

She scrambled to sit straighter, trying to put some distance between us as she pulled the sheet around her like armor, her cheeks flushed with anger. The sight was glorious! All that righteous fury directed at me was what I thought it would look like gazing at a Valkyrie. I couldn't help the smile that spread across my face, which only seemed to infuriate her more. It was a little disturbing to know how much I loved the vicious side of her.

She hit my chest none too gently, pushing herself away from me. I kept my expression neutral, though inside I was grinning like a fool. This woman was magnificent when she was angry. "No. I think you're a woman who knows exactly what she wants and isn't afraid to take it."

"Then why the hell are you laughing at me?" Lord, my cock now pointed due north, sniffing around her pussy like a dog scenting a bitch in heat. I loved this fire inside her. Stirring those embers into a raging inferno was going to be the highlight of my day.

I reached for her, but she jerked away, her eyes flashing with hurt and anger. Shit. Maybe I'd pushed too far. "I'm not laughing at you, Hannah, honey. I'm laughing because the thought of me wanting anyone else after having you is fucking ridiculous." I sat up too, making sure she could see my face clearly. "There are no club whores or any other women for me. There's just you. Only you. Always. *You.*"

She studied my face, searching for any sign of

deception. "You're serious."

I grinned again. "You think I wouldn't be?"

When she rolled her eyes, I could actually see the tension leave her body. "Well, I'll try not to bring home any wayward prospects if you can't get it up."

I barked out a startled laugh. "You keep givin' as good as you get, baby. That's what I want from you."

Her expression relaxed, and she smiled at me for a moment before it slipped from her face. "I don't know If I can be what you need, Knuckles." Her whispered words reflected the emotion swirling in her beautiful eyes. "I'm broken in ways I don't even understand."

"Ain't we all?" I traced the curve of her cheek with my thumb. "I spent years in a cage. You think I came out whole? We're all fucked up in our own ways. That don't mean we can't fit together. Maybe the way to fix each other is to not worry about filling in the missing pieces of our souls. Maybe those missing pieces of you are inside me. Maybe what I'm missing is with you. Together, I think we can be whole again."

Something softened in her eyes. "And what if I want to keep hunting? Not alone," she added quickly, seeing my expression darken. "But what if I still need to do this?"

I considered her question, knowing my answer might send her running if I answered wrong. "I'll never hold you back unless the risk is unacceptable. But you will do it with extensive planning, with me always in the background protecting you. And me. We do this together or not at all."

"I can live with that."

"And you ain't lettin' any of those bastards touch you. Never again. I absolutely will not bend on this."

"I figured." She leaned in and kissed me. I think

both of us needed the physical contact. I hadn't had anything other than stolen moments with any of the female guards or nurses on the inside. I'd only been with a couple club whores since I came home.

"I need to ask you something, Hannah."

Her expression was guarded, like she sensed a trap but couldn't see it. "What is it?"

"Have you been with a man other than the men you've hunted?"

She stiffened, but didn't pull away. "Why do you want to know that?"

"Because I think you're as starved for pleasurable physical stimulation as I am."

I wasn't sure she was going to answer me at first, but she surrendered the knowledge even if it was a little grudgingly. "No. There was never time. Besides, the sex I experienced wasn't something I wanted to repeat willingly."

"Why did you let me kiss you?"

Again, I didn't think she'd answer. The pause was longer this time, and I thought she might be weighing her options. I already knew she couldn't lie worth a damn so I was confident I could tell if she made something up.

Finally, she sighed, shaking her head. "Beats the hell outta me." She laid her arm over my chest and rested her cheek just above my heart. "You were different. When you pulled Dillon off me in the club, you were so angry. But not at me. At Dillon, because he was hurting me."

"Honey, angry don't even cover it."

"I know. I could tell in the raging bellow you let loose just before you beat the shit outta him."

"Didn't beat the shit outta him. If I had, I'd be in jail again. 'Cause I'd've killed the son of a bitch."

She kissed my skin, and I felt her smile against me. "It's not like you were gonna let him live anyway."

"No, but I always prefer no witnesses. Easier to dodge a murder charge that way."

That got a laugh from her. "Yeah. I guess it would."

"So, we good?" I held her gaze, letting her make the decision. Slowly, she lay back down, draping her body over mine.

"We're good," she murmured, nestling against me. "But I have one more question."

I tensed slightly, wondering what else she needed to know. "Shoot."

"This room." She gestured around the bare studio apartment. "What is this? You live here?"

I relaxed, running my fingers through her soft curls. "Just a place to crash. We all have one in the compound. Our own space." I looked around at my room. It had everything a person could need, but it was sparse. "Ain't had time to do more than get a bed and a couch. Thought we'd take one of the bigger apartments on the upper level in Gunnar's warehouse or one like it. All the buildings have them, but no one uses them." I snorted. "We always thought they were too comfortable, and we were manly men."

"Then why make them in the first place? If you all stay in the smaller rooms."

"That was Torpedo." I scowled. "Bastard said all the warehouses were empty and the club had money to burn, so he made fancy schmancy apartments on the top of all of 'em. Said *someday*" -- I rolled my eyes -- "we'd find women we wanted to spoil. I said any woman who wanted to settle down with a fuckin' biker needed to learn to live like a biker, to which he laughed in my face. Then Ambrosia, his woman, gave me 'the look.'"

"Ah. I get it."

"You do?" I narrowed my gaze at her. "What exactly do you get?"

She rolled over and stretched, her breasts on full display. Those beautifully puckered nipples pointed straight up, and I couldn't help myself. I rolled over to take one ripe peak into my mouth and sucked. I groaned around her breast, my cock pulsing against her thigh.

"All the old ladies at Bones have 'the look' in their arsenal. They take us aside when we find the man they think we're gonna end up with and teach us how to do 'the look.'"

"The one that says 'ain't you adorable, little fucker?'"

She burst out laughing. "Yeah. That's the very one." She snuggled in closer, took a deep breath, then let it out in a contented sigh.

"There are things we still need to talk about," I said, my voice low. "But they can wait."

"Mmm," she hummed against my skin. "Good, because I don't think I can form coherent thoughts right now." She stretched before settling down again.

My chuckle rumbled deep in the quiet of the room. "Did I fuck your brains out, baby girl?"

"Don't get cocky," she muttered, but I could hear the smile in her voice. "Though... yes. You absolutely did."

I pressed a kiss to the top of her head, breathing in the scent of her hair. The anger that had been simmering inside me since I saw Dillon hit her was finally quieting, replaced by something else. Something I wasn't ready to name yet but recognized all the same.

We lay in comfortable silence for a while, my hand stroking her back up and down. I felt her breathing even out, her body growing heavier against mine. Just when I thought she might have drifted off, she spoke again.

"What happens when Gunnar finds out?"

I chuckled, the sound rumbling through my chest. "He's gonna be pissed as hell. Might try to take my head off." I kissed the top of her head. "Worth it. So fuckin' worth it."

Chapter Ten

Hannah

The rest of the night was spent getting to know each other. Knuckles was an asshole in the extreme, but he was funny as shit. He constantly picked at me. He learned I was a jealous bitch and took full advantage. Without even leaving our little room, he managed to have me swearing to cut out the eyes from every club whore in the compound. He'd laughed so hard he had tears streaming from his eyes when I made the threat under my breath.

He wasn't mean about his teasing. He just liked getting a rise out of me. Not so much when I turned the tables on him. Before long there was a full-fledged tickle war going on, and Knuckles lost. Epically.

"That'll teach you to fuck with me." I gave a satisfied nod as I sat astride him, hands on my hips.

He stroked his rough hands up and down my thighs, the difference in our sizes a huge fucking turn-on. His muscled abdomen was so fucking delicious I wanted to taste every single inch of it. Again. "I guess it will, little hellion." His cock poked my ass interestedly as he continued to chuckle. "I'm gonna have to teach you a lesson about what happens when you tickle me," he threatened, though there was no heat in his voice. I was too caught up in the sensation of his hands on my thighs, the way his calloused fingers left trails of fire on my skin, to really pay attention.

"Oh yeah?" I arched an eyebrow, a smirk playing at my lips. "And what kind of lesson would that be?" I leaned down, my breasts brushing against his chest as I whispered in his ear, "Because I will retaliate."

"OK. Retaliation sounds interesting." The man

really was a hound dog. I loved it.

"The kind that involves me riding you until you beg for mercy."

His cock jerked against my ass, fully hard now. "Fuck, Hannah," he groaned, his hands moving to grip my hips. "You're playing with fire, woman." He growled, his fingers digging into my flesh.

I leaned down, my hair creating a curtain around our faces. "Maybe I like the burn." I nipped at his bottom lip, enjoying the way his breathing hitched. "Maybe I want to burn you too."

The shift was sudden -- one moment I was on top, the next I was beneath him, his powerful body caging me in. "You already have," he rasped against my throat. "Burned me to the fucking ground."

His beard scratched deliciously against my sensitive skin as he trailed kisses down my neck to my collarbone. I arched into him, my body already responding to his touch like it had been made for him alone.

The night faded into morning with neither of us getting much sleep. Not that I was complaining. When I finally did drift off, wrapped in Knuckles's arms, I slept better than I had in years. No nightmares, no restless tossing and turning. No waking up to a man touching or hitting me in ways I hated. Just peace.

I opened my eyes to find Knuckles dressing. His large frame moved around the small apartment with effortless efficiency. When he realized I was awake he gave me a smile filled with appreciation and welcome.

"Hey, baby." He crossed the short distance to sit on the edge of the bed. "Why don't you get some more sleep?" There was something in his face that warned me I should do what he said. Not because he'd be displeased, but because I didn't want to know what he was doing. Unfortunately, the part of my brain that hated bullshit knew curiosity would get the better of me if I didn't question him.

"Where you going, Knuckles?"

He held my gaze for long moments. I could almost see the wheels turning in his head, weighing his decision, going over words in his mind he thought might satisfy me. Finally, he gave me a curt nod before answering. "I confirmed Beth was the one who had my daughter kidnapped."

"Pippa?" I pushed myself up, sitting back against the wall where the mattress head was shoved against it. "Her mother did that?"

"Yeah, baby. She did. She thought she could put pressure on me to give up my control of the heroin trade coming through the city headed north. Specifically, the shipments headed for Terre Haute, where me and Gunnar were housed."

"So, she's the dealer inside the prison?"

"Nah. She's not that deep in. But she's the one who ensures the drugs make it inside the prison for the inmates to buy and sell, or simply to move from one prison to the next. She has her hands in several underground highways running through Kentuckiana. Terre Haute is a little out of the immediate area, but Evansville is on the fringe."

I nodded. "Yeah. Iron Tzars territory. I imagine Sting wouldn't appreciate you passing the drug trade to someone he didn't know and had no way to communicate with."

He gave me a wide grin. "Smart girl."

I rolled my eyes. "Please, Knuckles. Cain's my father. You do remember that. Right?"

He winced and closed his eyes, scrubbing a hand over his face. "Yeah. Fuck."

"You forgot. Didn't you?" I deadpanned my expression.

"Hadn't thought about it. Probably on purpose. Self-preservation and all that."

"Yeah. You think Gunnar will be after your head, you haven't seen anything yet." When he didn't say anything else, I prompted him. Because I was pretty sure he was hoping not to answer my previous question truthfully and completely. "So? What are you gonna do about Beth?"

"Kill her."

I blinked at him. "I... wasn't expecting you to cop to that."

"I ain't ever gonna lie to you, honey. Somehow, though, I don't think you mind."

"Not at all. Bitch deserves everything you want to dish out and then some. But if you think you're going without me, you better think again." I lifted my chin. "If you're making me your old lady -- and that better be what you meant when you said you were claiming me -- then she's going to be my daughter too."

He raised an eyebrow at me. "That make your brother your son?" His brows knit together. "You're his sister... so does that make him my brother-in-law?" The look of utter confusion on Knuckle's face made me laugh. "Laugh now, you little punk. You're just as confused as I am."

"That's also going to make Cain your fath -- OMP!" Knuckles clamped a hand over my mouth.

"Don't you fuckin' say it. No way that man is any relation to me." He looked so horrified I had to smile.

"You're afraid of my dad."

"I know what that man is capable of. Even

pushin' seventy, he's…"

"Terrifying?"

"A man not going to let his youngest daughter be given to just any fucker. He's gonna be super protective and picky about who he makes your protector from here on out."

I smirked. "You *are* scared of my father."

"Honey, in a fight where I was tryin' to kill him, I'd take him on without hesitation. It'd be close, but I could take him. Knowing I can't kill him or even hurt him too bad, he'd kick my ass six ways to Sunday. Add to that he's protectin' his daughter? Yeah. I wouldn't stand a chance and I ain't too proud to admit it."

"So, when do we leave?"

He studied me. "I'm not going to talk you out of this, huh?"

"Sorry, babe." With an unapologetic grin, I turned his words back on him. "We do this together or not at all."

His grin was magnificent. The times I'd seen him with Gunnar or around the clubhouse, I'd only ever observed a fierce scowl or indifference on Knuckles's face. With me, he was different, and it warmed my heart. I had the feeling he didn't smile often, and I was glad I could give that to him. "I'm gonna have to watch my step around you. You'll never let me get away with anything."

"You tore up about that?"

"Nope. Just keepin' it in mind for when I wonder how I ended up in a situation I'm not really comfortable with just to see you smile at me."

"Funny. I was just thinking the same thing about you."

He shrugged. "I suppose there are relationships built on worse."

"Look. I'm sorry if I was a bitch before. When you pulled me out after Dillon…"

"Yeah, honey. I know. And it's not somethin' that will ever happen again." He gave me a stern look. "We'll find another way to satisfy the kill. One that doesn't get anyone hurt."

"There was more to it than that. The guys I targeted I already knew were guilty as sin."

"I was right. Wasn't I?"

"Yeah." I sighed. "I was punishing myself for getting Gunnar in trouble. For not speaking up and admitting it was me. But most of all, for not bringing everything to my mom. My dad would have been the one in prison if I'd gone to him when Robert first hit me. I was too ashamed because Dad knew something was off with the bastard and forbade me to see him."

"Which was Cain's mistake. Not yours."

"Huh?"

"Honey, I didn't get to raise Pippa. Have never raised a child or been around them. Of any age. But even I know you do not forbid a teenager from doing something. It will backfire every fuckin' time, and you'll be in an even worse mess than you would be if you'd just let them do it so you could mitigate the damage."

"I still should have known better." I shook my head. "The really funny thing is, before dad wouldn't let me see Robert, I was thinking about breaking up with him anyway. He was always mean-spirited. But I was bound and determined I would be the one to decide if I wanted to see him or not. Not my father."

"You've not even tried to find your own happiness since that night. Have you?" Knuckles's expression was blank, but he reached out to brush my cheek with his thumb.

"I figured if Gunnar had to wait, then so would I. Besides, I was too busy making sure men like Robert were taken care of."

"The punishing yourself stops now, Hannah. You and Gunnar are both free now. And you're both absolutely gonna live your best lives."

Chapter Eleven

Knuckles

If there was ever a more satisfying feeling than flying down the interstate on my bike with Hannah at my back, her arms wrapped around my middle, her cheek pressed between my shoulder blades, I didn't know what it would be. Her grip tightened as we leaned into a curve, her body moving perfectly with mine. We'd been on the road for a little over four hours, headed toward Beth's place just outside Terre Haute, Indiana.

The woman thought she was clever, hiding in plain sight in a suburban neighborhood. Of course, I doubt anyone around her knew of her drug trafficking scheme. Or that she'd sold her daughter to a human trafficking ring to secure safe passage and exclusivity from Nashville to the prison in Terre Haute.

I'd called Gunnar before we left, letting him know I was handling the Beth situation. He'd wanted to come, but I'd convinced him to stay with Pippa. She needed Gunnar more than I needed him for backup, especially with Hannah riding shotgun and Hawk, Tiny, and Inferno with me. Besides, this was personal between me and Beth. She'd betrayed me, used our daughter as a pawn, and nearly gotten Pippa killed in the process. That wasn't something I could forgive. Ever.

We'd left the compound at dawn, after I'd made a few calls to set things in motion. Neither Torpedo or Bohannon were happy about me going behind their back and arranging this trip, but fuck 'em. I respected both men and was grateful for them helping me out when they did. But I didn't need their permission. They might have thought I did, but they were wrong.

And as soon as this run was done, we were going to have a chat about changing the guard. I was ready to take my fuckin' club back. Right now, though, I had more pressing matters. Like dealing with the woman who'd hurt my daughter.

We rolled to a stop in a small roadside park out of the way of the main traffic flow. Tiny wasn't with us. As the road captain, he'd brought a cage with a trailer on the back to haul our bikes. The big, black F-250 would be memorable if seen with the bikes, but if it was parked in an ATV park, not so much.

"You guys are about fifteen minutes from your target. Everything still a go?" Tiny was the biggest mother hen I'd ever met. God help him if he ever had a woman as fierce as Hannah.

I glanced around at the others. Inferno was impassive as ever, but Hawk had an almost gleeful expression. "Ready to watch the fireworks, aye, Inferno?" Hawk nudged the other man who only grunted.

Hannah had a small smile on her lips, and I had to stop myself from smiling too. There was nothing Hannah revered as much as she did family. Pippa was her family now. "Ready when you are, Knuckles."

"Looks like we're a go, Tiny."

"I've got another cage arranged if you need to remove her from the premises."

"I'll give you as much notice as I can if it comes to that."

"It won't." Hannah's small smile gave me chills. When she leveled a look on me, I recognized the anger inside her because I saw the same fire in my own eyes when I looked in the mirror.

"What are you plannin', woman?"

"Just going to give her some options. I think

she'll take option number one."

"What are the options?" Hawk looked interested, but he was also as much of a smartass as Hannah could be.

With a straight face, Hannah answered him, "Bad, and to-be-avoided-at-all-costs."

Hawk nodded. "I admit, I might be looking forward to this."

The neighborhood Beth lived in was very upscale. I was worried the bikes wouldn't fit in, but apparently, there was a weekend warrior "clubhouse" in the middle of the place. There were bikes going all up and down the neighborhood streets, which were nearly labyrinthine in their complexity. So we rolled up in front of her house and parked. There were eight other bikes parked on the street or in driveways in the immediate area.

"Protocol dictates we should let these guys know we're in their territory," Inferno muttered. "Don't mean no disrespect, but no fuckin' way." Though we'd all put our colors away before heading here, I understood how Inferno felt. Normally, we were a group governed strictly by the rules we'd put in place. Our habits were regimented as a way for some of the guys to cope. Breakfast, lunch, and dinner were always at six, noon, and six respectively. It was a constant in a sea of choices because, to borrow a phrase from a movie, when a man's been asking permission to take a piss for twenty or thirty years, it's hard to squeeze a drop without say-so.

"Got it," I said, snorting a little as I held still when Hannah braced her hand on my shoulder to steady herself as she got off my bike. "Ain't askin' permission today."

I got distracted as I watched Hannah saunter up

the sidewalk to the front of the house. Her ass swayed enticingly in the skintight jeans she'd put on when she'd insisted on coming with me. She wore a white tank over a black bra. Despite the absence of any tattoos at present, Hannah was every inch a biker's old lady. I had a feeling I'd be finding new tattoos -- and hopefully body piercings -- on her regularly.

"Uh, we goin' too, Knuckles?" Inferno's voice was soft, but I heard the hint of amusement there.

I scowled. "Yeah. Keep your eyes off my woman's ass."

"Wouldn't dream of lookin', brother." Hawk sounded too amused, so I gave him a death stare. Bastard wasn't intimidated in the least. But he didn't look at Hannah's ass.

I was expecting to lead this adventure, but my woman took point, which would probably work out in my favor later. Besides, I was curious to see what she had come up with for dealing with Beth.

Hannah didn't bother ringing the doorbell. She tested the door, found it unlocked, and strode right in like she owned the place. I followed close behind, Hawk and Inferno flanking us as we entered the pristine suburban home.

"Beth!" Hannah called out, her voice carrying through the house. "You have company!"

There was a clatter from somewhere in the back of the house, followed by hurried footsteps. Beth appeared in the hallway, her blonde hair perfectly styled, wearing designer jeans and a silk blouse that probably cost more than most people's weekly salary. When she saw me, her face went chalk white.

"Knuckles," she whispered, her eyes darting from me to Hannah to the men behind us. "What are you doing here?"

"Paying a social call," I said, my voice deliberately casual. "Nice place you got here. Must've cost a pretty penny."

Beth's gaze hardened as she regained her composure. "It's been a long time. You should have called first."

Hannah laughed, the sound cold and brittle. "And miss the surprise on your face? I don't think so."

Instead of addressing me, Beth chose to go with Hannah. Inferno gave me the side eye while Hawk looked positively gleeful.

"I don't believe we've been introduced." Beth's smile was cold like a shark. "I'm Beth. Knuckles and I have a daughter together."

Hannah didn't return the smile or offer her name. "I didn't come here to play patty-cake with *Real Housewives*. I came here to give you a choice."

"A choice," Beth scoffed as she crossed to the fridge and pulled out a bottle of sparkling water. "And what could someone like you possibly have to offer someone like me?"

"Oh, there's *a lot* to unpack in that statement." Hannah shook her head, chuckling lightly. "What can I offer you? That's easy. I can offer you a quick death. Now. Ask me about your choices."

"What are you talking about?" Beth looked from Hannah to me. "I'm calling the cops."

"Touch your phone and you lose option one."

"You can't bully me."

"Nope. But I can beat your ass into submission. You're already close to losing option one, and you haven't heard what those options are." Hannah clicked her tongue in sympathy.

"Knuckles?" Beth gave me the look a woman gets when she expects a man to defend her honor.

Usually for something that was entirely her fault.

"What?"

"Say something!"

I shrugged. "Not really sure what you want me to say."

"She's threatening to kill me, Knuckles." She sounded so outraged it was almost comical.

"She's giving you a choice, Beth." I straightened, taking a slow step toward her. "It's more than I'd give you. But Hannah and I are new." I grinned. "I'm still in the spoiling-her stage."

"You're out of your minds!" Beth's gaze darted from mine to Hannah's. "Crazy! You're both crazy!"

"Have a seat, Beth." Hannah had moved close to the other woman. Now, she grabbed a handful of Beth's hair and dragged her to the breakfast table in the big kitchen. Hannah pulled out a chair and shoved Beth into it before snagging her own and flipping it around so she could straddle it. Hannah sighed, giving Beth a kind smile. "I'm really sorry it's come to this."

"Come to what?" Beth's eyes were wide now. She knew she was in trouble, but still thought she could talk her way out.

"To you having to die today."

Beth's face drained of color, her hands clutching the edge of the kitchen table. "You can't be serious." The look on her face said she knew we were serious.

"Afraid so." Hannah leaned forward, resting her arms on the back of the chair. "See, you made a critical mistake when you sold your daughter to human traffickers. That's not something a mother does. Ever."

Beth was silent for a long time before she closed her eyes, finally realizing she was beaten. She shook her head once before pinning me with her furious gaze. "What do you want? Me to back off on pushing my product through your territory?" She threw up her hands. "Fine. Done. I won't move shit through your precious territory."

"This isn't about you not respecting territory. This is about Pippa."

"I told you I'd stay out of your territory, OK? I won't go after your product either. You'll never hear from me again." Her breath was coming in pants now, sweat beading her forehead and upper lip.

"Oh, I know we won't hear from you again. Now." I nodded to Hannah. "You don't have long before she makes the decision for you, so you better listen up."

Fear and dawning horror flooded Beth's expression. "I'm not going to sit by passively while you kill me."

"No, you're not," Hannah said brightly. "So why don't you shut up and listen." When Beth said nothing, Hannah pulled out a plastic baggie with a medicine vial and a skinny syringe. Being a nurse, Beth would know exactly what it was and what it was for. "Insulin. Taken from the clinic at the prison."

"You've lost your Goddamned minds! Both of you!"

"Your other alternative," Hannah continued, "is that you get taken. Same as Pippa did. They will do to you what they did to Pippa, then they will do to you what they would have done to Pippa had my brother not found her."

Beth's eyes were wide. "You can't --"

"Save it, sweetie," Hannah waved her off, interrupting what was going to be some royally indignant bullshit no one wanted to waste their time listening to. It wasn't going to make a difference anyway. "This is happening. I'm being considerate in giving you a choice."

"You're bluffing."

Hannah shrugged. "Suit yourself." She opened the bag and dumped out the vial and syringe onto the table before standing and putting the chair back under the table. "In case you change your mind. You won't have long, but I'm not forcing you to take the easy way out."

I saw the exact moment Beth realized she was in trouble. Her gaze flitted from Hanna to me. "Fuck you," she whispered.

"Nope. Fuck you. And they will," Hannah said with a bright smile. "They will."

Beth gave me a pleading look. "Knuckles." Her lips trembled and tears slid from her eyes. "Please. Can you really sit by and let her kill me? You're the father of my daughter."

I smirked. "That was the exact wrong thing to bring up if you wanted to live. You aren't anyway, but bringing up Pippa will only hurt you."

"Oh, God," she whimpered. The medicine vial and syringe sat on the table between Beth and Hannah. The elephant in the room. "Are you expecting a suicide note or something? Because no one will believe it."

Hannah put her hands flat on the table. "I couldn't give a good Goddamn if you leave a fucking note or not. You draw as much insulin as you can get out of that vial and inject yourself with it. Then you draw some more and do it again. You keep doing it until you pass out or you run out of liquid."

"I can't."

"Option two it is." Hannah picked up her phone and fiddled with it, placing it to her ear.

"No! Wait! Stop!" Beth's eyes were wide and she stood, reaching out to Hannah. My woman didn't move a muscle. She stood with the phone to her ear, the other hand cocked on her hip. Her expression was as hard as any MC president. "You have three seconds to get started, Beth."

With shaking hands, Beth snatched the bottle and drew up the liquid. She took several deep breaths before pulling up her shirt and inserting the needle into the skin at her belly. She kept doing it, sobbing uncontrollably. I'd never seen Beth like this. I wish I could say it made me feel bad, but fuck the bitch. She tried to have my daughter -- *her* daughter -- sold and whored out for men to do whatever they wanted to her. In my opinion, Beth was getting off too easy.

It took about thirty minutes to make sure she was done, but Hannah waited in silence. At some point, she'd sat back in the chair and crossed her legs. There was no conversation. There was no encouragement or berating. Beth finally laid her head down and didn't move.

Hannah led the way out the front door and back to the bikes. The rest of the neighborhood was going on like they had been since we rolled in. I'm pretty sure that asshole Hawk even waved at a few of them.

I wasn't losing a moment's sleep. Good riddance to bad rubbish.

Fuck the bitch.

Chapter Twelve
Hannah

I thought I might feel bad about what happened, Not because I'd been willing for Beth to die, but because I'd also been willing to give her to the very people I wanted to stop. I looked at it this way. As long as there were people who had too much money and too much free time. Beth had sold her own daughter to those people. I wasn't gonna lose a moment's sleep over her suffering now.

OK, so I did lose sleep. Just not over Beth. No. My man was insatiable. After we got back to the compound, he literally threw me over his shoulder, swatted my ass, and took me back to his room. He said it was just until we got the larger apartment a block over furnished. A couple of days at most. I told him that was fine as long as we didn't leave his apartment until the new one was finished, and clothes were not allowed. Yeah. I got Knuckles at his most primal after that little ultimatum.

"Two days," he growled against my throat as he pinned me to the mattress, his body a delicious weight on top of mine. "Two days of you naked and under me." His beard scraped deliciously against my neck. "I can get behind that."

We emerged three days later, both of us walking a little funny but with matching stupid grins on our faces. The club brothers who saw us either wolf-whistled or made gagging noises, but the knowing looks they exchanged said it all. They were happy for Knuckles. I thought he deserved to be happy for however long I could make it last. And I intended for that to be a very long fucking time.

The apartment we were given was the best thing

I'd ever seen in my life. Mom and Dad had enough money they could afford anything they wanted. They chose to live either at the compound or the ExFil base housing. So my tastes had always been pretty simple. This place wasn't fancy, but it was fucking *huge*. Wide-open spaces, four large bedrooms, and three bathrooms.

It was designed to be for multiple small families or couples. There was room for more than the four bedrooms. It wouldn't cut into the living area at all. The guys hadn't finished it yet because there was no need. The place was way too much apartment for the two of us, but I had the feeling it would soon become a hangout for the other club members. Just because everyone was happy Knuckles was back.

Right now, I was trying to get ready for a housewarming party. And yes, me and Pippa did it on purpose because the guys were getting too cocky for our liking. Torpedo and Bohannon had surrendered the club to Knuckles with their blessing, saying their goodbyes before heading back to Somerset, Kentucky. For his last official order as president, Torpedo ordered every patched member was to attend this housewarming party with a fucking smile. They were also informed not to forget to bring their side dish. I cracked up at the disgruntled looks.

Knuckles was sprawled out on the couch, watching me move around the kitchen. I was almost finished with the last of the food ahead of schedule so maybe I'd have time to run through the shower before everyone started arriving.

"If this is what you meant by 'domesticating me properly,' I'm not opposed." I moved around in one of his T-shirts, my legs bare, and my hair pulled up in a messy bun. It did things to him he didn't even try to hide.

"Quit staring at my ass and make yourself useful," I called over my shoulder, not even turning around.

"I am being useful." He grinned when I shot him a look. "I'm appreciating the view. Important work."

"Cut up the vegetables, you Neanderthal. I need to run through the shower before everyone gets here."

"Yeah?" He perked up at the mention of the shower, getting up and moving in my direction. "Been havin' some trouble with the hot water. I'll just go adjust the water for you. Make sure you don't burn yourself." He winked at me before pulling me into his arms and kissing me.

I laughed against his mouth, giving him a playful shove. "You're so full of shit. The hot water works just fine."

"Mmm, but you need someone to wash your back." He slid hands down to cup my ass. "Hard to reach spot, that."

"Quit trying to get me into the shower with you," I scolded against his lips, even as my body melted against his and I darted my tongue into his mouth with a contented sigh. I loved kissing this man. Loved sex in every form we'd explored. "We have thirty minutes before people start showing up, and I know what happens when we shower together."

"Thirty minutes is plenty of time," he growled. Knuckles deepened the kiss, thrusting his tongue inside my mouth over and over. Tasting. Tempting. I loved every blistering second of it.

"OK," I panted. "You convinced me."

"That's my girl."

Knuckles lifted me, urging me to put my legs around his waist as he carried me to our bedroom and the attached bath.

He kicked the bathroom door shut behind us, his mouth never leaving mine as he set me on the counter. The hard edge dug into my thighs, but I didn't care. Not when he was pushing my shirt up, exposing my breasts to his hungry gaze. And his mouth.

"Beautiful." He lowered his head to take one nipple into his mouth. The scrape of his beard against my sensitive skin made me gasp, my back arching to offer more of myself to him.

Impatient, Knuckles yanked the shirt over my head before fastening his mouth around one nipple and sucking strongly. I cried out, keeping my legs around his hips to hold him to me and threading my fingers through his hair.

The shower was completely forgotten as Knuckles worked his way down my body. He spread my thighs wide, his eyes darkening at the sight of my bare pussy. "Fuck, Hannah." His breath spread moist heat against my bare mound. "You're already wet for me." He stroked my wet folds with one finger before sinking two fingers inside me.

"Always," I cried out on a whimper. "All you have to do is look at me."

His answering smile was predatory before he leaned in, giving me one long, slow lick from entrance to clit. My head fell back against the mirror with a *thud*, a moan tearing from my throat.

"Twenty-five minutes." He winked at me before burying his face between my legs.

I'd never get enough of this man's mouth on me. The way his beard scratched against my inner thighs in an erotic rasp as his tongue worked magic between my legs had me seeing stars within minutes. My fingers tightened in his hair as my body tensed, that familiar pressure building low in my belly.

"Knuckles," I gasped, my hips rocking against his face. "I'm gonna --"

He growled against me, the vibration sending me over the edge. My orgasm hit me like a detonation, sudden and sharp. My body convulsed as waves of pleasure washed over me. Before I could even catch my breath, Knuckles was standing, unfastening his jeans and shoving them down his hips.

"Can't wait," he muttered, positioning himself at my entrance. "Need to be inside you right fucking now."

I nodded frantically, wrapping my legs tighter around his waist. "Yes, please."

He thrust into me in one smooth motion, filling me completely. We both groaned at the sensation, my walls still fluttering from my orgasm as they stretched to accommodate him.

"Fuck, Hannah." He pressed his forehead against mine as he settled inside me. Then he fucked me. Hard.

"Fuck!" I cried out, my body stretching to accommodate him. No matter how many times we did this, the initial penetration always took my breath away. Then when he rode me... It was teeth clattering. Mind-altering. And I loved every fucking second of it.

When he couldn't get the angle he wanted, Knuckles pulled out of me, lifting me from the vanity and spinning me around. He shoved me down so my tits were mashed against the counter. I looked into the mirror at the brutal expression on his face. This man needed me. He loved fucking me and I loved the fuck out of him fucking me.

I felt his hand shake against me as he hurried to guide himself back inside me. When he found my entrance and shoved inside me, we both cried out.

"So fuckin' wonderful!" I whimpered, meeting his gaze in the mirror. Knuckles's big body shuddered around me and my pussy pulsed in response. So did his dick. It was a vicious cycle.

Once we'd both adjusted once again, Knuckles fucked me with feeling. He gripped my hips, his fingers digging into my flesh as he established a punishing rhythm. The bathroom counter wasn't the most comfortable place, but, oh my God, I wouldn't change a thing! I loved watching his face as he lost himself in my body. It was almost better than the orgasms he gave me without fail.

The sound of skin slapping against skin filled the bathroom as Knuckles drove into me relentlessly. I met his gaze in the mirror, mesmerized by the raw hunger in his eyes.

"Touch yourself," he commanded, his voice rough with need. "I want to feel you come around my cock."

I slid one hand between my body and the counter, finding my clit and circling it with practiced fingers. The dual stimulation -- his cock filling me and my fingers on my clit -- was overwhelming, and I felt myself hurtling toward another orgasm embarrassingly fast.

"That's it, baby girl." His pace quickened. "Give it to me."

My second orgasm hit me even harder than the first, a scream tearing from my throat as my inner walls clamped down on him.

Knuckles's thrusts grew more urgent, his breathing ragged as he watched me in the mirror. His eyes were dark with lust, possessive and hungry as they locked with mine. He cursed, his rhythm faltering as he chased his own release. "You feel so fucking good." He slid his hand up my back to tangle in my hair. He tugged just enough to arch my back farther, changing the angle so he hit that perfect spot inside me with every thrust.

"Oh, God," I gasped, my fingers scrabbling for purchase on the slick counter. "Right there!" I screamed as one last orgasm ripped through me, making my knees go weak. If I hadn't been trapped between the counter and Knuckles's powerful body, I doubt I'd have been able to stay upright.

With a final, powerful thrust, he buried himself to the hilt, his body shuddering as he came. Deep inside my body. And I wasn't torn up about it.

For several long moments, we stayed like that, both of us breathing hard. Knuckles pressed soft kisses along my spine.

"That was…" I couldn't even find the words, my brain fuzzy from the multiple orgasms. And yeah, I felt kind of smug about that. I'd gone from never having an orgasm with a partner to having them all the fucking time. And it rocked so hard…

"Yeah," he agreed. "Definitely." He carefully withdrew from me and helped me stand upright. My legs trembled beneath me, and he steadied me with a strong arm around my waist. "Shower now? For real this time?"

I glanced at the clock on the wall and groaned. "We have fifteen minutes before people start showing up."

Knuckles chuckled, reaching past me to turn on the shower. "Then we better be quick." He helped me into the steaming water, following close behind.

We didn't make it. Not even close.

Totally worth it.

Marteeka Karland

International bestselling author Marteeka Karland leads a double life as an action romance writer by evening and a semi-domesticated housewife by day. Known for her down and dirty MC romances, Marteeka takes pleasure in spinning tales of tenacious, protective heroes and spirited heroines. She staunchly advocates that every character deserves a blissful ending.

Marteeka finds joy in baking and gardening with her husband. Make sure to visit her website to stay updated with her most recent projects. Don't forget to register for her newsletter which will pepper you with a potpourri of Teeka's beloved recipes, book suggestions, autograph events, and a plethora of interesting tidbits.

Marteeka at Changeling: changelingpress.com/marteeka-karland-a-39

Want more? Wanda Violet O. is Teeka's Dark Erotica side.

Bones MC Multiverse

Contemporary MC and Crossovers
- Bones MC
- Shadow Demons
- Salvation's Bane MC
- Black Reign MC
- Iron Tzars MC
- Grim Road MC
- Bones MC Legends
- Kiss of Death MC

Print and Audio
- Bones MC Print Duets
- Bones MC Audio
- Salvation's Bane MC Audio
- Iron Tzars MC Audio
- Grim Road MC Audio
- Kiss of Death MC Audio

Changeling Press LLC

Contemporary Action Adventure, Sci-Fi, Steampunk, Dark Fantasy, Urban Fantasy, Paranormal, and BDSM Romance available in e-book, audio, and print format at ChangelingPress.com – MC Romance, Werewolves, Vampires, Dragons, Shapeshifters and Horror -- Tales from the edge of your imagination.

Where can I get Changeling Press Books?

Changeling Press e-books are available at ChangelingPress.com, Amazon, Apple Books, Barnes & Noble, Kobo, and other online retailers, including Everand and Kobo Subscription Services. Print books are available at Amazon, Barnes and Noble, and by ISBN special order through your local bookstores.

Changeling Press, LLC

ChangelingPress.com